John F. Carr
& Mike Robertson

Pequod Press

THE LAST SPACE VIKING

A Pequod Press Adventure Novel

All Rights Reserved
Copyright © 2011 by Pequod Press
Original Cover Art—Copyright © 2011 by Alan Gutierrez

This book may not be reproduced or transmitted in whole or in part, in any form or by any means electronic or mechanical, including photocopying, scanning, recording, or any information storage or retrieval system, without prior permission in writing from the author and/or publisher.

Printed in the United States of America
First Printing, 2011
V 10 9 8 7 6 5 4 3 2 1

ISBN: 978-0-937912-12-6

Cover at by Alan Gutierrez

Pequod Press
P.O. Box 80
Boalsburg, PA 16827

www.PequodPress.com

Available from Pequod Press

Paratime Novels

Time Crime

Great Kings' War

Kalvan Kingmaker

Siege of Tarr-Hostigos

The Fireseed Wars

Terro-Human Future History Novels

Space Viking

The Last Space Viking

Fuzzy Ergo Sum

WAR WORLD

The Battle of Sauron

Discovery

CoDominium Take-Over

Space Viking Era
CHRONOLOGY

The Atomic Era is reckoned as beginning on the 2nd December 1942, Christian Era, with the first self-sustaining nuclear reactor, put into operation by Enrico Fermi at the University of Chicago. Unlike earlier dating-systems, it begins with a Year Zero, 12/2/'42 to 12/1/'43 CE. With allowances for December overlaps, 1943 CE is thus equal to Year Zero AE, and 1944 CE to 1 AE, and each century accordingly begins with the "double-zero" year, and ends with the ninety-nine year. –H. Beam Piper.

(*All dates in the Space Viking Era Chronology are based on Atomic Era dating. jfc*)

782	Foxx Travis born.
839	System States Alliance secedes from the Terran Federation.
842 - 854	System States War.
855	Ten thousand refugees from Abigor flee the Terran Federation for unknown worlds. They end up in a star cluster several thousand light-years from the Federation and settle an earth-like world, Excalibur.
895	Sword-Worlds Joyeuse, Durendal and Flamberge colonized from Excalibur.
915	Sword-World Haulteclere colonized from Joyeuse.
935	Sword-World Gram colonized from Haulteclere.
950	Aditya abandoned by the Federation, as it pulls back from the frontiers.
1000	The Interstellar Wars begin, a series of wars and uprisings which lead to the break-up of the Terran Federation.

1100 The final dissolution of the Terran Federation as war breaks out on Terra and the Sol System. The colony worlds turn on the mother world.

1200 The Interstellar Wars come to an end, more through exhaustion than desire. Only a dozen or so worlds still have the capability for interstellar flight.

1450 First Sword-World ship returns from the Old Federation. Aditya occupied by Morglay.

1533 Wulf Hellmut raids Baldur and a dozen planets in the *World Smasher* and brings home over a billion and a half stellars of plunder back to the Swords-Worlds.

1572 Captain Erlic Sanchez's raid on Isis is one of the richest Space Viking raids ever made in the Old Federation.

1595 After an unsuccessful raid on Aton by six ships from Haulteclere, Space Vikings no longer raid 'civilized' worlds in the Old Federation.

1602 Aditya is abandoned during a dynastic war on Morglay.

1615 Skathi, a Space Viking base world, is abandoned.

1650 Marduk-Odin "fake war." Both navies make a lot of fireworks, then each side goes home and claims victory.

1665 Planetary Nationalist Party takes control of Aton during the crisis after the war with Baldur.

1716 Lucas Trask, seeking revenge for the death of his new wife, leaves Gram aboard the *Nemesis* for Tanith in the Old Federation.

1718 The Battle of Beowulf.

1723 The Battle of Adhumla between Trask's allies and Andray Dunnan's Space Vikings.

1723	Dagon, a Space Viking base world, is raided by Otto Harkaman for attacking Ganpat, a Tanith trade world.
1725	Battle of Marduk between alliance of Lucas Trask's allies and loyalist Mardukan forces against Andray Dunnan's Space Vikings and Zaspar Makann's Mardukan rebels.
1730	King Lucas of Tanith and Prince Simon of Marduk establish the League of Civilized Worlds.

•

CIVILIZATION LEVELS

Civilization Levels (usually referred to as Civ-Levels) were invented by Otto Harkaman because he thought the former Federation Civilization Index, which only went to 5, was not descriptive enough for those worlds which had survived the fall of the Federation and the Interstellar Wars that followed.

Civ-Levels are used by Space Vikings throughout the Sword-Worlds and Old Federation to rank worlds and their stage of civilization, or decivilization, however that might be. Space Vikings primarily use Civ-Levels to rank Old Federation worlds in terms of fighting capability and potential loot. These are a holdover from the Federation Civilization Rankings that were included in the *Astrogator's Guide to the Worlds of the Federation.* Space Vikings find the ratings very useful as a shorthand when discussing past raids, future targets and dream scores.

Civilization Levels (Civ-Levels)

Level One—Blasted back to the Stone Age.

Level Two—A pre-mechanical world at a Dark Ages equivalent. Fighters use swords, bows and arrows and bone and leather for armor.

Level Three—early Medieval equivalent. Pre-mechanical world, but with steel plate armor and castles for defense.

Level Four—Late Medieval. Some hydraulic powered machines, gunpowder, and the printing press.

Level Five—Early steam technology, paddle wheelers, rifles and dynamite.

Level Six—Steam age with locomotives, heavy machinery, ocean liners and telegraph communications.

Level Seven—Gasoline engines, early autos, first airplanes, telephones, moving pictures and radio.

Level Eight—Jet planes, solid-fuel rockets, computers, chemical-explosives and television.

Level Nine—Semi-civilized world, atomic power, the atom bomb, television, super computers, interstellar travel.

Level Ten—A civilized world, with nuclear power, collapsed matter, hyperspace technology, with their own space ships for trading and protection.

PART ONE

AGNI

I

David Morland, Signals-and-Detection Officer aboard the *Nebula*, heard cries and the staccato sound of shots echoing inside the partially wrecked plumbing warehouse. The warehouse was a prime target because it was full of fabricated silver. On the planet Agni silver was as common as iron on most earth-like worlds. Here silver was used for everything from plumbing fixtures and pipes to building facades.

Agni's sparkling-blue sun pierced through the saffron sky like a lance. Its light was high in ultra-violet radiation and all the Space Vikings wore special goggles to protect their eyes. The natives had adapted to their hot-star sun with black pupils and a mahogany tan.

There was a loud boom and a burst of yellow light flashed through a rip in the half-collapsed warehouse roof. A heavily damaged groundcar was leaning against the portal doors as if trying to right itself against the building. He slowly worked his way to the door, when he heard a woman's scream cut through the noise of the fighting going on around him.

There were a dozen Space Viking ground fighters protecting the pinnace against a maniple of Agni regulars, wearing black uniforms with silver trim. One of the Vikings launched a heat-seeking grenade into the midst of the advancing soldiers, killing half a dozen and giving twice that many burn wounds. Their cries filled the air along with the smell of burnt flesh.

Having ascertained that their craft was safe for the moment, Morland led his five-man squad through the door of the large warehouse. Inside, the U-shaped counter had been hit by an explosive round and upended, leaving twisted wires and smashed computer parts littering the floor. The main door to the warehouse floor had been blown off its hinges and he led the squad into the large storeroom where large bins and boxes were overflowing with silver pipes and connectors.

"Slater," he ordered, "Bring a couple of contragravity lifters in here. We should be able to move a few tons of silver before it's time for lift-off."

"Yes, sir," the big man replied. He was dressed in typical Space Viking fashion, gray twill trousers with a short jacket heavily braided with the ships colors, red and black, and a combat helmet. He left with two of the squad.

From a back room he heard more screaming. It was definitely coming from a woman.

"Follow me!" Morland ordered, as he ran to the rear of the warehouse. According to the ship's code-of-conduct, rape was a violation of discipline and punishable by death. After the fighting was over, commercial transactions between Space Vikings and natives were encouraged, but even then there were strong penalties for taking locals against their will.

The scene on the main warehouse floor was chaotic, with plumbing fixtures, sinks, bathtubs and pipes strewn all over the floor. At the other end of the room was a growing fire. Morland spotted the woman and her attackers at the end of a long aisle of fittings and connector pipes of various sizes. The half-clad woman was fighting with one of her attackers with a pipe while the other acted as lookout.

He pulled out his pistol and started running toward the girl's attackers.

Seeing Morland, the guard raised his rifle and fired low. Morland was knocked off his feet and his left leg felt as if it had been hit with an iron bar. He had the usual body armor and leg and arm protectors or he might have been seriously injured. Taking out his pistol, he sighted on the fighter who had shot him, who was distracted by the two men coming to Morland's aid. He aimed for a face shot and got lucky, as the fighter fell over like a puppet whose strings had been severed.

One of his backup men, helped him to his feet and he limped to the rape scene. His leg was throbbing like an infected tooth.

The rapist was busy trying to yank up his pants when Morland got a bead on him. "Surrender, Parsons."

"You're not going to get me like you did Rydal." He dropped onto the girl, pulling out a gun.

Morland hesitated to shoot because he didn't want to hit the woman. He heard the *spaaang* of the shot as it went past his ear and hit the man helping him walk. As he started to fall, he aimed and fired off three shots. Parsons spun away from the woman, slamming into a bin full of silver pipe spilling them onto the concrete floor with a loud clatter.

The woman started screaming, there was blood on her shoulder from where she'd been struck by one of his bullets. This was the last thing he recalled as smashed into the hard floor.

He came too a few minutes later. The first thing he saw was a medic stripping the soft-armor pads off his left leg. There wasn't much blood, but he was getting shooting pains as the medic, a young man with a carrot red hair trailing out of his helmet and a straggly beard, manipulated his leg.

"How's the girl?" he asked.

"She took a bad hit in the shoulder, but she should be okay if they know anything about limb regeneration on this planet. Some trauma from the attack, that I can't offer an opinion on. The two you shot are dead—fitting end to bad trash."

He nodded.

"How about Smyth, the man covering my back?"

The medic shook his head. "Lucky shot! Right through the goggle into the eye—he never felt a thing."

That's what the poor bastard gets for coming to the aid of an officer. He hadn't been aboard the *Nebula* long enough to know many of the ground fighters, but Smyth had been there when he needed help. *That has to count for something.... When the ship gets back to Joyeuse, I'll have to make sure his family gets his death bonus. On some ships—and he had a strong feeling that the* Nebula *was among their number—records and death benefits had a habit of disappearing.*

It felt as if his leg was on fire as the medic put some medicinal unguent on his thigh. "How bad is it?" he croaked.

"A bad break is all, sir. The armor absorbed most of the impact, but something had to give. In this case, your femur. Some tissue damage, as well, but not too much bleeding. That was a big slug. You can thank the stars you were wearing leg armor; otherwise...."

I might have lost the leg, he thought to himself, finishing the medic's unspoken words. *Or worse, if it had hit an artery or vein.*

"Can you fix it?"

The medic shook his head. "Not with what I've got here. You'll have to spend a couple of days in the robomedic aboard ship."

"I can't leave until the holds are filled."

The medic shook his head in exasperation. "I can put a wrap on the leg, which will bind it together. Fortunately, for you, it's not a compound fracture. But you'll still need a crutch to walk."

"Fine," Morland said through clenched teeth. "Is there anything you can do about this pain?"

The medic pulled a hypo-sprayer out of his medpak and shot him in the thigh, which was the nearest exposed flesh.

Almost immediately he felt the pain diminish, then retreat to a faraway place. "Get me something I can use as a crutch. I need to see how the loading is progressing."

"Yes, sir."

Agni was their big score. The last two planets they'd raided had been nothing but petty theft. Most of the easily raided worlds in this sector of the Old Federation had been hit so many times the major cities were in ruins or were big slag-puddles. On too many planets the natives no longer bothered to improve anything, or just retreated into the jungles or other inaccessible places—providing thin gruel for Space Viking raiders.

Outside, the air was full of black smoke and the flash of gunfire. A large and heavily loaded contragravity lifter almost knocked him down as its driver steered for the pinnace.

Sergeant Xavier Burris, a thick-bodied man with piercing blue eyes and a pugnacious chin, ran over to him. "Where have you been, sir?"

He briefly reported the scene in the warehouse and his actions.

"Filthy swine!" Burris exclaimed. "You saved them from being spaced."

He nodded. "How's the collection going?"

"The holds are almost full. The locals are gathering for a counter-attack; it's time to bug out."

Morland agreed. He gave the "return to ship" signal and let Burris help him into the pinnace.

II

From a distance, the *Nebula* looked like a gigantic hot-air balloon. As his pinnace drew closer, David Morland could make out the warship's distinctive blazonry, a circular golden nebula impaled on a red sword. The *Nebula*, like most Space Viking ships, was a two thousand-foot spherical raiding vessel with a crew of three hundred along with five hundred ground fighters. The *Nebula's* primary mission was to travel into the Old Federation, which had collapsed into anarchy over eight hundred years ago, to raid and loot unsuspecting worlds. Of the thousands of planets in the Old Federation, not more than twenty retained the technological civilization of the former Federation. The rest were potential targets for ships like the *Nebula*.

Within seconds the hull of the ship filled the viewscreen. The pinnace had reversed thrust in time to come to a complete halt, resting in place through its contragravity lifters. Morland involuntarily winced as the collapsium deck cover slid up to allow the two-hundred-foot pinnace to be caught by the grapplers and yanked inside the *Nebula's* docking deck. This maneuver, which only took seconds, was one of the most dangerous operations undertaken by collapsium-armored warships. For a few brief seconds, it provided the enemy with a window for a clear shot into the innards of the immense warship. Although the inside of the docking deck was protected by collapsed-matter shielding, even a two-megaton blast inside the ship could cause irreparable damage.

Fergus Byrne, Third Officer aboard the *Nebula*, was waiting inside to greet him as he disembarked from the pinnace. Byrne's presence was in clear violation of ship's regulations. In a combat situation, with the

Captain, First, and Second Officers away from the ship, Byrne's place was on the bridge.

"Mr. Morland, I'm going down to the surface. I want you to assume temporary command of the *Nebula.*"

"Is everything okay, sir?" he asked.

"Stillwater is secure. I'm going to join Captain Orrick. I want to see this strange world for myself. Dismissed."

"Aye, aye, sir," Morland replied. He wanted to ask Byrne why he was violating ship regulations, but knew he'd get a good chewing out if he did. The *Nebula* was widely regarded as an unlucky ship and there were questions about the leadership abilities of its captain and senior officers. Its last half-dozen or so voyages had gone poorly; some were barely profitable while others had lost money, presenting the owners with big losses, which meant that the current trade-and-raid journey was a make it or break it trip.

Morland might have joined the *Nebula* just in time for its last voyage, which would inevitably color his chances of finding a berth on another ship when they returned to Joyeuse. The last thing he wanted to do was to rile one of the officers who might be in a position to offer him a post on another ship sometime in the future. Therefore, he swallowed his objection to Byrne's jaunt to the surface.

Agni was the only known habitable planet in a blue star solar system and worth visiting. Usually blue stars were so short-lived that life rarely had a chance to develop. Agni was the exception; it had been discovered at a time when the human race was desperate for more worlds to colonize, and so it had been settled.

When the Old Federation fell apart, Agni had lost hyperdrive capability and contragravity, but had preserved a certain level of civilization and had retained primitive nuclear power plants. When the planet had been rediscovered and raided by Space Vikings first venturing back into the Old Federation, those raiders had quickly learned that the inhabitants of Agni were not easy marks. They fought ferociously in defense of their world.

Over the centuries Agni had remained a tempting target to marauding Space Vikings. Since the Agni locals had good weapons and fought so well, the planet was only raided by the most daring, or desperate, of ship captains. No one ever returned from Agni without a damaged ship and serious casualties.

Lately, raiding Agni had become even more dangerous. They had either rediscovered—or, more likely, captives taken alive from past looting parties had schooled them in—the direct conversion of nuclear power to electricity. This allowed them to develop even more lethal weapons. It also made raiding Agni more lucrative, for besides silver there were plutonium and power unit cartridges to be looted as well.

Maybe this is why the Nebula's officers are celebrating their most successful raid ever planetside? Morland wondered. Regardless, he found it strange. The ship had taken a lot of damage during the raid and there was always the possibility of more hidden missiles. Or what if a ship was lying in wait near one of Agni's moons?

His crew began unloading the pinnaces, which were packed as full as possible with silver, small machinery and the usual odds and ends from the raid. The medic gave him a worried look. "Sir, that's a nasty break. You really should be in a robomedic."

"That will have to wait until everyone gets back," he said, trying to remove his armor while standing on one leg with the medic's assistance. Morland couldn't very well command a ship, even temporarily, from a robomedic. The anesthesia was already beginning to wear off and he had the medic spray his leg with something that numbed it, bringing the pain down to a manageable level. Then he slapped on a temporary brace.

Morland still couldn't walk unassisted, but he could certainly sit in a chair on the bridge and give orders—if necessary.

Then, the outer decked opened again as a troop carrier entered the docking port, triggering a warning siren. There were new scars on the craft's hull, and flashing yellow lights indicating wounded were aboard.

He turned to the medic who was helping him toward the elevators. "Go help with the wounded."

Morland used his hand-phone to call the deck chief. He told him to unload the two pinnaces as fast as possible and have the crews on standby in case they were needed again. The chief looked as if he were about to disagree, but instead nodded and left. The crews coming off the pinnaces obviously wanted to start celebrating what was clearly a lucrative raid.

They can wait until the ship is safely off-world, he thought. *They'll have plenty of time to celebrate and recover before their next stop*. Realizing he was coming near the end of his ability to stand on one leg, he waved over a crewman to help him make his way to the bridge.

There were only a few members of the ship's company on the bridge. Morland carefully settled himself into the captain's chair. He found that once he propped his leg up, it didn't throb so badly. He knew the two junior officers on the bridge, Konrad Veazey and Silvia Ryan well. They had been his main companions on the ship since neither of them belonged to any of the cliques surrounding the senior officers. He sighed quietly, reminiscing over the much friendlier atmosphere on his previous ship, the *Prince of Thieves*. However, it was Captain Allison who had told him that he was ready to be a senior officer and time to learn how other ships did things when he had sent him to the *Nebula* to interview for Fourth Officer—which now seemed like a long time ago.

According to the latest status report, the raid on Stillwater was going better than the raid he had led in Svaha Port. After some hard fighting they had taken a nuclear manufacturing plant located on the fringe of Stillwater and were still loading plutonium and power cartridges. They had lost some men during the take-over, but not enough to impair the raiding expedition.

There was still some fighting going on around the fringes of the plant according to the last communication report, but it didn't seem to be anything more than occasional sniping. There was only one pinnace left at the nuclear plant which was still being loaded. The pinnace commanded by the Second was several miles away from the plant.

Suddenly one of the crew swore. "Missile fire! One of our craft just disappeared. The bastards hit it!"

"Which craft was it?" he asked.

They all turned and looked at Ryan, who was handling the communications station. Her face had gone pale as she looked up from the board. "The Captain's combat car," she said, her voice suddenly hoarse.

Morland gaped at her for a second, his face turning as pale as hers. "Double check on that," he ordered. He felt his heart sink—the Captain! He hadn't liked the man much, but still he was the *captain.* Orrick was a hard but fair officer, and the only one of the ship's high command who didn't play favorites.

The entire bridge crew turned to their instruments. A lady, whom he'd suspected was the Captain's mistress, was openly crying. One by one their heads swung back to look at him, each one nodding confirmation.

He ordered the news sent to the Second, who was now the acting Captain.

"Confirmed," said Byrne's voice over the speaker. "I'll return to the *Nebula* shortly. We've detected the launching site. We're attacking that area now."

His telescopic-screen showed Bryne's pinnace launching a number of missiles at a part of the city that seemed to be mainly industrial buildings. The missile barrage continued long after the entire area was engulfed in flames.

It was serious overkill as far as Morland was concerned, but he wasn't going to relay his disapproval to the new captain. Byrne was not a man who tolerated being second-guessed, nor did he have any hesitation about showing his displeasure to subordinates who didn't follow orders to the letter.

He heard Byrne ordering everyone at the nuclear plant to cease looting and to start evacuating the planet. He checked the personnel tell-tales on the main board. Besides the five dead crewmembers that had been in the captain's combat car, there were half a dozen casualties on the ground. Another two squads of ground troopers were away from the nuclear plant site looting other areas of the city.

Morland turned to one of the other screens, punching the combination for the deck chief. When he came on he told him to launch whichever pinnace had the least amount of freight left in it to help Captain Byrne pick up the troops remaining on the planet.

He had that information sent to Byrne and thought over his new position. He hadn't liked Captain Thomas Orrick, but he had been a fair, if distant and formal presence. On the other hand, Fergus Byrne had treated him rudely from his first day aboard the *Nebula*; he wasn't looking forward to serving under him. For all he knew, Byrne might feel the same way about him. *I'll be cashiered when this voyage ends,* he thought. *No use worrying about the future, though; best to focus on the tasks at hand.*

"Bring the *Nebula* down to within a quarter mile of the surface to provide support," Morland ordered.

Everyone looked at him in surprise, but complied with his order.

Captain Orrick had always kept the *Nebula* miles above any fighting. He claimed they could see the fighting better and use their reserves more efficiently that way. But he'd also confided once to Morland that this strategy reduced potential battle damage to the ship.

He looked up from his instruments in annoyance. The pinnace still had not been launched. He called the deck chief and asked what the problem was. The chief looked as if he would rather be anywhere else at the moment.

"Sir, most of the crewmen have left. None of the pinnace pilots are available."

"Did you relay my orders to them not to leave the dock area?" asked Morland.

The Chief looked very uncomfortable and didn't reply. Morland waited, saying nothing.

Finally the Chief spoke. "Aye, aye, sir. I did."

Morland thought for a moment. "Who is the ranking officer down there, Chief?"

The chief looked around for a few seconds, "Officer Duggan, sir."

"Tell him to grab whatever crew he can roundup and take out a pinnace to support Captain Byrne and assist with troop pickup. Can you do that, Chief?"

"Yes, sir," the Chief said, looking embarrassed. "I'll tell him."

"Don't tell Duggan, order him. Understood, Chief?"

"Aye, aye, sir." This time he sounded like he meant it.

Morland reported the incident in the bridge log, though he had no idea how Byrne would react to it. *It all depends on whether or not any of the crew disobeying orders are his personal favorites,* he thought sourly.

The pinnace had just launched from the ship, when suddenly one of the signals-and-detection officers reported, "Bogeys being launched from the surface! Two sites, three, four."

Byrne's pinnace was at the center of most of the missile fire and began firing counter-missiles as it tried to dodge the incoming rockets. As Morland watched, one got through, rocking the pinnace. *The armor isn't very thick on those pinnaces,* he thought. *They can't take too many hits like that.*

He punched up the code for Duggan's pinnace.

"Reese, where are you?"

"We're moving to intercept," Duggan replied.

Though they were descending as fast as they safely could in an atmosphere, the *Nebula* was still miles from the site. The pinnace could get there much faster.

He watched Duggan's ship on the screen. They were firing counter-missiles, trying to intercept the missiles being fired at Byrne's pinnace. Both pinnaces were also launching offensive missiles at the launching sites. Veazey had taken over the *Nebula's* missile station and had also begun firing at the launch sites on the planet.

"More missiles coming from new sites!" Ryan cried. "Some of them are aimed at the nuclear plant!"

Another signals officer was informing the pinnace at the nuclear plant about the incoming missiles. Veazey began targeting the new launch sites.

Morland looked at the screens. There were no counter-missiles being launched from the pinnace on the ground. Ryan called the pinnace again, but on one replied. As the bridge crew watched in horror, it vanished in a series of explosions.

Someone was swearing at the top of their lungs. Once he'd calmed down slightly he realized that it was coming from him. He would have thrown up if there was anything in his stomach. *I can't remember the last time I ate,* he thought, as he gagged on stomach acid.

Groundside the nuclear plant vanished in a mushroom cloud. He watched numerous tell-tales on the main board switch from green to red. Some of them blinked for a few moments, indicating failing life signs. Then they all turned solid red. Everyone on the ground at the nuclear plant was dead.

Some contragravity units remained in the air high above the nuclear plant; there were several troop cars and a number of one-man cavalry mounts. They were tossed around by the blast winds and several of them disappeared in the broiling clouds. More red lights.

He ordered everyone who was low on ammunition back to the *Nebula*. The other survivors began to move toward the nearest of the two groups of troopers still on the ground. The air was suddenly clear of missiles.

"Duggan," Morland said, calling the two pinnaces. "There are still two bodies of troops on the planet." He gave their locations. "Are you able to pick them up?"

"Yes," Duggan replied, then promptly headed for the troops farthest away from the *Nebula*. There was no reply from Byrne's pinnace and he repeated the message.

Finally, "Captain Byrne, here," came in on audio; there was no visual transmission. "We are badly damaged, out of offensive missiles and unable to make pickup." The pinnace was moving slowly toward the ship. "I am returning to the *Nebula*."

"We will come get you, sir," said Morland, slowing down and altering course toward Byrne's position. There weren't any signs of additional missile sites, but Veazey was firing the short range guns toward any activity their probes could detect down below.

Byrne's pinnace came into view. There were several additional scars on it from missile strikes. When he checked, the tell-tales showed only three people on board. That was why it had responded so sluggishly to the attacks. It was short most of its regular crew. He asked Byrne why.

"Never mind," Byrne snapped back, though his voice quavered in a way Morland had never heard before. "Did you take care of all the missile sites?"

Before he could reply someone yelled, "More bogeys coming up! Both at the pinnaces and us."

He heard Veazey ordering counter-missiles launched.

"Hurry, Captain!" he said. "Get behind us and we will protect you."

"I'm trying!" Byrne said desperately. "Duggan, get back here and help cover us."

Morland activated a private channel between the *Nebula* and Duggan's pinnace. "Disregard that order, Duggan," he said.

Byrne wasn't thinking straight. Duggan couldn't possibly get there in time to make any difference. Furthermore, he was in command of the only ship close to the troops on the ground.

Watching on the big screen he saw a missile catch Byrne's pinnace, explode, then spin it around. Counter-missiles fired wildly from the pinnace. Morland looked helplessly at the instruments. The *Nebula* was going as fast as it safely could in an atmosphere.

Then another missile hit the pinnace, opening up a gaping wound in its side. Ryan looked back powerlessly, shaking her head; the pinnace was still almost a minute away. He felt a slight jar and became aware of red lights blinking on the board. Two missile impacts.

He turned back to the main screen just in time to see another missile slam into the pinnace. He watched in horror, along with the rest of the bridge crew, as the ship disintegrated in a fiery cloud of shrapnel and debris.

III

When he realized that Silvia was speaking to him, he asked her to repeat herself.

"What are your orders, Captain?"

Her question didn't really connect for an instant. Ship captains were veterans in their forties or fifties with decades of experience. They weren't twenty-eight year olds on their first voyage as a senior officer. He realized everyone was staring at him and shoved his thoughts to one side.

Missile fire had ceased and Duggan's pinnace had weathered the storm, taking only one hit. He had landed and was loading one of the squads of ground troopers.

He directed everyone to carry on searching for any other missile sites and to continue protecting the surviving ground-fighters. Duggan was likely to get there first, as the *Nebula* had to readjust its course and get the Abbot lift-and-drive engines back up to full speed after trying to save Byrne. He thought about launching the last pinnace and decided not to. It would just be another target without adding significant firepower.

It was difficult to see the city underneath them, even with the telescopic-screen. There was so much smoke from fallout and burning buildings that it felt like night was falling. He was surprised to realize it was only early afternoon. Somehow it felt like they had been fighting all day.

Duggan's pinnace had finished loading and was headed toward another squad of ground troops.

"Any signs of more missiles?" Morland asked.

Several of the bridge crew replied simultaneously in the negative. Everyone seemed to have their attention focused on locating missile launchers. They'd already paid a big price for being caught unawares.

He wondered what ever had possessed Byrne to take a pinnace out with only two crewmen. He shrugged mentally, *I'll probably never know.* He began issuing orders, moving personnel around to fill the spots vacated by those crew members who had been killed. A healthy share of this voyage's profits were going to be paid out in death benefits.

After a few minutes he became aware that one of the ship's officers had not responded to his orders. "Where's Astrogator Didzia," he asked, puzzled. He didn't see his name listed on the main board as being aboard ship.

There was a pause while several people examined their instruments. A few shook their heads indicating that they couldn't find anything. Then Silvia Ryan turned to him, her face drained of color. "David," she almost whispered. "Didzia was on Byrne's pinnace."

He leaned back in his chair, stunned. In a day of almost inexplicable errors and misjudgments, this was the climax. It was an iron law among Space Vikings that at least one astrogator always had to remain aboard ship during a raid. There were too many things that could go wrong on a raid, as had been amply proved today. The Second Officer was the main astrogator. Didzia was his backup. Without him the *Nebula* had no way to get home!

One by one, everyone on the bridge reached the same conclusion. They all turned and looked at him. He looked back at them, trying to hide the fact that he didn't have any answers. After everything that had happened today, he just felt numb.

It was Veazey who spoke first. "Wasn't Reese Duggan studying navigation?"

The *Nebula* had finally reached a position over the pinnace and the remaining ground troopers. The troopers had insisted on remaining long enough to load the gold and jewels they had found in a large bank vault. He wanted to order Duggan to leave immediately but couldn't think of any plausible reason to do so, since there were no further signs of any resistance. He didn't want to tell Duggan that he was their only chance of leaving the Agni system alive. He might as well save him from worrying any more than he had to.

That came an hour later, after the pinnace was safely back inside the ship. Morland ordered the bridge crew to place the *Nebula* in high orbit around Agni and went to the landing deck to meet Duggan. He had debated whether to tell him immediately or wait a while. Given that Duggan liked to celebrate a successful raid as wholeheartedly as any crewmember, he decided he'd better tell him now rather than wait a few days until he sobered up.

Duggan went pale when he heard the news that he was the ship's sole astrogator. Morland waited patiently. After a few seconds he saw that Duggan was coming to grips with the situation.

"I don't know that I can do this, David."

"Sure you can," Morland replied with more emphasis than he felt. "You've taken some classes and watched Didzia numerous times."

"Yes, but that's not the same as *doing* it."

"Whatever you need," Morland said. "I'll give you *carte blanche.* Personnel, whatever."

Duggan thought for a few moments. "There might be some charts and books that I don't have in the Second's, sorry, former Second's quarters. If I could look for them, Captain?"

It felt strange, almost otherworldly, to be called captain. He shook his head to clear it; then waved over a few troopers and told them to escort Duggan to wherever he needed to go. The act of standing for just a few minutes had worn him out. Stabbing pains, almost like electric shocks, were racing through his leg. He was about to take the elevator to the med room and climb into a robomedic for a few days when squad leader Xavier Burris came over to him.

"Sir, message from Officer Ryan," he said, handing him his personal communicator.

"Captain," Ryan said. "Hill in Weapons Control has armed the Planetbuster and says he's going to launch it. I've ordered him to stop, but he won't listen to me. He says the wogs need to pay for the deaths of the Captain and all the others."

Morland swore wearily. This was all he needed; a Planetbuster was capable of leveling an entire city, as well as starting a major earthquake.

He told her to relay orders to Hill that under no circumstances was he to launch any missiles at Agni and that he was on his way to Weapons Control.

As he started to limp toward the Weapons room, Burris reached out and stopped him. "Captain, Officer Ryan said I was to escort you wherever you went. She figures with some of the things that went on today some of the crewmen might be a little on edge."

Morland protested for a moment then acquiesced gracefully. *She might be right,* he thought. He didn't object at all when the squad leader called over a dozen troops and a one-man air-cavalry mount and promptly placed him on the mount. Whatever the medic had sprayed on his leg a few hours ago was beginning to wear off. The leg was throbbing again as they headed to Weapons Control.

IV

He paused at the doorway. Weapons Control was a hotbed of activity. Several people were clustered around the main computer terminal. Others were opening a cabinet. That puzzled him for a moment until he realized there were personal weapons inside.

"Override the bridge controls," Hill ordered. He was a short, slender man in his early forties. Morland didn't know Hill well. In his few encounters with him he had been like many of the older crewmembers who had been with the *Nebula* for a long time—sullen and unfriendly to the point of rudeness. Former Captain Orrick had been lax in both discipline and ship maintenance.

"Disregard that order!" Morland exclaimed, as he entered the room, still on the one-man cavalry mount. "Everyone resume your stations."

Hill quickly turned around, snarling a response. "Who are you to give us orders? You're brand new on this ship."

Before Morland could reply, Burris spoke for him. "Because he's the Captain, that's why." Burris was warily watching the crew still near the arms cabinet. Some of them had moved away, clearly wanting to avoid any confrontation.

Morland trained his twin 15mm machine guns at the remaining men.

Several remained with faces frozen in anger.

"The Captain and all his senior officers are dead," Burris added.

"I don't care who's dead," Hill cried out. "I've served the *real* Captain over twenty years. And I'm going to avenge his death." He turned back to the computer and started punching buttons.

"Mr. Hill, I am ordering you to step away from that computer and return to your station," Morland said firmly. *Even if he does stand down, I'd better not leave him on duty,* he decided. *He's likely to try it again. I should confine him to his quarters.*

Hill swung around quickly, his eyes even more enraged. "I'm not taking orders from you!" he shouted, turning and gesturing to the crew by the cabinet.

As one of them reached toward the cabinet Burris stepped forward and raised his rifle. "Don't even think about it," he said.

Hill's eyes swung from Morland to the troopers standing behind him. "Are you going to listen to him?" It wasn't clear at that moment whether he was speaking of Morland, Burris, or all of the squad. "You don't have to take orders from him. We can run our own ship!"

Morland didn't dare turn around to see what effect Hill's words were having on the troops behind him. That would be showing them that he thought his orders might not be obeyed. There was a pause that seemed to go on forever. From the look on Hill's face, his words hadn't been successful. Hill tensed, looking as if he were going to spring at him. He held his eyes on Hill's, willing him to stand down. He wondered if there were any bullets left in the cavalry mounts' machine guns if that wasn't successful, because he had removed his pistol when he returned to the ship. "I'm ordering you to stand down!"

Just then Burris brushed by Morland, pulling out his side arm and sticking it in Hill's face. "You've disobeyed two direct orders from the Captain," he said in a harsh voice. More conversationally, and without turning around he said, "Sir, do you want me to shoot him?"

Morland hazarded a glance toward the crew by the cabinet. None of them had moved. They were staring at Hill, waiting for a decision from him.

"No one has to die, Mr. Hill," Morland said softly.

Hill tensed again.

This is it, Morland thought. *I'll either have to kill him or I'll have no authority whatsoever on this ship, and maybe none ever again as a ship's officer.*

After a long nervous moment, Hill suddenly sighed and relaxed, his eyes going dull.

Mentally, Morland heaved a sigh of relief, then he turned to Burris. "Have Mr. Hill and these crewmembers," he said, pointing to the crewmen by the cabinet, "taken to the brig."

Burris gestured to a sergeant, who took everyone indicated into custody and escorted them out of the room.

Morland turned to the rest of the people in the room. "Does anyone else have a problem with taking my orders?" he demanded.

The remaining crewmembers looked at each other shaking their heads.

One man, looking around and seeing that he was the ranking crewmember, said "No, sir. I understand Mr. Hill's actions—I'm damn mad at the Agnis myself. I'd like to see them get some payback for the Captain.... But, we will obey your orders, sir."

Morland nodded, not showing how relieved he felt. "Despite the losses, we've made out pretty damn well on this world." Indeed, the latest estimate was that they had close to half a billion Sword-World stellars worth of loot, and that was before the uranium and plutonium metal had been weighed. From what he had seen, he suspected another billion stellars. "I don't want to shoot this old cow. Who knows, we might want to come back and milk her again some day."

Everybody laughed at that, happy at an opportunity to relieve their tension. He allowed himself a brief smile and left the station.

V

"I'm sorry, David." The dark face of Konrad Veazey was a little anxious. Morland tried to rouse himself fully to answer Veazey's summons. It felt like he'd just lain down in the robomedic. He was somewhat relieved when Veazey told him he had spent over half a day there.

As the feeling started coming back into his limbs he learned why Veazey had awakened him. Word had spread among the crew about the two men he'd executed on Agni for rape; they were popular crewmembers and no one was happy about it. It appeared that the crew had also come to the realization that Reese Duggan, who had never plotted a hyperspace jump before, was the *Nebula's* only ticket back home.

There were several hundred agitated crewmembers gathered in the main dining room. Needless to say, the free-flowing alcohol available after any raid had not helped things.

"That's not all," Veazey concluded. "The word has spread that you told Duggan to plot a hyperspace jump to Imhotep. Most of the crew want to go straight back to Joyeuse."

Morland ran his fingers through his hair at the news. "Why did Duggan have to shoot his mouth off about that?"

"It wasn't Duggan, Captain," Veazey corrected him.

That's right, he thought. There were several crewmembers assigned to Duggan to give him whatever help he needed. They had been present when he had given Reese the destination. One of them must have opened his mouth, spilling the news, which apparently had spread like wildfire through the crew.

He heaved himself out of the robomedic and with Veazey's help unhooked himself from all the tubes and IVs. Then he put the leg brace back on; it still hurt, but the pain wasn't as bad as he remembered. "Have an armed squad, under Sergeant Burris, report to the infirmary and escort me to the dining room."

After what had happened in Weapons Control, he now accepted that he might need serious backup to ensure the crew complied with his orders. "I will go and talk to the crew."

"I already have two squads standing by in the corridor," Veazey said, naming the squad leaders. They included Burris, who had backed him in Weapons Control, and another squad leader he felt he could trust. If he couldn't, both he and the *Nebula* weren't likely to make it home.

Suddenly he looked around at the bare room. "Where are my clothes?"

They searched, but couldn't find anything. The most important meeting of his short career as captain was delayed because he couldn't find his pants. He sent a crew member to his quarters, who returned with his uniform. Someone had taken the effort to put on the proper insignia, while Burris presented him with the former captain's hat.

The dining room was over a third full when he entered it. The walls of the room looked as dingy as ever. Now that he was captain he was going to see about getting the ship cleaned up. It would give the crew something to do rather than sitting around wondering if they were going to make it back home alive.

He had ridden an air-cavalry mount from sick bay, but insisted on walking when he entered the room. The squads with him spread out as unobtrusively as possible. He had told the squad leaders he didn't want it to look as if he needed armed guards surrounding him. He did have a few troopers with him and they helped him up on to a table where he could be heard by everyone. Veazey had gotten him a cane so he could support himself.

As the crowd gathered around he was glad to note that there weren't that many unhappy faces. There were some that looked a little inebriated, and a few more who were just plain falling-on-the-floor drunk. He decided he'd better start them out with the good news.

"I am happy to report," Morland said. "That we have estimated our loot to have a value of between one and a half billion to two billion Sword-World Stellars."

That caused some joyful exclamations from people who hadn't heard the news yet. This was a huge haul, not the biggest in history, but big—very big. Many even applauded. There were a few raucous comments about what people planned to do with their share of the wealth.

He got their attention and went on to describe their situation, trying to paint it in the best light, including Reese Duggan having to navigate them home. There were no exclamations this time. Everyone seemed to have already heard the news.

One man asked him politely why they were going to Imhotep rather than straight back to Joyeuse? Before he could reply, several men, who'd clearly been celebrating a while, spoke up and repeated the question, making it sound more like a demand. He was happy to see that several of their fellow crewmen immediately took them to task for their behavior.

"We are not going straight back to Joyeuse because I do not intend to give up a billion stellars of our money by selling our cargo at half price on Joyeuse."

That got their attention, even if it was exaggerated.

"We have so much silver that if we try and sell it all on one planet, the price for silver would crash and we'd be lucky to receive a tenth of its true value."

He went on to explain the original plan of the voyage, which was to stop at Imhotep and trade silver, which for some reason the natives valued more than gold, for that planet's prized furs. Imhotep was less than eighty hours from Agni. From there they would then go to Hoth, one of the largest of the Space Viking bases in the Old Federation, and trade more silver there, along with the plutonium they picked up. Once they had traded enough silver, they would head back to Joyeuse.

Morland didn't say anything more because he didn't want to promise anything he couldn't deliver, but he thought a few trading stops could easily drive up the value of their loot closer to two billion stellars. He could see that he was getting through to most of the crew. Even if they didn't understand the economics of what he was discussing, they were comforted by the fact that their Captain seemed to have a plan.

There were a couple of loudmouths who were determined to spoil the good mood.

"What about Bill Wilkie?" one of them yelled.

"Yeah," said another. "And what's Mr. Hill doing in the brig?" The speaker named several others of the crew in Weapons Control, asking about them as well.

Morland could see several of the troopers moving toward the troublemakers. He waited a few moments for them to get closer.

"That will be enough of that," he said sharply.

He waited a few seconds for that to sink in and continued. "Everyone who is in the brig is there because they refused to obey orders. We had problems yesterday because people decided to ignore orders and do whatever they wanted to. That kind of disobedience will not be tolerated on *my* ship."

He had their attention now. He knew that word of all the mistakes made during the raid, from the alternate astrogator leaving the ship, to the pinnace on the ground being unmanned, and the undetected missile launcher that killed the captain, had spread throughout the ship. "If everyone had obeyed Captain Orrick's standing orders, we would not be in any trouble."

The friends of the more agitated crewmembers were doing their best to shut them up.

The man who had first asked the question about their destination spoke up again. "Captain, I'm not concerned about the shares; I just want to get home."

Morland was pleased to see that he didn't seem to have much support. He decided to lighten the mood.

"You all know Reese Duggan." He paused. "Do you think he is good for only one jump?" he asked with a big smile.

People grinned at that, some laughing aloud. Others began yelling out comments about Duggan's party exploits.

Sensing it was time to leave on an upward note, he gestured to the troopers to help him down from the table. As he climbed down he inwardly winced at the pain in his injured leg. He still needed a few days in the robomedic, but he wasn't likely to get it anytime soon. It would be better to wait until they were in hyperspace. Until then, the crew needed to know that their Captain was on the job, even if he was propped up in a chair on the bridge unable to walk.

VI

The grey of hyperspace had faded to the black starlit void several minutes ago. The brilliant light of the stars pierced the darkness. No one on the bridge said anything, waiting for him to speak first. They had stopped the *Nebula* for a sight-stop so they could see where they were since there was no way to do a course reckoning while in hyperspace—just the endless gray-wash of hyperspace on the viewscreens.

It was standard operating procedure for a hyperspace ship to take a sight-stop about a light-year from their destination, especially if two or more ships were traveling together, so they could coordinate their microjumps and planet arrival times. In this case, with an untested astrogator, it was to determine if they were where they were supposed to be.

He sat quietly, watching the tense back of Reese Duggan, knowing that Reese was searching for familiar star references for Imhotep. The sparkling bridge, which reflected a newly cleaned *Nebula*, wouldn't mean a thing if they were lost in space with no hope of returning home.

Suddenly Duggan relaxed and turned to him with a smile. "Captain, request permission to begin hyperspace microjumps to Imhotep."

The crew burst into cheers.

He smiled back. "Good job, Reese."

"Ryan," he said, turning to the new Second Officer. "Tell the crew to prepare for landing on Imhotep."

HOTH

The stop at Imhotep had gone better than expected; they'd gotten more in trade for some of the silver than Captain Morland had expected. Plus, they'd been able to unload a lot of the surplus machinery they had on hand in trade for several hundred lots of beautiful pelts. Imhotep was a Civ-Level 6 world transitioning into a Level 7, with electricity beginning to replace steam power; therefore, they had a good appetite for primitive machinery, like what they'd stolen on Agni.

Now he was aboard one the pinnaces traveling down to Hoth. Nikky Everrards was Prince of Hoth, or at least he had been when Morland was last on Joyeuse aboard the *Pay Dirt.* Of course, rulers of Space Viking base worlds were often subject to change so he wouldn't know for sure who was in charge until they landed. They were not giving out any information on the radio which was standard procedure for security purposes. They'd been met by warships and boarded twice by Inspectors from Hoth's Navy; once right after their last micro-jump and the second time just before they reached the fourth planet of the Iverson's System's gas giant, Loki. Both ships carried the Everrard's family emblem, a white skull impaled by a red sword, so he felt safe assuming that the Everrards were still in charge.

Still, it wouldn't be unprecedented to find out that one of Nikky's siblings, like his younger brother Johann, was now in charge. " Uneasy lies the head that wears the crown," was one of Otto Harkaman's favorite quotes and said it all in his opinion.

Hoth's major businesses were acting as a clearing house for ship cargos and ship repair. Their clients were a dangerous and demanding bunch of Space Vikings. It wasn't unheard of for several Space Viking ships to band together and take over a base world. It was cheaper, but more dangerous, than founding a new one.

The last base take-over Morland had heard about was on Seshat, where three Space Viking ships had defeated Seshat's two-ship navy, then ransacked the planet. Instead of leaving with their loot, they'd taken over and created a short-lived triumvirate. As was typical of such ad hoc governments, the triumvirate hadn't lasted long before Ivan Gherhart had taken over and proclaimed himself King of Seshat; in quick order he had promptly run the planet into the ground. Now only a ship on its last legs would deign to raid the place.

Hoth's ruling family, the Everrards, were originally a noble family from Curtana, who had first raided the world some two centuries ago. They'd liked the mild climate and hard-working natives and made it their home. Originally, they had used it as a base of operation for raids along the outer rim of the former Federation. It hadn't taken long before the Everrards realized there was more money and less danger in repairing battle-damaged ships than in raiding, so they had brought in a crew of shipwrights from the Sword-Worlds and gone into the ship repair business. They had done quite well, too, until Lucas Trask showed up and built his own ship repair facilities on Tanith that were both cheaper and more up-to-date than what the Everrards' offered.

Still, Hoth was an important stop for buying and selling plunder; many Space Vikings, who didn't like the Trasks or what they stood for, used it as a dumping ground for goods they didn't want to haul back to the Sword-Worlds which wanted mostly high-end luxury goods. However, most Space Viking cargos—reflecting the Neobarbarian worlds they raided—were low-tech goods, machinery and slaves. Often items of little value in the Sword-Worlds were quite valuable to the more technologically backward planets of the Old Federation. The Sword-

Worlders and most Space Vikings looked down on slavers, but there was a good market for them on certain worlds.

Since face counted a lot at the Hoth Mercantile Clearing House, Morland had brought along a squad of ground fighters in their *Nebula* dress uniforms, gold and blacks. He had put Sergeant Xavier Burris in charge of the squad. The only ship mate he'd brought along was the *Nebula's* Ship's Services Officer, a dour little man named Sigard Olthar. He was a chronic complainer, but no one on the ship knew value or was better at horse-trading than Sigard.

As the pinnace approached Hoth's major city and spaceport of Khmun, Morland used the telescopic-viewscreen to study the city for signs of war or civil unrest. The buildings were ramshackle with towering contragravity towers and spires mixed in with ground-hugging buildings. Still, overall things appeared calm and there were no damaged buildings. He noted six spaceships were docked in the eight-pointed star of the great spaceport. At the center was an octagonal building, the Hoth Mercantile Center with a tower rising out of the center that rose to a height of two thousand feet. The Royal Tower was the Everrard's palace and center of administration.

Khmun Spaceport wasn't as large or as impressive as Tanith's Rivington Spaceport, but it was a substantial port and sign of Hoth's prosperity and importance in the Space Viking universe.

After landing the pinnace, they were greeted by the Port Inspector and a squad of local troopers. After the usual greeting, the Inspector said, "Captain Morland, as with all first time visitors, Prince Everrards requests your presence at the Royal Tower Audience Chamber."

Since their vessel contained only samples and was empty of cargo, the inspection was perfunctory and Morland and Burris, his bodyguard, were quickly escorted to the Royal Tower. Along the way, he wasn't surprised to see a coffle of bedraggled slaves working on clean-up duty. One of the biggest problems facing most Space Viking base worlds was how to control the native population: some did it by rigid control and punishment, others by enslaving the local populations and working them to death, while the Trasks did it by ruling over their subjects, Space Viking émigrés and locals alike, on a merit basis.

The Everrards were in the middle. They gave limited freedom to the locals and brought in slaves from other worlds to do the dirty jobs no one else wanted to do, which seemed to please just about everyone except the slaves. It was a better system than the one on Jagannath where the Grathams held sway over the locals with an iron fist and everyone else, but those of Space Viking blood, were considered second-class citizens or slaves in all but in name.

Morland knew that when he founded his base world that he would follow the Trask model. Not only had it proven its worth on Tanith, but it was philosophically in line with his own minority—among Space Vikings—held egalitarian beliefs. Not that he wasn't a believer in firm discipline, but he also recognized everyone had the right to rise to their own highest level of being regardless of birth. Like Lucas Trask and Otto Harkaman before him, he believed that an enlightened monarchy was the best of the limited number of workable Terro-human governments.

The Federation had certainly proven the fallacies of republican government. Of course, it could be said that tyrants, like King Alwyn of Joyeuse, just as clearly showed one of the major deficiencies of a monarchy. Maybe a workable system of government for humans was like the quest for the Holy Grail—unobtainable but a worthy undertaking.

They took a pseudo-gravity lift to the fiftieth floor and were seated in the outside anteroom to the Presence Chamber. There were two other Space Vikings, one a captain with a grizzled countenance, and several well-dressed businessmen or industrialists.

The other captain, with a twinkle in his blue eyes, introduced himself as Captain Guthram of the *Star Smasher*, a fifteen-hundred foot warship. "Don't take offense, but you look a little young to be a Space Viking captain."

Morland nodded ruefully; his question wasn't unexpected. He briefly explained how he came to be Captain of the *Nebula*.

"If you left Agni with a shipload of plunder, you're a better man than I!" Guthram exclaimed.

He shrugged. "Just lucky."

The older man nodded. "Luck is as vital to success as being prepared; and you don't have one without the other. You're from Joyeuse, right?"

"Yes, how did you know?"

"Your accent. Besides, I met Captain Orrick of the *Nebula* before at the Charlemagne Ports of Call on Durendal a few years ago when he was doing a job for Prince Elmesan, and don't ask me which one because there are a parcel of them. He struck me as a pretty sound captain; he must have been desperate to get himself tied up with King Alwyn."

Morland said. "He had a couple of bad runs."

Guthram nodded knowingly. "He's not the only one. Pickings are getting mighty slim in this sector of the Old Federation. I'm hoping to take a loan from King Nikky so we can try our luck again."

Morland knew better than to expect Guthram to give away his itinerary, since Space Vikings were as secretive about their target worlds as fishermen were about their favorite fishing holes.

The older captain moved in closer so they wouldn't be overheard. "I'm thinking about joining up with a couple of friends. The only chickens worth plucking these days are the civilized worlds and you don't do those by yourself. Might you be interested?"

"I would be if I weren't going back to Joyeuse after this stop," he replied.

"Hmm. You might rethink that, young man. Do you really think that old tightwad Alwyn is going to let you stay on as captain of the *Nebula* once you hit Joyeuse?"

Morland thought no such thing, but he was honor bound to return to Joyeuse. He nodded.

"If I were in your boots, I'd sell off my cargo" —he smiled wickedly—"and I'd set off for some Neobarb World a few parsecs from here and declare myself king. Let the old skinflint chase you down—" He guffawed. "You wouldn't be the first, or the last. That's how the Everrards got setup here on Hoth."

Before Guthram could go on in this vein, the Palace Chamberlain called him through the intercom to the Presence Chamber.

"Good luck to you, lad. I have a feeling you're going to need it." They bumped fists and the older captain added, "I hope to see you again, Captain Morland. Anyone who can leave Agni with an intact ship and her holds filled with loot, is all right in my muster book."

Morland had a short wait before he was called into the Presence Chamber. He saw Guthram leaving out the back portal with slumped shoulders.

The Presence Chamber was outfitted grandly with beautiful wall hangings, tapestries and art masterpieces adorning the walls. The entire wall opposite the Throne of Gold was one huge mosaic, made entirely of precious gems and metals, showing the original conquest of Hoth, from the Everrards' point of view, of course. Above the Hoth Throne of Gold was the Everrards' blazon, a silver skull impaled by what appeared to be a sword made entirely of rubes. King Alwyn's audience chamber looked pathetic in comparison; no wonder he was jealous of his Old

Federation cousins.

King Nikky in person was as impressive as his presence chamber. He was a big man with a broad girth who looked like he could acquit himself with honor in a sword fight or a street brawl. He had a full brown beard and wore a gold crown that might have bent the neck of a lesser man. The King was younger—probably late thirties—than he'd expected.

After the Chamberlain announced him, the King said, "Welcome to Hoth, Captain Morland."

"Thank you, Your Highness."

"I understand you've just returned from Agni with your holds full, is that correct."

"Yes, sire. We had both great success and great failure."

"Explain?"

"We pulled off a successful raid, but unfortunately we lost most of our senior officers, sire."

"Including Captain Orrick, I believe."

"Yes, sire, he took a combat car out to view the battle and got hit by an Agni nuke. We also lost our Executive Officer and Astrogator. We were lucky to make it out of that system."

The King nodded. "Orrick was a good commander. You're lucky to have learned under his command. But he was an unlucky son-of-a-bitch! His first big score in a long time and he takes one up the tailpipe.

"But enough of that, young man. I believe you may be in a position to solve one of my problems." He paused and gave Morland a penetrating stare.

"If there's anything I can do to help Your Highness, please let me know?" Morland felt uncomfortable, since he wasn't very practiced in dealing with kings and nobles in general. Nor did he like it when they implied favors he neither owed nor was obligated for, since he was not a subject of the Hoth. On the other hand, a nobody like himself didn't lightly anger a monarch who might throw a spanner in your works if you didn't give him what he wanted.

"I understand you were able to obtain some radioactives during your raid on Agni, is this correct?"

Morland didn't know whether or not this was a good guess or if there was a leak among his crew. It wasn't all that hard to make a quick radio transmission from orbit to surface. Regardless, the cat was out of the bag. "Yes, sire. We were able to obtain approximately fourty-eight tons of radioactives. Two-thirds is enriched uranium."

King Nikky drew back in surprise, his mouth an open O.

"We hit their refinery at the right time, and a couple of nuclear plants as well." The going price was one thousand stellars per ounce for enriched uranium and ten times that for plutonium metal.

"You have certainly come to Hoth at the right time, my young captain. I'd like to purchase half of your enriched uranium at the going price. If that is agreeable."

Nikky's face took on a hard cast that promised dire consequences should his deal be thwarted. No fool he, Morland quickly agreed. He didn't know what Captain Orrick's *deal* was with King Alwyn so he could plead ignorance if it turned out that Alwyn wanted all the radioactives for Joyeuse. Although he couldn't imagine him being too unhappy with almost a billion stellars in profit.

"I'll leave it to my Chamberlain to work out the details. I take it you'll want payment in precious metals, not Hoth banknotes?"

Morland nodded.

The King expelled a deep breath. "Unknowingly, you may have saved a kingdom. Of course, my words go no further than this room, *understood?*"

"Of course, Your Highness," he said, thinking: *I'd much rather make a friend and ally than shoot off my mouth.*

"Right now there's a dearth of radioactive materials in this sector of the Old Federation. The planets who have the ore have either lost it, don't know how to mine or refine it, been bombed back to the Stone Age or are too well protected. This whole sector is played out as far as I can see. We're either going to have to go deeper into the Federation, or band together and take out the civilized words which will be costly. I'm beginning to think we're at the end of the Space Viking era…."

Don't say that, Morland thought, *hell, my career is just beginning!*

After shaking on the deal, he left on good terms with one of the most powerful men in the Space Viking community of worlds. He wasn't sure if he could bank King Nikky's goodwill, but he believed he was a man of his word.

He left the place to join Sigard inside the Hoth Mercantile Center which was as busy as a beehive; there were four ships with full holds to be sold and lots of merchants going over sample lots and cargo manifests. Plus hordes of government inspectors and tax collectors since Hoth took a three and a half percent duty fee on all import and export commercial transactions. A few of the Space Viking base worlds had gotten greedy in the past and raised their duty fees to as high as ten percent, only to see their income drop precipitously as ships stayed away. Three and a half percent duty tax was the norm set by Tanith and now almost universal among Space Viking base worlds.

The current silver to gold ratio was twenty one-ounce silver crowns to a single one-ounce golden Sword-World Stellar. The *Nebula's* holds carried over fifteen hundred tons of silver bullion and scrap. The trick was to sell only as much as the market would bear, otherwise they'd take a loss. No one world could handle so much silver which was why he'd declined to return directly from Agni back to Joyeuse.

Once again, they got lucky. There was a party of freebooters from one of the Sword Worlds—from their accent, he suspected Tizona—who were seeking gold and silver bullion. He suspected they were going to use the precious metals to hire an army or a fleet to conquer a planet. In return they received rare art masterpieces, a thousand cases of Tizona vodka, power unit cartridges, machinery and robot servers; all of which would bring a good price on Joyeuse. He was tempted to do some needed repairs, but he wanted to get back home and let the investors see for themselves what a bad beating the ship had taken on Agni.

Thanks to Sigard Olthar's bargaining skills they were able to unload over half their silver on the freebooters and another quarter to the King's purchasing agents. When they got back to the *Nebula*, it took a week to unload all the uranium, silver and furs they'd sold and to bring back all the trade goods they'd traded for and purchased. During the two-day celebration that followed, Morland was regaled by both the crew and ground fighters for salvaging what could have been a complete disaster on Agni. Nor were they unhappy at the prospect of their share of what looked to be a two billion stellar haul. Morland only hoped King Alwyn was one-tenth as pleased.

JOYEUSE

I

Captain Morland found himself standing behind his Astrogator's seat at the bridge. He was staring into the gray void of the outside viewscreen, which had been displaying the same bland surface for the last four thousand hours, or one hundred and sixteen Galactic Standard days since they'd left Hoth. Suddenly the viewscreen flashed into a whirling kaleidoscope of color as the hyperspace field collapsed. Everyone saw it differently, but no one could fully describe its full beauty. Thousands of artists over the millennia had tried to capture its magic in many mediums, but none had succeeded. Maybe it was because each mind saw the swirling colors through its own filter.

Suddenly the viewscreen displayed a jeweler's black backdrop studded with bright diamonds shining in all their glory. Morland expelled the breath he'd been unconsciously holding. He could watch this starry transformation a million times and always be entranced.

In the center of the scintillating stars was the yellow orb of Maxwell's Star, the sun of Joyeuse. It was about the size of a gold Sword-World stellar held at arms-length. The light was twelve hours old.

"Good work, Reese," he said.

Congratulations were coming in from all over the ship. Surprisingly, some of the accolades were for him as well as Reese Duggan. Duggan announced that they were twelve light-years from Joyeuse. The praise was well-deserved. With just a slight miscalculation by their untested astrogator, they might have found themselves in an unsurveyed sector of space, spending the next couple of years searching for a way back home until either their fuel ran out or their food.

From here they would make five or six microjumps until they were a light-second away. Any closer to something the size of Joyeuse and the collapsing field itself would kick the ship back half a million miles.

Reese Duggan was ignoring the congratulations; he was already busy pressing data buttons and checking calculations for the next series of jumps. "We'll need six microjumps now, and I'll try to get within ten hours normal-space distance."

Twelve hours later they were approaching the surface of Joyeuse using their normal-space drive. Morland stepped down from the command chair, extending his hand and adding his congratulations to those coming over the radio and being said in person.

"Well done, Duggan," he said, as they shook hands. "I'll be recommending you for a bonus," he added.

Duggan colored slightly as he murmured his thanks.

I hope my recommendation is worth something, Morland wondered. He had no idea how the Nebula's owners would react to all the deaths and damage to the ship that had occurred on Agni. They might decide to use him as a scapegoat, holding him responsible for the previous officers' action—stranger things had happened when a captain was lost without a reasonable explanation. However, the big haul they'd made on Agni would certainly go a long way to ameliorating any bad feelings.

As he mentally ran through what had happened during the long hyperspace voyage, Morland couldn't see what he might have done differently. And Sword-World law was well established regarding what happened to people who assumed new positions duc to deaths on a voyage, so he had the Captain's share of a lucrative raid to look forward to.

Momentarily allowing himself to daydream, he thought about what he could do with his portion of the profits; pay off his parent's house; provide help to his sister and brother-in-law's business—there were many possibilities. Maybe he'd even splurge and get a few fancy Space Viking jackets like those worn by successful captains. He mentally shook his head at these dreams of improved status in the world. He didn't know if the Nebula's owners would keep him on as captain but he was certain that his experience as captain would allow him a chance at better opportunities in the future.

Suddenly he found himself stifling a yawn. He had been up almost twenty-two hours straight. He wanted to be on the bridge when the Nebula returned to the Joyeuse system from Hoth.

"Captain," Sylvia Ryan said peremptorily, after seeing him yawn, She pointed toward the bridge portal. "We're in normal space now. You're overdue for some sleep."

She turned and grabbed Duggan by the arm. "And take him with you."

Duggan chuckled with the rest of the bridge crew and turned to leave, asking Ryan to wake him up when they were an hour from the surface.

The ringing in his ear roused him from sleep and at first he wondered where he was. Morland relaxed when he realized it was the alarm in his new captain's quarters. He had not moved into the cabin until after they arrived at Imhotep, and only then after the other officers insisted that he needed to, as a symbol of being captain. The room was palatial compared to his former quarters, and the furnishings were fit for a king. He didn't have much to add, just some personal items and a few family photos.

He pressed the button which opened the door and sat up in bed. Konrad Veazey, now First Officer, entered the room. "Captain, there's something not right groundside on Joyeuse. It looks like serious fighting around the capital city."

He continued explaining as Morland splashed water on his face and hurriedly dressed. Two hours from the surface, the radio tower at the Longinus Spaceport had stopped broadcasting. A few minutes later, it began broadcasting again, stating that the tower was under control of forces loyal to Count Benedict and calling on everyone to rise up against the regicide, King Alwyn.

As they hurried up to the bridge Morland tried to remember everything he knew about Count Benedict. Beyond that he owned Boarshold, the largest industrial complex on the planet, he couldn't recall much. As they entered the bridge Ryan updated them.

"There's fighting all over Longinus," she said. "And Duke Wiltham has joined the rebellion on Benedict's side."

Duke Wiltham he did know. He was Duke of Corsuble, the second largest port on Joyeuse. Some of the ships he had worked for had traded at Corsuble.

"King Alwyn has requested that all loyal troops and ships come to his aid. And Captain," Ryan said, apprehension covering her narrow face, "He specifically asked for us."

Morland sat down, running his hand through his hair, absently taking the cup of coffee handed him by one of the staff. Alwyn was one of the owners of the *Nebula*, as well as his king. There was only one way he could honorably respond.

"Are there any major ships involved yet?" he asked.

Ryan re-seated herself and checked some instruments. "There are four ships fighting near the King's palace, two on each side. There are two others coming that should reach them in about two and a half hours."

"Full speed ahead, all hands to battle-stations," Morland commanded.

The last order was probably unnecessary as the battle-stations board was a bedazzling glitter of red lights displaying full combat readiness. The system boards in front of him were all lit up as well, showing the battle readiness of every system on the ship, but Veazey repeated his words over the *Nebula's* internal comline.

"The other ships are asking our intentions and identity, Captain," said Ryan.

"Who are they?" he asked.

"The ships fighting for the King are," she said, then paused for a moment to collect her thoughts. "The large one is the *Crusher of Worlds* and the small one is the *Houndstooth*. The two ships fighting against them are the *Falcon* and *Rocio's Prize*. The two approaching are the *Caloundra* and *Mighty Max*. All four of the rebels are fifteen hundred footers."

It was time for an announcement, Morland decided. At least they had a size advantage. "All ships," he said. "This is Space Viking ship *Nebula* declaring for King Alwyn. All ships supporting the rebellion are directed to stand down and surrender, or face destruction."

Both the *Caloundra* and *Mighty Max* changed course, heading for the *Nebula*. Time seemed to slow down until they reached extreme missile range. He felt a tightening of tension throughout the bridge. After a lucrative voyage the last thing anyone wanted was to die before they could spend their stellars.

Suddenly they were upon the two ships, missiles coming and going from each ship: Offensive missiles aimed to damage or destroy the opposing ship. Defensive missiles intended to intercept the offensive missiles before they could impact a ship. The skies between them were filled with bursts of flame as missiles met. He felt a jar telling him that not all of them had been intercepted. Flickering red lights on the board showed where the *Nebula* was hit. Automatic systems and repair crews would be racing to patch up any damage before it could get worse. They would have all been so much vapor if the *Nebula* hadn't been armored in collapsium. The thin shell of dense collapsed matter limited the damage of a nuclear missile impact to a few decks.

Then they were through the two-ship gauntlet with all three of them still intact.

As the *Nebula* turned, Morland shifted his attention to the battle between the remaining four ships. Something nagged at him as he watched them maneuver. He looked at the screen showing the two ships they had been fighting. Even though the shooting had stopped over a minute ago they were still in the process of turning around.

"We're fighting armed merchantmen," he yelled to the bridge crew. Several turned around from their stations to stare at him. Then gradually it sunk in.

Veazey crowed "We can outmaneuver them!"

Everyone went back to their tasks heartened by the suggestion. As Morland racked his brain for how to take advantage, his viewscreen showed the *Crusher of Worlds* down at the surface suddenly come apart in flaming chunks of metal. The *Houndstooth* turned and fled, leaving the *Nebula* to fight four ships by herself.

Looking at the screens he saw that the *Caloundra* and *Mighty Max* were still too far away to engage them. He was going to keep it that way. Fighting four ships at the same time, even armed freighters, was suicidal. If they ganged up on the *Nebula*, there was no way they could stop the enemy ships' combined missile fire.

"Head toward the *Falcon* and *Rocio's Prize*," he directed Ryan.

A minute out of extreme missile range, he ordered a change of course. One of the ships started to turn but the other was much slower. Even as he started to give the order Ryan was already turning to engage the first ship, which was moving sluggishly and showed serious damage on the telescopic-screen. Again missiles went out and the skies between them lit up with fireworks.

Then they were past the *Falcon* and closing in on *Rocio's Prize*, which had not been able to fire on them because they were too close to their sister ship. Ryan directed them right at the *Rocio*, missiles spewing again. They were close enough now that the short-range guns began blazing away; he could see great rips in *Rocio's* hull.

"Weapons, it's time for one of our fifty-megaton missiles."

"Aye aye, sir," Weapons said.

He watched as a fifty-megaton missile, viewscreen-piloted, head straight for a large tear in the hull. Suddenly the screens went white as the auto-filters went on and *Rocio's Prize* disappeared in a ball of fire, throwing out a shockwave that rocked the ship.

In an outer-space battle, you didn't have to worry about atmospheric effects such as shock and sound waves. This right here was a good old-fashioned slugfest. Everyone on the bridge was shouting and yelling. One of the junior officers had been thrown against a bulkhead and was bleeding from his forehead. There was the astringent smell of burnt electronics and vaporized steel.

Morland hastily checked the screens for the other ships but they were still some distance away. He looked at the board which seemed to be made up of nothing but flickering lights showing where missiles had impacted. Even more ominously much of the board was green, showing missile tubes and weapons control rooms so severely damaged that repairs hadn't even started.

"Captain," said one of the bridge crew. "The *Falcon's* turned tail."

It was true. The other ship was slowly turning away from them. Screens showed her to be heavily damaged, far more than they were. The other two ships were headed in their direction but were still far enough away to ignore. Weapons sent off a brace of missiles after the *Falcon*, then he decided to let her go and hope that she was permanently out of the battle.

"Captain, we have plenty of missiles but not enough available tubes to shoot them," one of the weapons officers reported.

"Weapons Control rooms two, three, five and seven have been damaged and are out of commission," Veazey said, concern on his face. "One and eight are back on line, but their crews aren't responding. Only four is fully functional."

We can't fight a battle with only one weapons control and a few dozen missile tubes, Morland thought, doing his best not to show his mounting frustration. They had to have more time to make repairs. But if they left the battle scene, the two remaining ships would probably attack the king's palace which was in the middle of Longinus. A glance below through the viewscreen showed that already most of the city seemed to be burning. He forced thoughts of his family's safety to the backside of his mind.

"Sylvia," he said to the Second Officer. "Head toward the *Caloundra* and *Mighty Max* but at an angle. Change course periodically but always a little further away from the intersection point. Try to draw them away from the city while our repair crews restore our weapons systems."

"Aye, sir," she replied.

"Konrad, order repair crews to one and eight," he said.

Veazey turned to comply, skepticism in his face. He knew what he was thinking. They had lost so many crew members on Agni that they were already shorthanded. Many of their backups had already been at the stations that had been damaged—probably dead.

As he examined the damage further Morland began to realize he had made a huge mistake. He had purchased new missiles on Hoth to replace those lost on Agni. However, he had not repaired the damage done to the outer hull. He had told the crew the damage wasn't severe, but that wasn't the real reason. He had wanted the ship's owners to see the kind of wounds the ship had taken, which would go a long way in explaining the deaths of the captain and the other officers. Now, they might all have to pay for that miscalculation.

Some of the incoming missiles had already hit existing weak points in the hull. Unlike the more primitive Agni missiles, which just penetrated two or three decks in, these were full powered missiles. With the collapsium hull armor already gone they had ripped deep into the *Nebula.* Critical bulkheads and compartments were also collapsium-lined; otherwise, no ship could fight once it was hulled. The nuclear blasts would blow right through the core of the ship, leaving behind an empty husk. These were not wounds that could be repaired while in flight; they needed a full-fledged shipyard for repairs.

Ryan turned suddenly, interrupting his thoughts. "Captain, Sergeant Burris insists on speaking to you."

Puzzled, he told her to put him through. Xavier Burris was a ground fighter who didn't have any backup skills useful in a ship-to-ship battle. He should be down in crew's quarters with the other noncombatants. No doubt they were all more than a little nervous. Experienced space hands would know from all the jolts and klaxons that the *Nebula* had taken numerous hits and was in trouble.

"Captain," said Burris without any ceremony. "Mr. Hill has a proposition you should hear."

Morland suddenly realized Burris was inside the brig. Before he could think that through, Hill began to talk.

"Captain I swear allegiance to you and I will follow your orders without question." Hill spoke rapidly, afraid of being interrupted. "I've been following what's going on and I know you need experienced weapons crews. All of my crew swears allegiance as well. Please release us so we can fight for our ship."

Morland thought feverishly. He didn't have much choice if he wanted the *Nebula* to survive this battle. "Sergeant Burris," he said.

"Yes, sir," Burris replied.

"I'll be sending Officer Ryan down to you. Assist her in taking charge of the missile crews. After the battle, escort them back to the brig."

"Understood, sir."

Ryan was already out of her chair by the time he spoke to her. "Divide the crews as you see fit, but get one and eight operational."

She nodded. She looked over at Veazey then turned and left the bridge. Veazey looked very uncomfortable, but didn't say anything. Morland knew the two of them were lovers, although they hadn't advertised their relationship. Nothing mattered now but survival.

He looked around to direct someone to replace Ryan in the pilot's chair. With a shock he realized that there weren't any pilots left. He thought about putting Reese Duggan in the chair, but Duggan had almost no experience as an atmospheric pilot. Aware that all eyes on the bridge were on him, he stepped out of the Captain's chair and limped over to the pilot's seat. Amazingly, until he got up, he hadn't even been aware of his leg injury.

"Continue repairs on the missile tubes," he ordered. "Everyone else prepare for some maneuvering."

11

For the next half hour Captain Morland maneuvered the *Nebula* back and forth, feinting attacks and then turning away before the enemy ships got within missile range. In ship-to-ship battles, missiles were carefully rationed; shooting them off too soon allowed the other ship's anti-missile batteries and short-range guns an excellent opportunity to take them out. The idea was to maneuver your ship within missile range and then fire your missiles. Of course, the missiles still had to thread their way through the enemy's counter-missile fire, but the odds of striking the other ship went way up the closer the two ships were to each other. Maneuverability was the *Nebula's* sole advantage over her opponents, which were souped-up freighters—not warships.

Morland was surprised that one of the ships didn't drop out of the fight and attack the palace. As he listened to the radio chatter however it became clear that the King's forces were slowly losing the ground war in Longinus, although the palace still hadn't been breached. The two ships probably thought they were doing their part by keeping the *Nebula* out of the battle.

They may be right, he thought. He didn't dare send his remaining two pinnaces out to harass the enemy, since they'd be quickly picked off by the enemy ships. In addition, the hundreds of ground fighters still alive on the ship, armed with weapons designed to handle serious opposition planetside, would make a substantial difference in the battle. However, if he tried to land the *Nebula* now he'd be a sitting duck if the two ships attacked.

Two calls came almost simultaneously.

"Missile tubes one and eight are repaired, Captain," Ryan announced.

"Weapons Control rooms one and eight are ready to go, Captain," Hill said. "We also have the Planetbuster armed and ready to launch."

"No, Mr. Hill," Morland replied quickly. "We are only a mile or two above the surface. A Planetbuster would destroy the city along with any ship it hit."

And probably a lot more besides, Morland thought.

"Yes, sir," Hill answered, without any hint of disagreement.

"All right let's go," Morland ordered, and he increased speed and directed the *Nebula* towards the two remaining enemy ships. He had determined after the last fight that besides maneuverability, the other advantage the *Nebula* had was her short-range weapons. It made sense. When converting a freighter into a warship, it was a lot easier and cheaper just to add some missile tubes through the corridors, rather than taking out a few decks to build short-range weapon emplacements.

He had hoped to catch the two ships off guard but their missiles launched almost simultaneously with the *Nebula's.* He changed course slightly, increasing speed as he headed between the two ships. That did have an effect, he noticed, as the *Caloundra* lagged behind the *Mighty Max* in making the turn with them. Then they were less than two miles away and the short range guns cut loose. They were past before he could see what kind of damage had been done.

"How'd we do, Konrad?" he asked as he swung the *Nebula* around for another pass.

Veazey, normally not too excitable, was grinning as he looked away from the sensors. "We got them good. Serious damage to both ships, Captain."

Morland turned in his seat to examine the board. There were plenty of new green lights, showing more missile tubes permanently out. As he watched, some of the flashing red lights steadied, showing they were repaired. This was it; the *Nebula* had only one more good run left in them. He felt a growing battle frenzy and forced himself to calm down.

"Let's finish this," he said. "Tell everyone to tighten their harnesses."

He turned back toward the two ships while Konrad repeated his announcement over all the ships com lines. The ships were a little more separated than usual and he wanted to see if he could engage them one at a time. The *Mighty Max* started to slow, waiting for the *Caloundra* to get closer. Morland began punching buttons rapidly. His coffee mug tipped over and an alarm started blinking as the *Nebula's* stabilizers struggled to keep up with his maneuvers. Those crew members who hadn't been seated grabbed at safety lines or tumbled over.

The *Caloundra* was at a much higher altitude than the *Max*; he headed toward her as fast as they could go. Once again missiles shot out and there seemed to be nothing but fire and smoke between the *Nebula* and the smaller ship. Then it loomed ahead and the short range guns hammered away. As they passed, he saw orange and red flames blossom all over the *Caloundra* and he knew she'd taken one too many midship hits.

"She's a goner!" someone cried, as the *Caloundra* disappeared in a pulsing ball of red fire.

They didn't have time for any celebration as the *Mighty Max* was coming up rapidly and he heard Veazey yelling to Weapons to give her everything they had. He felt several big jolts and the *Nebula* wiggle-wobbled, then stabilized. When they reached short-gun range, the other ship suddenly veered away.

He concentrated on turning the *Nebula* to close with the *Mighty Max* in case she was trying to escape. The ship responded slowly. Clearly the *Nebula* had taken a lot of damage in the last round. He studied the main viewscreen to see where the *Mighty Max* was headed.

"She's running away!" a crewman cried out.

"No," Veazey said. "She's going the wrong way. She trying to land!"

Morland finally located the *Mighty Max* on one of the screens. He could see several large holes on her hull with black smoke pouring out. She was swinging back and forth, indicating that her drive thrusters and contragravity were not working in unison. She did slow her descent enough so that her landing, if you could call it that, did not result in any explosions. However, her landing legs collapsed underneath her and the ship rolled over. It was clear the *Mighty Max* wasn't going to lift off again. He doubted that many of the ship's crew would walk out of that crash landing alive.

He turned and looked at the board and gasped. He blinked his eyes a few times but nothing changed. There were so many green lights he wondered how they could still be up in the air. When the haze of battle began to clear he saw that the engines were fine, but that he had only a dozen missile tubes and just one weapons control room remaining intact.

Morland maneuvered the *Nebula* slowly, hovering over the telecast station so that they could jam it. The station was still broadcasting support of the rebellion, which he was now going to use against it. Despite all evidence to the contrary, it was claiming that the *Nebula* had been destroyed. They turned on their jammers for a few seconds, which put the station temporarily out of commission without permanently damaging anything.

Then he opened all radio channels and broadcast across the spectrum, announcing the survival of the *Nebula* and the destruction and retreat of all of Count Benedik's ships. When that was done he called Xavier Burris and ordered him to prepare all the available ground troops for launch.

Suddenly a transmission came through the radio.

"Joyeuseans, this is Count Benedik. My ships still survive and I call on you to continue our fight against the regicide and false king Alwyn."

Morland signaled to Veazey to locate the source of the transmission. It helped that Benedik stayed on the air for quite a while, enumerating the many failures of Alwyn as both man and king.

"Captain," Veazey said. "He's not down below in Longinus and he's not back in Boarshold. He seems to be transmitting from somewhere in between."

That doesn't make sense, Morland thought. Benedik would either be leading the attack or sitting in his stronghold, depending on his personality. Then it hit him.

"Konrad, is the transmission coming from the *Falcon*?"

Veazey quickly put the *Falcon's* position up on the forward screen. It took only a minute to confirm it as the source of the transmission. It was headed back toward Boarshold.

Morland looked at the board, where lights were slowly—too slowly damn-it—changing from green to red. The *Nebula* had much more speed than the *Falcon.* Nor did the *Falcon* have the repair capabilities that a Space Viking warship had. They could catch her in a few hours.

Then the radio sputtered to life again.

"This is King Alwyn calling. *Nebula,* I order you to land all ground fighters and take control of the transmission tower."

Morland gestured peremptorily to Veazey, who was about to reply. He thought furiously. The order was moronic. The telecast tower wasn't anything important. Protecting the King and capturing Count Benedik were the keys to stopping the rebellion.

He looked around the bridge. As was typical of a Space Viking crew, the personnel were from many of the Sword-Worlds. At the moment none of the crew on the bridge were Joyeuse natives. That would make this easier he thought as he got up from the pilot's chair and strode over to the communications area.

Pressing a button he said "This is Captain David Morland of the *Nebula.* We have received a transmission from the palace but it is so garbled from outside interference that we are unable to reconstruct it. We are landing troops to support the King and we will pursue and capture Count Benedik."

He paused a moment for effect.

"Your Majesty, if you can hear this transmission, please hang on. Your loyal subjects are coming to your aid."

He then switched to an internal channel and called Burris again, telling him that he wanted half the remaining ground troops launched along with all of the armored aircars. Benedik had probably committed most of his troops to revolt, so Boarshold was not likely to be heavily defended and he thought he could take it with just the one-man cavalry vehicles. *If they don't surrender quickly,* he thought, *a few well-placed missiles might be enough to get them to surrender without risking any ground troops.*

"And Mr. Burris," he continued. "Tell Officer Ryan to return to the bridge."

"I'm sorry Captain," replied Burris. "Officer Ryan was in Weapons Control One with Mr. Hill. They've both been killed."

He heard a choked sob from the direction of Konrad Veazey. He turned and looked at the board. The light for Weapons Control Room One is bright green. *Poor Sylvia,* he thought. For a moment he felt sick, wishing he'd never taken service on the *Nebula.* He took a deep breath, forcing himself to calm down. *This was not the time for grieving.*

"Thank you Mr. Burris," he said. "When you reach the surface, make contact with the King's forces and help them any way you can."

"Aye, Captain," Burris replied.

He looked at Konrad Veazey, who was struggling to keep his emotions under control. He considered relieving him of duty, but knowing Konrad he would be insulted and refuse. *He can just stay where he is,* Morland thought. *We aren't going to be shooting at anyone for a while. Besides, I don't have anyone else.*

There was another disagreeable task he had to perform. He rose from his seat and stopped, realizing he couldn't leave the bridge at a time like this. He motioned for Reese Duggan to follow him to a corner of the bridge where they could not be overheard. The rest of the crew didn't seem to be paying them any attention at the moment, either busy with other tasks or caught in their own private grief over the death of their comrades.

"Reese, I want you to go down to Records," he said, looking at him intently. "I want you to personally destroy the transmission records of King Alwyn's order. Can you do that for me?"

Duggan's eyes widened as he realized what Morland was asking. Then his usual good humor reasserted itself and he smiled.

"Aye, aye, Captain." He turned and left the bridge.

"Captain, the pinnaces have departed," someone reported.

He limped back to the pilot's station and ordered signals-and-detection to track Count Benedik and the *Falcon's* course.

III

Boarshold wasn't just one centralized industrial complex, but many spread out over miles of gently rolling land, with industrial buildings mixed in with residential ones. They had tried to follow the *Falcon*, but it had started a series of microjumps the moment she realized the *Nebula* was tracking them. In another ten hours, Count Benedik and whomever was with him would be entering hyperspace and beyond capture.

The *Nebula's* ground fighters had turned the tide back in Longinus. Benedik's forces still held the telecast station but that was about it, and would probably surrender once word reached them of Benedik's escape. Nothing had been heard from Duke Wiltham or any of the other lords supporting the rebellion since the enemy ships had been defeated.

Morland was tired of fighting; in fact, he was tired period. It was one thing to have to fight pitched battles on the worlds he raided; he expected people to defend their homes and property. He would do the same if someone had tried to take something from him. But now the political instability that seemed endemic to the Old Federation had spread to the Sword-Worlds—right in front of his eyes. He wanted nothing more than to return to Longinus and see if his family was still alive. As he looked down at this wealth of land and buildings, he felt his anger grow.

He couldn't understand why Benedik was so desperate to attain more, considering all that he already owned. *He's just power hungry*, he decided. *No cure for that except a bullet to the head.*

Let the King deal with that; I'm no executioner. He knew that if the

King were present, Alwyn would order the complete destruction of Boarshold—innocents be damned—all to punish the rebel's power base. *To Nifflheim with him!* he decided.

Morland turned in his seat, intending to order the *Nebula* back to Longinus. Then he realized he was in the pilot's seat and punched the course out himself. It would be almost an hour before they reached Longinus. He was torn between touring the ship to see the damage and going to his room for a brief but needed rest. As if he was being observed from afar a voice rang out over his hand-phone.

"Captain, Duggan here. Could you come to Records please? I have something you should see"

He wearily acknowledged and left the bridge.

"Well that explains some of what happened that day," Duggan said, shutting off the machine.

Morland sat there, too stunned to reply. Third Officer Fergus Byrne's pinnace had fired the missile that killed Captain Orrick and the other officers. It had been right there in the automatic records. The bridge crew had missed it because they were looking in other areas, as ordered by Byrne before he left the ship. After a few moments, what Duggan said sunk in.

"What do you mean?"

"Didzia and Byrne were this tight," Duggan said, holding his two fingers pressed together. "I'm sure Byrne would have made him First Officer. It would have been a natural choice with him becoming ship's navigator."

"Roger Galves," he continued, naming the other man on Byrne's pinnace, "was equally close to Byrne. I'm sure they were both promised plenty for going along with Byrne."

Morland ran his hand through his hair. "Records were in Galves' section, and no one covers that station during a raid. It would have been easy for him to go there when they returned and delete any incriminating evidence." He shook his head, "Whatever possessed Byrne to do it? How did he think he could get away with it without anyone investigating?"

"He did get away with it," Duggan pointed out. "I only found this by accident while I was going through the records for King Alwyn's transmission to be certain I had deleted everything."

"Things were pretty chaotic during the Agni attack," Morland said, remembering all the personnel he had to shift around and how shorted-handed the *Nebula* had been on the trip back from Agni. "He certainly couldn't have planned on so many people dying on Agni."

Duggan looked meaningfully at Morland. "That means he probably had someone else's support."

He felt himself trailing half a beat behind Duggan, but then he reached the same conclusion. "The King had to have been behind it! That is the only way Byrne would have known that there wouldn't be any serious investigation. The King must have put him up to it."

"It makes sense," Duggan said. "King Alwyn is new on the throne. He had already offended some of the investors by asserting his claim on the *Nebula.* And Captain Orrick had been around a long time, he was pretty independent. Alwyn probably felt he needed his own man as captain."

Duggan shook his head. "This would have given him a hold on Byrne. But Byrne obviously didn't mind, he just wanted to be captain and didn't care how."

"And he was...." Morland added. "But not for very long." He drained the drink in his hand, looking around for where they had set down the bottle.

Duggan handed it to him and continued, "It was the King who

pushed for the raid on Agni. He must have figured with Agni's tough reputation no one would have been surprised if the captain didn't return. And Captain Orrick was known to take a command-car out to inspect things after a raid was over. However, there was one wild card—the Agnis. No one counted on the locals gumming things up with their own missiles."

Morland didn't really register all of Reese Duggan's comments. King Alwyn had already radioed, congratulating him on his victory over Count Benedik and asking to meet with him the minute he got back to Longinus. He was going to have to watch his every word while meeting with the King. If he gave a hint that he was aware of Alwyn's treachery, he was likely to be the next one to die under unusual conditions.

IV

Chancellor Kronigblertz tapped lightly on the inlaid door that barred the way into King Alwyn's audience chamber. Those doors were as hard as steel, made from imported Irminsul heartwood, and ferried at great expense from halfway across the Old Federation to Joyeuse. The King of Joyeuse was at best, touchy and somewhat—well, maybe a lot—paranoid; although, truth be known; he had every right to be. He was an unloved monarch ruling over a planet in serious economic trouble, which many of his subjects believed was in no small part his fault.

Nor did it help that many believed he had aided his cousin's entry into the void so that he could claim the crown for himself. King Olov had been another weak king in the Guntharl lineage; there hadn't been a strong one since King Svenn had died almost a hundred years ago in an attack against the League of Civilized Worlds.

It's my misfortune to have been born in such troubled times, Kronigblerz thought wryly. *And, my misfortune, to serve under such a wretched ruler.*

Alwyn's former Chancellor had strongly suggested lowering taxes, building more schools and universities and encouraging his subjects to stay on Joyeuse, rather than haring off on mad schemes to plunder the Neobarbarian worlds of the Old Federation. His insistence had almost cost him his head until he'd been dismissed.

Instead of rebuilding, Alwyn tried to buy his way out of Joyeuse's troubles by sponsoring Space Viking raids. Unfortunately, the King's first two expeditions had ended in failure: on the first, the Captain had made a series of rich hauls only to disappear, never returning to Joyeuse and repaying the hundreds of millions of stellars he had borrowed to outfit his ships. The second expedition of three ships had met with disaster when it had attempted to raid the Marduk trade world Lilith and instead ran into a Mardukan fleet, hidden on one of Lilith's moons. Two of the Joyeuse ships had been hulled, and the third taken prisoner.

It had cost Alwyn fifty million stellars to ransom the crew, which included his nephew—or, as one wag said, he'd have left them all to rot on Abaddon, the moon Marduk used to hold prisoners of state. The other two ships had been a total loss. The third expedition into the Old Federation had been his only success, but it had lost most of its crew including the captain. King Alwyn had been under siege when the third Space Viking ship had returned from Agni with a hold full of loot.

The timing had also been good. Morland had destroyed two of Count Benedik's ships and led the counterattack on Boarshold, although the *Nebula* was heavily damaged in the process. Impressed with his loyalty as well as the enormously rich haul he brought with him, Alwyn had confirmed Morland as Captain of the *Nebula*, even though he was two years shy of thirty.

It wasn't difficult to see why the King's own subjects were beginning to regard any Space Viking enterprise as sheer folly. Now, Alwyn was sponsoring another expedition with a Captain not even into his third decade. As far as Chancellor Kronigblertz was concerned, by sending out another expedition, the King was tossing his fate to the winds.

The doors suddenly swished open and the two guards, dressed in Alwyn's black and gold livery, stepped aside to allow him entrance.

"Your Majesty," he said, as he bowed down to one knee before Alwyn.

"Sit down, 'Blertz," the King ordered. His long face was framed by two great dew-lapping jowls. Alwyn's crown hid his bald head and gave his countenance some semblance of majesty.

The Chancellor hated it when the King shortened his name like that, and Alwyn knew it. So he kept his expression impassive as he took his seat on the hard leather chair, a great contrast to the stuffed and form-fitting chair the King sat in.

"I have an important matter of state to discuss with you."

The Chancellor felt his heart quicken. Was the King finally going to make a serious decision about the economy or begin the spaceport repairs?

"I'm not happy about the name of Our Viking ship."

"What? What's wrong with the name, *Nebula*, Your Majesty?"

"It doesn't have the right swagger for a proper ship name. Maybe it's good enough for some scow out of Odin or Gilgamesh, but not a Space Viking raiding ship. I've been reading Captain Hellmut's book, *The Black Swan*, and none of his Viking ships had such a pusillanimous name."

"Yes, Your Majesty, but Wulf Hellmut was a Space Viking in the early days of raiding the Old Federation. Those days are long gone, thanks to Lucas Trask and others of his ilk."

"True, most of the glory is gone. The civilized worlds, like Aton, Baldur, Odin, Isis and Marduk, all have their own fleets and spheres of influence. It's getting so there aren't many Old Federation planets worth raiding within three thousand hours of Joyeuse. Still, it's up to Us to set the bar high, keep appearances up. I suggest we rename the ship the *Skull Splitter*."

The Chancellor moved his bottom to find a more comfortable position, while he tried to frame a response. "How does Captain Morland view your proposal, sire?"

The King barked out a laugh. "If he doesn't like it, he can work alongside his father at the robot factory."

His father teaches robotics, he's not a repair man, he thought to himself. However, one did not become Chancellor by correcting the King. "But, you do owe him, sire."

"I guess it could be seen that way...." Alwyn paused to stroke his beard, a sign that he was doing strenuous thinking.

The man saved your Crown, for God's sake! Once the thought was out, he was glad he'd not said that out loud. The Christian sect, the Old Anglicans, he belonged to was a minority religion in the Sword-Worlds and the King was not well-disposed toward Christians in general, even less in the specific. Not that he thought much of any other faith; God help the man who brought up the Gilgameshers.

"Morland's getting his just reward; after all, I let him remain in command of the *Nebula.* Besides, he allowed Count Benedik to escape."

The Chancellor bit down on his tongue. True, Benedik had escaped on the *Falcon,* but if Morland—who'd had no way of knowing Benedik was aboard—had chased after it, instead of fighting the other two ships attacking the palace, all might have been lost and the King dead.

"This expedition is costing us more than the Crown can afford, Your Majesty."

"Have to spend money, to make money." The King laughed at himself, as if he'd said something witty or original. Then he frowned. "Are you suggesting my policy is in error, 'Blertz?"

"No, no, Your Majesty. I just worry that you've placed so much responsibility and possibly the future of your crown on such young shoulders." The sweat was beginning to collect in all the wrong places underneath his robe of office.

"I have all the confidence in the world in Captain Morland; after all, I will have his family in the palm of my hand while he's off raiding in the Old Federation."

"Do you think that will be enough, Your Majesty? It wasn't enough for Captain Sveynsans. His younger brother is still a resident in the keep's dungeon."

Alywn frowned.

"What happened to his sister, sire?"

"She's still working off his losses at one of the Docktown brothels. I don't see young Morland putting his sister out on the street."

The Chamberlin nodded in agreement. "He's a rare sort; he actually holds to his own words." *Yes, and his honor is going to cost him plenty, if anything goes awry on his journey into the Neobarbarian Worlds.*

V

Captain David Morland sat at the Muster Table with his Astrogator, Reese Duggan and his First Officer, Laz Rivera, the oldest of the three and an unusually short man for a Space Viking. However, Rivera had a wiry frame and was fast as a meteor and surprisingly strong; the silver streaks in his hair and the lines that gouged his space-burnt face had fooled more than one man. He was also a good judge of character. A trait Morland wished he had more of, but—as his father had counseled—it would come with time and experience.

They were seated to the right of the bar in the Ports of Call inn, the Space Vikings' unofficial union hall; there was one, usually run by a grizzled Space Viking veteran, in every Sword-World spaceport as well as on any respectable base world. Ports of Call Longinus was run by a one-legged ex-Space Viking named Olgof Barthalyn; he didn't look like much, with his graying thatch of hair, a full beard in the old-fashioned style and his gnarled and lined face, but what Chief Olgof didn't know about the trade hadn't yet been written.

Every Ports of Call inn had a Muster Board posted in the back, next to the Chief's office, where new ship arrivals could list themselves and any positions open for hire. Morland's list had been up for a Galactic Standard week and he'd filled most of remaining ship's positions left vacant after the ship's losses at Agni and in the ground fight that followed the Battle of Joyeuse.

Now he was looking for ground fighters, one thing every Space Viking ship could never have enough of. Olgof had told him the *Devil's Due* had just spaced in from Balmung where there were always a lot of men looking for work. Balmung was a hard-scrabble world, if there ever was one, and anyone who could get off—left. Sometimes ships stopped there to pick up good ground fighters, and would ferry excess recruits, for a fee, to another Sword-World so they could find work.

Families on Balmung were large and sometimes several families, or an entire clan, would scrape together whatever stellars they could raise to send younger sons off to the proper Sword-Worlds for work. Then, the sons would send back funds to Balmung if they prospered. However, many of them died on forgotten worlds, while others found places for themselves on base worlds, or even on Neobarb worlds in the Old Federation. Few ever returned.

"I don't like this last-minute name change for the ship," Reese Duggan said. "It smacks of insecurity." Reese was a holdover from the crew of the *Nebula* and had been promoted Chief Astrogator when they had lost all their superior officers during a vicious missile counterattack on the planet Agni.

"The King's desperate," Laz Rivera said knowingly, "and for good reason." His words were punctuated by another mortar barrage just outside Longinus.

Morland thought about that while the robot-bartender brought over another pitcher of Durendel draft. The cost would be computed by the robot and added to his tab. Usually, a recruiting captain would buy a drink for the house every time he signed on a new crewman. The custom explained why the tavern was filled to bursting with rough looking men and the usual mix of tarts and doxies.

A sound like that of a string of firecrackers going off filled the tavern when the Ports of Call's door was opened to admit a young man. *The fighting is getting awfully close to the city,* Morland thought. He couldn't help but worry about his parents. One of the rumors running through Longinus was that the rebels had two strike teams outside of

Greensward, one of the outer suburbs, and another battalion of ground troops following behind. He wished he could take his parents with him, but King Alwyn demanded that they stay on Joyeuse as hostages to ensure his return. With the war going on, there were no guarantees; Alwyn, himself, might be dethroned or assassinated during the years the *Skull Splitter* was off raiding in the Old Federation trying to establish their New Base Venture.

A typical Space Viking raid ran anywhere from four to five years, depending on how deep they went into the Old Federation. Twice as long as a typical Viking raid eighty to a hundred years ago. It was getting so that all Neobarb worlds worth looting were more than twenty-five hundred light-years from the Sword-Worlds Cluster. If the League of Civilized Worlds and the Mardukan Kingdom kept expanding, the Space Vikings would soon find their way of life coming to an end. Maybe it was true, what Ship's First Historian, Ulrik Selner, said: "Civilization is on the rise; it's time for the Sword-Worlds to start looking inward, rather than outward into the Old Federation."

Morland hoped not. Being a Space Viking was one of the few ways in which a Sword-World youth, without a patent of nobility or family connections, could get ahead. It was either join a Space Viking crew or follow in their father's trade.

David's own father was a robotics teacher and an intuitive master mechanic, a trait which he hadn't inherited. His own dream had been to explore the universe, especially the worlds of the Old Federation of legend, as the captain of a Space Viking ship. Now, his dream had suddenly—and surprisingly—come true.

However, the reality was nothing like the dream: He had demanding investors, like King Alwyn, pestering him. As Captain, he was saddled with big debts he'd have to pay back at inflated interest rates. He had too little intelligence regarding targets and far too much unknown territory to cover. Sure, the planetary raids and trading visits were exciting, but in his last trip he'd got into a gunfight, had to execute two rapists and face down a mutiny with a broken leg and no pistol. Otto Harkaman never had those difficulties, or if he had he kept them to himself and out of his autobiographies.

The young man who'd just come into the tavern approached the Muster table. He had a long face with a bushy beard like a fan, and two of the brightest blue eyes he'd ever seen.

"Captain Morland, sir."

He rose to bump fists in the standard Sword-World greeting for two men of fighting age. "What can I do for you?"

"I'd like to join the crew of the *Skull Splitter*," he said, with a thick Balmung accent.

Morland liked the way he held his gaze, and didn't shy away as if he were insecure or hiding something. "Your name, son?"

The potential crewman was probably only a couple of years younger than himself, but the weight of his new office was aging Morland quickly.

"My name is Rovard Harvan, sir. I was a junior signals-and-detection officer aboard the *Devil's Due*. I know I'm young, only twenty-six, but I'll work hard if you give me a chance."

"At what?"

"Oh, I just put it on the Board. I'm applying for your open position of Assistant Signals-Detection Officer."

Morland's first thought was to say no, but instead he said, "Have a seat, and let me see your Ship Registry Papers." *Where would I be if Captain Orrick hadn't given me a chance?*

Harvan reached into his jacket and removed a dispatch folder holding a sheath of papers. The papers were made from rag-linen and Hoth heartwood which made them just about indestructible to anything but a blast furnace. They had all the proper seals and stamps. His personnel record said that Harvan had shipped out of Balmung as a cabin boy at twelve and had slowly risen through the ranks as he went from ship to ship during the next fourteen years. *Great Gehenna, this kid's spent more time in space than I have!*

"From your records, I read that you've served on eight different ships. How come so many?" It was a sign that he was either restless or a troublemaker, although there were no disciplinary hatch marks on his deportment reports.

Harvan shrugged his shoulders. "I leave a ship when I determine that I've risen as high as I can go, sir. Most captains pigeonhole a crewman pretty quickly."

He paused and Morland knew he could supply the missing thought tag: *especially when they find out he's from Balmung.*

"It's tough to rise in rank unless you transfer aboard another ship."

That was true. Most ships returning from a raiding expedition were chronically short of good men, especially if they landed on a good port like Excalibur or Quernbiter. On a planet like Joyeuse, that didn't see more than fifty ships come and go in a year, a man could get stranded for a long time. He figured that the *Skull Splitter* would be the last ship spacing out of Port Longinus for the rest of the year.

"Recruit Harvan, report aboard ship and see the Master. He'll give you the paperwork for the signals-and-detection exams. Have him report the results back to me ASAP, and we'll see if you pass muster."

"Yes, sir!" Harvan said with a smile.

As the recruit turned and went toward the door, Morland rose up and said, "Drinks on the house!"

Everyone in the inn cheered, except three big men who pushed their way through the crowd heading for the bar.

"It's a good thing, David, that we got shipboard promotions," Vann

Stenger said. "I don't know if I could pass the Second's exams, especially the star navigation portion—even if I took them now."

Morland was about to answer, when he recognized one of the three men pushing their way to the table. The big one was a former crewman, a friend of Hill's, the man who'd almost sparked a rebellion on the *Nebula.* He saw Vann Stenger about to draw his side arm, and put out a restraining hand. "Let me take care of it."

When Hill's friends were about five feet away, Morland rose up to his feet. The other two drew back when they saw that he was about six foot two. He was short-waisted and a lot of people, when he was seated, thought he was much smaller than his true height. The big man ignored his friends and charged forward, pulling a knife from behind his back.

Without thinking Morland coldcocked him as hard as he could, knocking the man down to the floor. Vann Stenger and Duggan had pistols in hand to make certain that the other two stayed out of the fight. Meanwhile, a crowd had circled behind the two men.

The former crewman slowly rose to his feet, spitting teeth and blood out of the side of his mouth. "You lousy Son-of-a-Khooghra! I oughta kill you…" He turned to the crowd, "This snot-nosed kid here cost me my berth. He had no right—"

One of the older crewman who'd been aboard the *Nebula* during the Agni raid, yelled, "Marks, you're a troublemaker, always have been. The story I got, you was about to draw a gun on the Cap'n. If it were me, I'd have deep spaced 'ya!"

There was a chorus of agreement from the crowd.

Morland pointed to Marks. "Get him out of here, but leave him alive." He had to add that in, otherwise someone would have slit his throat in the back alley to curry favor. After all, he was dealing with Space Vikings, not dirtsiders.

TANITH

I

Captain Morland looked out the viewscreen of the pinnace as they approached Tanith's largest spaceport. Rivington City was a teaming metropolis, with aircars flitting across the sky like tiny silver birds and rainbow-hued dragonflies. According to the latest population figures, Rivington held more than three million inhabitants. As they descended to the spacedock, he could see thousands of ground cars filling the streets. It was hard to believe that less than a century ago this bustling city had been just another demolished Neobarbarian town with no future but famine, disease and death.

His appointment with King Rodrik wasn't until the next day, but he had arrived early to see if there were any other Space Viking captains in town who might be interested in joining forces. If it wasn't there already, the day was coming when single Space Viking ships would be regarded as prey rather than predators. With space navies popping up everywhere in the Old Federation these days, it was smart to arrive in a flotilla if at all possible. If he could add one or two more ships to his command, their combined firepower would effectively quadruple the number of target worlds they could successfully raid.

Tanith was the mostly likely world in the Old Federation to join up with other Space Viking ships with the same idea in mind. While the Trasks officially claimed to eschew Sword-World raids, they privately welcomed their business, encouraging Space Vikings everywhere to sell their stolen hauls on Tanith and use their spaceyards for repairs and refurbishing damaged ships. Since the Sword-World Cluster was several thousand hours away from the fringes of the Federation, it made sense for their raiders to sell their cargos on Tanith and find new shipmates closer to their prey.

In the early days of his reign, Lucas Trask had discouraged Space Vikings from refitting and organizing expeditions on Tanith and in the League of Civilized Worlds sector. This had worked well until competing merchants from Marduk and Beowulf had driven down prices and made interstellar trade far less profitable. Tired of the competition and portage costs, Trask's descendants became more forgiving and took full advantage of the cornucopia of opportunity and wealth their special relationship with the Sword-Worlds offered. For the last sixty-some years, Tanith had been the ultimate Space Viking base world and had prospered accordingly.

But that time was rapidly coming to an end, what with competing sovereignties like Marduk, the Odin Confederacy, Baldur, Osiris and Aton all annexing nearby smaller and weaker worlds. To Morland, this meant that Space Vikings had to develop a new strategy, find other sectors of the Old Federation not dominated by the civilized worlds. This was what the New Base Venture was all about. Now, if he could only convince three or four other captains of this....

Tanith did not have an "official" Ports of Call inn, for obvious reasons of statecraft; instead they had a spaceport bar called the Riff-Raff Tavern, where Sword-Worlders and other spacers congregated for news and company. The first captain to approach him was an older man with red-rimmed eyes, who claimed to have plied the trade for some forty years. "I've never seen the pickin's so sparse," he complained, "not since the Baldur and Isis War. My ship the *Rubber Ball's* been stuck in the Rivington spaceyards for nigh onto a year. With some help—I only need two hundred thousand stellars—I can pay off my repair bill and docking fees and recruit a new crew."

Morland bought him a round of Baldur honey-rum and sent him on his way. Rumor had it that he was a rummy down on his luck and that the *Rubber Ball* would see the scrap yard before it saw space again.

The next two captains he spoke to were already committed to their own small flotillas. "Bunchin' up, that's the only way to survive in the Federation today," one captain complained. "A lone-wolf Viking can't make a living out here," another added. "The Marduk Navy likes to have a small squadron of two or three ships lying in wait at some of the more tempting targets; they'll ambush ya', hull your ship and deep-space yer crew."

He looked over at Ulrik Selner, who was loading his pipe with Jagannath tobacco. Selner had been Ship's Historian under former Captain Orrick and one of the few from that crew he trusted.

"Things are even worse than they were on our last trip."

Selner nodded back. "Back in Lucas Trask's time, there were typically some two hundred Space Viking ships roaming the Federation at any one time. Today, there are less than eighty ships plying the trade. Sure, there's a few Neobarb pirate ships, but they're usually scows left on-planet when their Space Viking crews turned native, or got captured when they drank too much. I even read of one case where the crew was poisoned by tainted wine when the so-called friendly natives showed their true colors. If our New Base Venture is going to turn a profit we're going to have to range far off the beaten track."

"I agree, but we're still going to need more ships."

"I talked with the owner and he said there are eight Viking ships in port," the Historian said. "The *Grim Reaper* just got back two days ago from Hoth. Maybe you should talk to the captain; he's the one in the corner sitting behind the Gilgameshers."

The Trasks had always had a soft spot for the Gilgameshers, maybe because of the help they'd provided to Lucas Trask when he had no other allies. The truth was they were clannish, wore full beards without mustaches, knee-length coats buttoned almost to their chins and small white caps. They also wore heavy boots with steel spikes in the front that they could activate with a tooth-trigger. Most wore self-righteous and condemning expressions on the lean faces and they foreswore hard drink of any kind and looked around with disapproval upon those that did imbibe.

There were rumors that the Gilgameshers stole children late at night and slipped them aboard their ships before their parents even knew they were missing. Others claimed they drank the blood of virgins in their pagan ceremonies, or made human sacrifices to Yah—their so-called god. Of course, these same traits, the historian inside told him, had been attributed to other religious minorities throughout recorded history on Old Earth and even the Federation.

Only on a few planets were the Gilgameshers prohibited, but most places gave them a begrudging welcome for the trade goods and news they brought to otherwise lonely worlds and isolated outposts. Tanith, other than Gilgamesh—and he had never read or heard of anyone who'd visited that world and come back to tell the tale—was the only world where they were actually welcomed and had their own hostels where their special foods were prepared and served. From here, Gilgamesh was at the far end of the Federation; otherwise, he would be tempted to make a visit: Even if it was just to ascertain whether or not they were the most heavily defended world in the Federation.

On the other hand, they'd been trading within the Federation even before the first Space Viking raids some four hundred years ago. *Great*

Satan, he thought—and not for the first time—*Gilgamesh must harbor the greatest motherlode of treasure and loot in the galaxy!* The idea of sacking Gilgamesh had set every Space Viking salivating since the times of Wulf Hellmut the World-Smasher, the first of the great Space Viking raiders.

Catching his eye, he waved the captain of the *Grim Reaper* over to their table.

He stood up to introduce himself, "I'm Captain David Morland of the *Skull Splitter.*"

The other captain, a bald-headed man, who was as tall as David and twice as wide, but with muscle and beef—not fat, said, "Pleased to meet you, Captain. You're probably the youngest captain I've seen in some time. By the way, my name is Anse Shawley off the Space Viking ship, the *Grim Reaper.*"

They bumped fists and sat down.

Now, this was the kind of man he had envisioned as the archetypical Space Viking when he was a boy, but had only met one or twice since he'd taken up the trade. To include this skipper among his flotilla would be a dream come true.

He hit the button summoning the robot-tender and asked Shawley what he wanted to drink.

"Since it's on your tab, I'll have a shot of Jack Daniels Black."

He ordered his usual, Durendel draft, and a Jack Daniels to see if it was even available. He'd read once that legendary Old Federation liquor had been distilled only on Terra.

The robot squawked and returned to the bar, after pouring his draft. Like most tenders it personally carried only refills for the most popular orders. Special orders had to be gotten at the bar. The robot came back a minute or two later with a black-label bottle and it poured Captain Shawley a shot.

Morland shook his head. "You got me. When did they get it in?"

Shawley laughed. "Wait until you see your bar tab! I heard the owner saying he'd gotten a couple of cases off a Gilgamesher ship. It appears there's a Jack Daniels distillery on Isis."

"Do they trade with us?"

"No. They don't allow *any* Space Viking ships, including those from Tanith, within the Isis system. Me, I'd raid 'em just for the Jack—if Isis weren't so damn well guarded. They've got at least ten ships, five of which are always on system duty. You'd need a real fleet to crack that nut."

"That's the problem we've run into, too. On my last ship we hit Agni and ran into a buzz saw—"

"Oh, you're that captain. Good job! I heard about the *Nebula* and how your captain was killed by a missile. So they gave you your own ship as a reward for bringing her home?"

"No, it's the same ship; just a new name. King Alwyn didn't think the name was Viking-esque enough."

Shawley laughed. "It's some fearsome reputation we Space Vikings have; I just wish it translated better into stellars."

"Maybe I can help you on that account. My Letter of Marque is to raid anywhere in the Old Federation. My intent is to do just that, but not in the same over-tilled fields. I want to go farther into the Federation than any ship has since Harkaman's famous raid on Osiris."

"You're ambitious, for a youngster, I'll give you that. Unfortunately, my ship's already committed. I've joined up with the Black Band, a four-ship flotilla. Most of us captains have had a rich world or two that we've kept an eye on over the years, but haven't had the manpower to risk taking. Now we've put all our brass rings into one hat, so to speak, and we're going off on our dream grabfest."

"Well good fortune to all of you."

"You, too, Captain Morland. Let's drink to lots of loot and willing lasses! Maybe someday we can work together."

"I'd like that, Captain; I really would." A large part of visiting these taverns was to meet other captains, get to know them and sometimes pick up valuable information. Also, it didn't hurt to make a few friends along the way. Captain Shawley was the kind of Space Viking captain he'd always wanted to emulate. On one level, he supposed, he'd always be a failure; he had a "nice face" and people usually liked him. He'd probably never have the grizzled visage of the proper Space Viking, as he'd imagined as a youngster, but there were advantages, too, in being able to put people at ease.

After two more depressing interviews, he was about to call it a night when a middle-aged man, with a pot belly and clearly in need of a shave, approached the table.

"Captain Morland, I presume?"

"Yes, and who do I have the pleasure of meeting?"

"Captain Javen DeBorder of the Space Viking ship, *Pay Dirt*. I understand you're looking for a backup ship."

"Sit down, Captain," he said, hitting the button to recall the robot-tender.

"Don't mind if I do. I own my own ship, well—to be honest, King Rodrik and I own it together."

Morland nodded to show his interest.

"That's one reason I'm sympathetic to your plight…."

"Meaning?"

"One ship against who-knows-what-all's-waiting-out-there! That's how I got my ship hulled; we went on a grab-and-slash raid to Ithavoll. We'd heard from some Gilgameshers that it was a Civ-Level 8 world, you know, jet planes, computers, televisions—lots a good grab. We get in-system and find out it's now Level 9, with nuclear bombs and interstellar fighters. To make a long-story short, we took out a whole fleet of interstellar fighters without any serious damage and we were about to send out our pinnaces, when all of a sudden—a Mardukan battlecrusier shows up! Well, we took damage, but hightailed it and made an immediate microjump at about 2 AUs out…yeah, I know that's dangerous, but we didn't have any choice—not with the battlecrusier on our arse!

"Fortunately, we got out with minimal loss of life, but with some serious hull damage. Landed here and the King offered to refit the ship in exchange for shares." DeBorder shrugged his shoulders. "What else could we do?"

Morland shook his head. The Space Viking nightmare….

"Anyway, I'd like to join forces with the *Skull Splitter*, with your permission, of course."

Morland didn't know what kind of hold the king had over DeBorder, but he could smell the desperation. He was gulping down vodka like it was mother's milk. His inclination, based on the captain's disheveled appearance and alcohol intake, was to turn him away. On the other hand, he'd met with just about every other Space Viking captain on Tanith and there just wasn't anyone else, unless he wanted to park in orbit and wait a few hundred hours. No, he had his own investors to worry about; King Alwyn was not a patient man, either.

"I'll take you on, Captain DeBorder, but only under the following conditions."

"Yes sir, you just call them out."

"I want it in writing that I'm senior captain and that you will follow my orders to the letter. Is that agreeable and understood?"

"Aye, aye, sir."

"My plan is to travel far beyond the beaten path. We will be traveling as far as Odin, maybe farther in search of new worlds that haven't been robbed into terminal poverty."

"Is that agreeable?"

"Aye, aye, sir."

"In regards to shares, as senior captain I get an extra five percent of all captured goods, specie, jewels, machine goods, and all ransoms over and above your share. Is that agreeable?"

DeBorder didn't look so eager anymore, but he capitulated.

They shook hands to seal the deal.

"Welcome aboard, Captain."

"I'd like to make a toast."

"Yes," Morland said.

"To hot guns, great pillage and willing girls!"

"Aye, aye."

11

"Captain Morland, for the second time," the annoyed voice announced, "His Highness, King Rodrik, will see you now."

David Morland, Captain of the *Skull Splitter*, looked up at the attendant in surprise. He must have missed the earlier announcement, because he had been in the anteroom less than a Galactic Standard hour. At least a dozen men had been waiting longer. He had been picking up a lot of information from various traders, Space Viking captains, politicians, and other supplicants in the room while trying to cover his nervousness. Even the Gilgamesher had been somewhat friendly for a member of that cult, perhaps because he was the only one of his kind.

Morland rose up and followed the attendant through a crenellated door and down a corridor lined with a variety of paintings and sculptures from a myriad of worlds in the Old Federation. There on a pedestal was a fertility goddess from Amaterasu, a funerary mask from Liothe hung on the wall next to a complex light sculpture from Aton, and there in a gold frame he saw what appeared to be a Rembrandt painting from Old Terra.

He felt a little bit of pride that he actually recognized where some of the pieces came from. *I might even have stolen that one,* he thought as they passed a piece of statuary from Imhotep. They'd sold the ship's share of the loot from that raid on Excalibur; what he couldn't explain was how the piece could have gotten from the Sword-Worlds to Tanith in such a short time.

"Through here, please." The attendant directed him through an unmarked door, then took his leave.

Morland entered a small, well-appointed room to find it occupied by a man in his early fifties sitting alone at a table and smoking a cigar. He was in front of a large picture window and he could see a flock of white clouds grazing in the blue-gray sky over the occupant's head. They were on the five hundredth floor of the Trask Tower, the tallest building in Rivington, the capital of Tanith.

He paused uncertainly. The man was about the right age as the king, but he was dressed like an ordinary man of leisure, with a tunic and trousers, but wore neither crown nor cap of maintenance.

"Captain Morland," the man said, rising to grasp his hand. "Please sit down."

He tried to hide his astonishment but did not succeed.

"Oh, I'm not given to the fancy airs they have back on the Sword-Worlds," King Rodrik of Tanith said with a smile. "I prefer to visit with most people alone without formal court proceedings."

"Thank you for seeing me, Your Highness."

King Rodrik Trask was a handsome man of just above average height, vigorous looking with a Vandyke beard shot with grey. His informal manner put Morland, who had not grown up around royalty back on the Sword-Worlds, somewhat at ease.

"It's not often," he said, "that I get to see someone from the old home world. Cigar?"

Morland, who didn't smoke, declined. "Thank you, sire, but while my family was originally from Gram, I have only been there once. I've lived on Joyeuse all my life, when I haven't been out raiding, that is."

"Yes, I've heard about your raiding prowess," Rodrik said with a chuckle.

Morland reddened. "Thank you, Your Highness. I just did what I had to do. It wasn't nearly as impressive as people insist on making it out to be."

King Trask smiled wryly and said, "The world is full of people who couldn't do what they had to do when it needed to be done. So they're rightfully impressed when they run into someone who does. But, enough flattery for today: tell me, why did you request information on our trade worlds?"

He poured himself a glass of some Janicot whiskey and directed Morland to help himself. "You're young for a captain, but so was my father, Arthur Trask, when he set out to make his name."

Figuring that he'd be better off accepting hospitality from the king, Morland complied, reminding himself to go easy on the drink. He'd never had Janicot whiskey before, but he'd heard from other crewmen that it was the finest sipping whiskey in the Old Federation. It went down easier than Baldur honey-run, but lit a fire in his stomach.

"King Alwyn of Joyeuse has directed me to found an Old Federation base world for raiding purposes," Morland said. Actually, he was the one who had persuaded King Alwyn that forming a base in the Old Federation would strengthen his economic position and the security of his reign—and the New Base Venture was born. The plan was to found a new base, deep into the Old Federation, far beyond where any Space Viking had ventured. The problem was that most of the worlds, especially those of a Civ-Level 6 or above, within three thousand light-years of the Sword-Worlds were played out. Or were civilized planets, like Isis, Odin or Marduk, with their own fleets and ground fortresses and damn near impossible to raid without an armada.

Morland intended to establish a base world deeper into the Old Federation than any other Space Viking had done before him. "I don't want to raid any of your trade worlds by mistake. I am also looking for advice."

The King nodded. "Advice?"

"Yes, sire. Your grandfather has always been someone I have admired greatly ever since I read Otto Harkaman's book about him. Now that I'm going to be doing something similar to what he did, I would be grateful for any advice you can give me."

Rodrik's grandfather had been Lucas Trask of Gram and the legendary Space Viking, Otto Harkaman, his best friend. Trask had turned Space Viking, after the murder of his wife on their wedding day, by Andray Dunnan. Trask had come to Tanith thinking that Dunnan might be there, and he had stayed to rebuild civilization. Trask had later become involved in a civil war on Marduk when he found out that Dunnan was the power behind the revolutionary government that had seized power on Marduk, one of the few planets that had remained civilized after the collapse of the Federation.

Trask had assisted Prince Simon Bentrik and his son Steven in the reconquest of Marduk, resulting in the death of Dunnan. Prince Simon had become King Simon I of Marduk, and together with Trask, as King Lucas I of Tanith, they had formed the League of Civilized Worlds.

"So you've read Otto's book on my ancestor."

"Actually I have read all of his books, sire. They were what inspired me to become a Space Viking."

Harkaman had written several books about his experiences as a Space Viking; his most famous, besides *The Bestiary of Old Federation Worlds*—which was as vital on a ship's bridge as a copy of *The Astrogator's Guide to the Worlds of the Federation*—was *The Trials and Tribulations of Gentleman Privateer.* He had also written a history of the Space Vikings that was scorned by professional historians, but eagerly devoured by the inhabitants of the Sword-Worlds and made into three different films.

The King chuckled again. "The poor economy didn't have anything to with your choice, then? I understand that the economy on the

Sword-Worlds is so bad that even girls are taking positions on Space Viking ships. I've even heard of a ship, *The Rapier*, that has so many children on it they've had to organize a school."

Morland stifled the grin that threatened to break out. Rodrik was known to be a traditionalist and had very conservative positions on social issues. Indeed, more than one sociologist had commented that the Space Viking bases established in the Old Federation tended to preserve social values that were actually a generation or two in the past on the Sword-Worlds. The irony, in regards to the King of Tanith, was that he wasn't so conservative when it came to his own personal values.

"That is true, Your Highness. In fact, my signals-and-detection officer is a woman, and my sister is one of my best junior officers. She is in charge of ship's systems."

Rodrik scowled, clearly not in agreement. Changing the subject, he asked, "So Otto Harkaman inspired you to become a professional robber and murderer?"

"Yes sir, although I do my best to minimize the murdering."

The King, trying to hold in his laughter, started to choke. He paused to fill his glass with another shot of whiskey from a crystal decanter. "I've heard you keep your crew on a tighter leash than many Space Viking captains nowadays. What else did you copy from Otto Harkaman?"

"History is my hobby sire, although I haven't developed the knack for it that Harkaman had." The more imaginative Space Vikings developed hobbies to combat the boredom of long voyages, as there was little aboard ship to occupy one's time during the long periods of time it was in hyperspace, which could run into thousands of hours. Laz Rivera, his First Officer, was a well-known artist. He had known crewmates who were sculptors, musicians, writers, miniaturists, scientists, wargamers, model-makers and painters, although most of the ordinary crewmen played cards or other games of chance.

As Captain, he limited gambling on the *Skull Splitter* to low stakes so that crewmen wouldn't end a successful tour flat broke. It caused some resentment among the semi-professional card sharks and gamblers, but he brooked no disobedience. Anyone who openly disobeyed orders would be dropped off at the next landing—even if it was a Neo-barb Level-1 world.

Morland's hobby was to read whatever he could get his hands on. He had only a technical school education in basic ship operations and was always self-conscious about his lack of education. He had continued his self-education as a junior officer on Space Viking ships by volunteering for whatever duty was needed.

"You're young, you still have time," Rodrik said, looking into his whiskey as if he carried the weight of empires on his shoulders. "I've never been on a raid myself so I have little advice to impart. The Trask days of raiding and fighting pretty much ended with my father. However, the one thing I did learn from my father is that there's no such thing as too much information."

Morland nodded. "Now that I have my own ship, I brought several historians along to assist me." The poor economy of Joyeuse had been helpful there as well. He had been able to choose from dozens of unemployed or under-employed academics. The three he had chosen, beside his Ship's First Historian, had all been specialists in Old Federation history.

"Are you raiding alone?"

"I was just talking about combining forces with a captain in your audience chamber, Javen DeBorder of the *Pay Dirt.* What do you know of him?"

The King roared with laughter, "I know that working with you would be a very good thing for him, and for me. He owes me money for repairs to the *Pay Dirt.* That's why he's waiting outside, he can't make his loan payment and he's hoping I'll extend it."

"Would you, Your Highness? I would like to team up with a more experienced captain."

"If he teams up with you, I will. But you don't need a partner. You made more on your first raid as captain than any expedition DeBorder has ever led."

"I appreciate your kind words, Your Highness. Still, having two ships provides a lot more flexibility in raiding." Indeed, with a second ship he could take on more advanced, and therefore more lucrative, worlds. Plus he needed the extra ground fighters. A Space Viking ship, the size of the *Skull Splitter*, normally carried a crew complement of three hundred to run the ship along with five hundred ground fighters. He had brought only three hundred, along with over two hundred engineers and technicians to help him set up a base; so he was short ground fighters which limited his raiding ability.

They spoke about politics on Joyeuse for a while. King Rodrik was surprisingly knowledgeable about all the personalities and rivalries, although he was dismissive of the Sword-Worlds in general. "The Sword-Worlds' days in the sun are on the wane. Is there any Sword-World, other than Excalibur, without a war going on?" he asked, refilling his goblet.

Morland agreed with the King about the Sword-Worlds. Though the non-civilized worlds of the Old Federation were referred to as Neo-barbarians, many of the worlds he had raided had struck him as more civilized than parts of Joyeuse or many of the other Sword-Worlds he had visited. The continuing dynastic wars on almost every Sword-World contributed to the instability and cultural stagnation. Though his father constantly said that everyone always claimed that the old days were better, in all the histories he had read it was clear that the

Sword-World economies had been stagnating or deflating for over a century.

He had often considered immigrating to Hoth or Xochitl, or Jagannath or any of the other Space Viking base planets in the Old Federation, because they seemed a lot more stable and better run than any Sword-World other than Excalibur. Only the realization that he would be abandoning his family had stopped him. Now that he had become Captain of the *Skull Splitter* his goals had become a lot more ambitious—whether or not he would be able to achieve them was another matter.

"Haultclere and Quernbiter are pretty stable right now," Morland said, "and the war on Morglay has quieted down. Various factions on Curtana and Durendal were advertising for mercenaries on Joyeuse when I left. Of course most of Tizona's been destroyed. And Gram...." he paused. Gram hadn't had a stable government in over fifty years. It had split into two dozen different states over the last two generations.

King Rodrik stretched. It was obvious he was uncomfortable about the pathetic state of Gram and its subjects. "I'm surprised any Sword-World king is financing another base world in the Old Federation after the double-cross Sanchez pulled off."

Morland nodded. Elric Sanchez had already been a famous Space Viking a generation ago when he led an expedition financed by the King of Flamberge to found a base on Melkarth. After a few successful raids he had declared his independence from Flamberge and set himself up as the King of Melkarth. Flamberge's subsequent credit collapse had led to the King's overthrow and plunged Flamberge into a state of anarchy from which it had not yet recovered.

Still, having an established base in the Old Federation had many advantages for Sword-Worlders. The Sword-World Cluster was over two thousand light-years from the rim of the Federation. With base worlds, ships could restock supplies and make repairs without traveling back to the Sword-Worlds after each voyage, which saved them anywhere from five months to over a year of travel time, depending on what part of the Old Federation they were operating in. Since the amount of damage a Space Viking ship took was often directly proportional to the amount of loot it obtained, successful Space Viking ships usually needed frequent repairs and were not often in good enough repair to return home to the Sword-Worlds.

Furthermore, Elric Sanchez had brought with him much more of the industrial equipment and machinery necessary for a base than parsimonious King Alwyn had provided Morland for their New Base Venture. On the other hand, Joyeuse's poor economy had allowed Morland to recruit as many industrial engineers and technicians as he needed. The end result was that Morland would have to find a planet with much of its industrial infrastructure still intact. The need to find such a base necessitated traveling far beyond the usual haunts of the Space Vikings in the Old Federation.

"My brother and parents have remained behind on Joyeuse as... *guests* of King Alwyn."

Rodrik nodded. "That makes sense. From what I've heard, Alwyn has never been considered a trusting soul."

Morland nodded. *Guests, is one word for it,* he thought, *a polite word for hostages.* His parents and brother were allowed to live in their home and continue their normal lives; they were just not allowed to leave Joyeuse. If he didn't return, he had a pretty good idea of what King Alwyn would do to them. As even a middling historian knew, the past was the best indicator of future events.

"Well then," said Rodrik, "as I said, I can't give you much advice, but I can give you our list of trading worlds, such as it is."

"I would also like the most current member list of the League of

Civilized Worlds so I don't raid any of them by mistake, either." From its humble beginnings under Lucas I of Tanith and Simon I of Marduk, the League of Civilized Worlds had grown to over thirty members, including many, like Tanith, that hadn't been remotely civilized until recently. One of the political goals of the League was the revitalization of the entire Old Federation.

"You mean you don't know?" Rodrik asked.

"Know what your Highness? I only arrived on Tanith a day ago. I spent most of yesterday at the Riff-Raff Tavern and didn't hear anything about the League."

"It hasn't been officially announced," Rodrik said, shaking his head. "But the Space Viking grapevine is usually more current than even palace gossip. You're the first to hear these words from my mouth—the League of Civilized Worlds as of now is defunct."

"Doesn't exist?" Morland couldn't have been more surprised if someone had told him that an intact ship with crew from the Terran Federation had landed at Rivington spaceport.

"Yes," Rodrik stated flatly. "Marduk has pulled out of the League and declared itself an empire."

He sat stunned as Rodrik went on.

"It's been coming for a while now. Steven the First was the last Mardukan king with any connection to the founding of the League. When he died, things started going in a different direction. I always hoped we could keep the League together, but I failed," he finished, his expression bleak.

"Then it was Lucas…?"

"Yes. The man named in honor of my grandfather is now Emperor Lucas the First of Marduk. He was the one who killed the League of Civilized Worlds."

"But why did Marduk leave the League?" Morland said, rising to his feet.

Rodrik took a few moments to remove a cigar from one of his pockets, "Because too many of the Leagues' worlds were scattered about at the rim of the Old Federation. It's harder to trade with us due to longer travel times. The inner worlds have bigger markets and are more populated, despite my own efforts in that area with regard to Tanith," Rodrik ended dryly.

Once again he suppressed a chuckle. King Rodrik had fourteen legitimate children and was rumored to have a few bastards as well. He had created a scandal by divorcing his first wife, a descendant of the Sword-World émigrés who constituted the nobility of Tanith, because she did not want to have more than five children. Rumor had it that the reason he had taken a local woman as his second wife was so that he would not face the same objections. Many of his first wife's family, the Koreffs, had left Tanith over the public embarrassment.

"We have only one hundred and thirty million people on Tanith," Rodrik said. "Most of the outer worlds aren't much larger. There are simply more people on the inner worlds."

This move by Marduk was more than just trading, he decided. *There's a lot more going on than what Trask is telling.*

"How is this new League organized?" Morland asked, running his hand through his hair and pacing unconsciously as he considered how this news would alter his plans.

"However Marduk wants to organize it," Rodrik stated. "It's an Empire, the Mardukan Empire—not a partnership of equals. Marduk's made that clear. Most of the League's richer worlds, like Beowulf and Amaterasu, have already joined them. Didn't really have a choice. I suppose Tanith will have to do the same, eventually." He paused for a moment. "Or...."

He didn't finish, but Morland could form those unspoken words into thoughts. *Or go to war with an opponent who has more ships and better system defenses.*

"I'll see that you get an updated list of the worlds allied with Marduk, although it's probably dated. Given the temper of their Navy these days, I suggest you don't raid any of their worlds. The consequences could be dire."

"So that means a journey to Marduk...I'm glad I don't have to explain that decision to King Alwyn."

Rodrik shrugged. "By the way, I'd suggest you do something about your name and emblem. Emperor Lucas has orders to detain any Space Viking ships in Mardukan territory. Technically, once you leave Ertado's System you'll be in violation and subject to seizure and confiscation."

Morland hit his head with his palm. "Things sure weren't this complicated when we left Joyeuse."

"I've got a suggestion. Let me register the *Skull Splitter* as a Tanith ship; that way you can freely enter Marduk space. Lucas has *generously* declared Tanith a neutral state."

"Thank you, Your Highness. That will be a big help."

The King frowned. "I'm not the least bit happy at how highhandedly Marduk is throwing its weight around. It's too early yet to tell if Lucas is on the side of the devil or the angels. But, We don't owe him a thing."

"Thank you, Your Highness, for your generous offer. It would be best if we changed the ship's emblem back to the Nebula design while we're still in dock."

"I have another suggestion," the King offered. "One of our materials engineers has come up with a new lighting system that will adhere to collapsium plating. If you use this, you can keep your old emblem and, with a flick of a switch, you can convert it to the other one. The lights will adhere to the hull and conform to any design they're programmed with."

"That could be very useful, Your Highness. I suspect it will become a popular trade item with all the Space Vikings who visit Tanith."

The King made a small smile. "We do what We can. Be sure and tell your Sword-World friends. I know I should have seen this coming...."

Morland sighed, "So the League of Civilized Worlds is no more."

"Yes, no violence, no civil war, no economic disaster. Not out with a bang, but with a whimper."

MARDUK

I

The tavern had a very relaxed, comfortable feel. The bar occupied only a small portion of the room. Most of the place was taken up by long tables, encouraging people to talk to strangers. It also gave room for more patrons, which was why it was set up that way. Everyone was dressed informally, some in regular ship dress, others in Mardukan Imperial Navy uniforms. The women were dressed like exotic birds of all shapes, sizes and colors.

Morland was sitting at a small table with his Second, Evard Vann Stenger. He and Vann had been close friends ever since they were junior officers together aboard the *Prince of Thieves*, before he had been hired as Fourth Officer on the *Nebula*. When King Alwyn had appointed him Captain, Vann Stenger had been waiting on standby on Joyeuse and eagerly accepted his offer to join him as Second Officer. He had served in a variety of junior officer positions in the past, from weapons, to communication, to engineering, to ship's services. Besides his experience, his relaxed personality made a welcome contrast to Morland's intense one, and he was a valued confidant. He had eagerly joined him on the New Base Venture.

Van Stenger was not executive officer only because King Alwyn had insisted that Morland take Laz Rivera as his exec. That Rivera was Alwyn's man and had orders to remove him if he tried to go independent was implicitly understood by both parties. Rivera was a veteran officer and had proved so far to be a good exec, nor had he showed any resentment at serving under a man young enough to be his son.

A watering hole like the Dragon Inn was a great place to obtain information; it was close to Malverton Spaceport, the largest spaceport on Marduk, and often frequented by Mardukan Naval personnel. It didn't hurt that the beer was good, too.

The *Skull Splitter* had come to Marduk to obtain a list of its trading worlds, so they didn't end up raiding one by mistake, as well as to gain information on how the new Empire was defended. If information on future expansion plans was obtained, so much the better. Now that the Emperor, Lucas the First, had dissolved the League of Civilized Worlds and declared the Empire of Marduk, everything in this quadrant of space was topsy-turvy. Nothing was certain.

He wondered how the Odin Confederation was reacting to the news. The Confederacy believed themselves to be the successor state to the former Terran Federation. Even during the darkest hours—during the Federation's descent into chaos and the Interstellar Wars that followed—the Confederacy had kept the flame alive.

The latest news from the palace was bad, very bad for Space Vikings everywhere in the Old Federation. Emperor Lucas had just declared that the Mardukan Empire's sphere of influence extended five hundred light-years in any direction.

That this policy would anger many of the Old Federation worlds within the Mardukan sphere of influence didn't bother Morland. Nor was he concerned that many of those worlds would soon be forced into making some hard decisions about their sovereignty. What concerned him, was the declaration that any Space Viking ship that raided within the Mardukan sphere of influence would be "hunted down as pirates, their ships destroyed and all captured hands deep-spaced."

Consequently, his crew had found it prudent to remove their helmets, emblems and insignias as well as exchange their Space Viking jackets for drab coveralls. Orders were to identify themselves as traders from Tanith. He had half his command—after taking alcodote-vitamin pills—visiting bars throughout the city to learn news about how this policy was being enforced.

What they had found so far was disconcerting. Marduk had been on a ship-building binge for years. They had obviously been planning this step for a long time. After the failed Makann revolution a century ago, the King and the Navy had been the only institutions to emerge with their prestige intact. Former King Simon had ruthlessly suppressed not only the socialist followers of Makann and the nobles who had supported him, but also many of those members of the upper class who had remained neutral. He had also rescinded many of the ancient privileges of the nobility. The end result was that the Navy had become the ultimate meritocracy.

They all heard the same story repeated, over and over again—about how some common crewman had worked and studied hard, making his way up through the ranks all the way to captain—that it was getting downright boring, regardless of how the details changed. Although a few junior Mardukan officers in their cups complained that the nobility were more likely to be promoted to officer status, all agreed they were just as likely to be demoted, if they demonstrated that they couldn't pass muster. One thing all the Mardukan Naval people were in accord with was their new Emperor and their Empire. Everyone, to a man, enthusiastically supported his expansionist policy; after all, they were Naval officers and wars meant ship-to-ship actions and promotions.

The remaking of Marduk into an empire by Emperor Lucas I had also fired up the economic boom, which had begun during the reign of Steven I and showed no signs of stopping. This had not hurt the new

Emperor's growing popularity. Scores of ships had been coming and going in orbit when they arrived, the majority of them were hyperspace freighters.

"Now I understand why King Rodrik said that fringe worlds like Tanith weren't populated enough for Marduk," Morland said. "You could count all the people on thirty Taniths together and you still wouldn't come up with a number that equals this planet's population."

Evard Vann Stenger shook his head as he sipped beer from his glass. "We've seen how crowded Malverton has become. Now I can understand why the Mardukans are actually starting new colonies."

The century-long economic boom had increased Marduk's population to almost four billion people, a number unheard of since the Third and Fourth Atomic Wars had culled Terra's teaming billions. At the same time, Morland hadn't seen more than a handful of indigents. Certainly nothing like the bums, bindlestiffs and tramps that despoiled every major city on Joyeuse.

Morland laughed. "I wouldn't call them real colonies."

Seshat, Obidicut and Tetragrammaton had been trading partners of Marduk that had undergone heavy nuclear bombardment during the Makann revolution and lost most of their population. Mardukans had been immigrating to those worlds as their home world grew more crowded. Though the word on the street was that some of the immigration to Seshat was involuntary. Perhaps that's why there were so few indigents around; Marduk shipped them to other worlds. Maybe he should recommend that policy to King Alwyn.

They overhead a couple of naval officers describing the recent annexation of Baldur into the new Empire. Baldur was another world that had remained civilized after the fall of the Federation. Word of the severity of the political infighting between various parties on Baldur had reached even as far away as the Sword-Worlds. One faction had sought Mardukan help and with their financial aid had seized power. According to the officers, it was nothing but a puppet kingship since the Mardukan navy had appropriated almost the entire Baldur space force.

Their new king gets to do what he wants on Baldur, one of the officers said, as long as Marduk runs what happens outside the Baldur System. They were also full of speculation as to which trading companies would gain the greatest share of the Baldur trade bonanza, and which officers might be promoted to new commands on former Baldur ships. "Mardukan Empire," one officer had said loudly as he left, "His Majesty should declare us the Galactic Empire."

11

"There's Tylor," Vann Stenger announced, his height allowing him to see Third Officer Tylor Ragnarsans enter the bar. With him were Lord Yorick Ladbrok, Astrogator Reese Duggan and Morland's sister, Ship's Systems Officer Zandra Konigstrum. Ragnarsans had been recruited on Joyeuse due to his reputation as a crack ship's officer, and so far Morland had not been disappointed.

Reese Duggan had been on the *Skull Splitter* when Morland first came on board, he'd been promoted after the death of the other senior officers on Agni, and was happy to stay on when Morland became captain. Besides being a good Astrogator his carefree and optimistic attitude made him a well-liked officer.

Lord Yorick Ladbrok was the son of Duke Teodor Ladbrok, one of the major agricultural landholders of Joyeuse. He was tall and well-built, with thick brown hair and a goatee. A prominent hawk nose and deep brown eyes dominated his face. He had an inborn sense of command that inspired loyalty from the rough and tumble ground fighters.

Ladbrok wasn't actually a Duke yet, and as the fourth son, wasn't likely to be, either. He was along on the voyage because his father was very influential and one of the investors in the New Base Venture along with the King. There wasn't much for him to do back on Joyeuse and he saw this expedition as an opportunity to distinguish himself within the family, learn a new trade and gain some fame. Formerly, he'd been a captain in the King's Guard, but it had mostly a ceremonial position and he was anxious to make a name for himself as a Space Viking. Ladbrok had proved to be very good at getting along with all levels of the crew so, despite his youth, Morland had made him ground force commander.

There were several similar representatives of the younger Joyeuse nobility among the crew, who hadn't proved anywhere near as useful as Ladbrok. Those varied from Count Kendrell Decan, who was an arrogant jerk, to Lord Nevil Wallace, who was a nice enough guy, but couldn't be trusted to do anything right; his family had sent him away for just that reason. Ladbrok had done a good job of keeping the remaining nobility from disrupting the ship during hyperspace downtime.

Ship's Systems Officer Zandra Konigstrum was David Morland's much older sister. She was fourteen years his senior and they had never been close. Her husband had been killed in the civil war on Joyeuse and their home and business destroyed; one minute she was in a happy marriage with a prosperous business, then all of a sudden life whirled around, turned everything upside down—and she had nothing and nowhere else to go.

Zandra was a tall women with a stocky, motherly figure and her hair worn short like a man's. With a few less pounds, she could have been attractive, but her only interest was in her son. She had brought her fourteen-year old son Richard along, as cabin boy, because her husband had died and she no longer felt safe on Joyeuse with their parents being held hostage to Morland's good behavior. When she had asked her younger brother to find a place for her on the *Skull Splitter*, there was no way he could turn her down.

In actuality, Morland had been glad to add her to the crew, since the rest of his family was hostage to his good behavior on Joyeuse. It was only due to her married name that she escaped from Joyeuse. With her background, Zandra had been qualified to be ship's systems officer and was doing a good job, despite the dark cloud that occasionally blackened her moods. All he asked was that she kept their relationship secret so that he wouldn't be accused of nepotism. Little things like that could wear on a ship's crew, especially when they were thousands of hours from home.

Morland grabbed a pitcher and poured glasses as the four officers seated themselves while Vann Stenger filled them in on the news about Baldur.

"That fits what we've heard, as well," Ragnarsans said. "Marduk may claim suzerainty over five hundred hours in every direction, but their main push is toward the inner worlds, particularly the civilized ones. We overheard several groups, both officers and crew, say that soon they'd be halfway to Odin."

Duggan drained his glass and held it out for a refill. "Others say Isis is next."

"That would be the next closest civilized world," Stenger replied, refilling the glass. "The Captain heard Ithavoll has enthusiastically joined the Empire."

Reese Duggan shook his head. "This is going to seriously curtail where our expedition can travel."

"Anyone hear anything from the *Pay Dirt*'s crew?" Morland asked.

Gytha Valkanhayn made a face. "Like I'd pal around with any of those lechers."

The partnership with the *Pay Dirt* on the New Base Venture had not started out well. Right after they'd hit port, the *Pay Dirt*'s Fourth Officer, Hereld Norwell, had pressed his advances on Gytha to such an extent that she had knocked him to the floor. In most Space Viking haunts that would have been worth a big laugh with some jibes for the bruised suitor.

Unfortunately, Norwell and several of the *Pay Dirt* crewmen had started to attack Valkanhayn, and only the swift intervention of Vann Stenger and *Pay Dirt*'s XO Will Haversham had prevented bloodshed.

Morland's discussion of the incident with Captain Javen DeBorder had not satisfied him either, which may have been due to DeBorder's state of mind. DeBorder had not been sober whenever he saw him on Marduk, nor had most of his crew. So far, neither he nor his crew had obtained any information beyond what the *Skull Splitter*'s people had already learned.

Ladbrok was relating a long story about the *Pay Dirt*'s crew competing to find the cheapest bar to drink in when Ragnarsans interrupted him. "We've done all we can here. We're not getting anywhere sitting around this bar. What's our next move, Captain?"

"We're going to Odin."

The Astrogator said, "Captain, you're talking about a two-thousand hour journey with little or no payback. Maybe if we went farther out on the rim of the Old Federation, we could find a world worth looting."

Morland shook his head. "Most of the Old Federation rim worlds are Civ-Level 2s and 3s, with an occasional Civ-Level 5 world. There's damn little profit there for our investors, and very little for our New Base Venture. Nor can we afford to antagonize Marduk by poaching in her territory, whether we agree she has the right to it or not."

Lord Yorick put down his stein of beer. "Might makes right, my father the Duke always says. And Marduk's fleet has a fistful of might."

⊕DIN

I

Just as they had done before reaching Marduk, *Skull Splitter* and *Pay Dirt* came out of hyperspace a light-year from Odin for a site-stopping. After informing Captain Javen DeBorder that this time they were going in alone, they made a series of microjumps toward the Valhalla Star System. At fifty Galactic Standard Astronomical Units, the camouflaged *Skull Splitter* was directed by two Confederacy Naval cruisers to report to the Naval Station at Hugin, one of Odin's two moons. Both Hugin and Munin, which were in conveniently opposing orbits, were honeycombed with fortifications and hardened missile and anti-missile missile bunkers.

Even Weapons Officer, Reginald Mathes, admitted that Odin would be a tough safe to crack. The Naval Station was easily identifiable, being in the shape and color of Odin's planetary insignia, a green world ribbed with blue, surrounded by two-dozen stars; in Munin's case, a green circular building housed the spaceport, while the stars were missile launching pads.

"From what my detectors can scan, Captain, it's not the visible fortifications we need to worry about," Weapons reported. Mathes, was the oldest crewman on the ship, but he wore his silver hair proudly and comported himself the same as a man half his age. He was also a serious pipe smoker and had a tobacco tin rumored to have been blessed by a space sprite—therefore being bottomless. He was also the only man Morland had ever encountered who had mastered Gilgamesh trade-talk, an insider language the Gilgameshers used to communicate among themselves while among outsiders—which included everyone within human-occupied space who hadn't been born on Gilgamesh.

"Fortunately, Reg, our intentions are good."

"Let's hope that's the read the Base Commander gets," Weapons replied.

The Captain took a pinnace down to the surface accompanied by his Second and First Historian, Ulrik Selner, the second-oldest man aboard the *Skull Splitter.* They didn't see much of the Base interior; instead they were directed to a holding room just on the rim of the huge landing port. There they were interrogated by a young Lieutenant who asked to see their Tanith Registry and citizenship papers before selling them Odin landing passes for a thousand Odin stellars, or ten Sword World stellars, per man.

It was nothing more than a disguised landing tax, but Morland had no choice but to pay. Interestingly, the Lieutenant didn't query them about where the stellars came from; he was just happy to get the payment in specie instead of inflated paper like League dolars, Mardukan marks or Confederate credits. Stellars were the only coins made of 24-carat gold; even the bank notes were backed with gold ingots by the Royal Banking Office of Excalibur. With bank notes from any of the other Sword-Worlds, you took your chances. Sword-World Stellars were the preferred currency even in the Old Federation.

When they were back aboard the pinnace, the Historian muttered, "Highway robbery, Captain. That Lieutenant, if I know his type, will pocket those gold stellars you handed over and replace them with his own worthless Odin credits." He shook his head in disgust. "He'll make a year's pay with those in the blackmarket."

"Yes, I agree. King Rodrik gave us enough League tender that I could have easily paid it in dolars, but I knew that when the Lieutenant smelled gold—well, you notice he didn't ask us anymore questions?"

"Quick thinking, Captain. I'd have never seen that angle in a hundred years; maybe that's why I'm just Ship's Historian."

The Captain's face reddened. "Don't ever disparage your contributions to this expedition, Ulrik. The greatest of all Space Vikings, Otto Harkaman, considered himself a student of history above all else."

The Historian winced, realizing he'd just unwittingly gored his captain's favorite hobbyhorse.

The landing at Asgard Spaceport was picture perfect; the city stretched out before them in all dimensions, from squat urb-mounds to towers and spires stretching upward into the blue sky. Trails of silver aircars, like insects on gossamer wings, wove through the skies in lines that might have been choreographed by a master director rather than the city air-traffic computer.

During the Federation period, before the collapse, Odin, with its wide grasslands and evergreen forests, had mandated a planet-wide covenant requiring that all major buildings were to be contragravity towers and spires. From the 3-D pictures Morland had seen in pre-collapse books, the entire world had looked like a park with the occasional crystal-like growths reaching tenuously for the sky.

During the System States War, Odin had taken in many refugees and been forced to ramp up its own industries with the collapse of the tourism industry. And, while many of those covenants had been overturned; the traditions had remained and Odin was not only one of the most magnificent and powerful worlds of the Old Federation, but the most beautiful.

They repeated their Marduk strategy on Odin, cruising all the bars near the main spaceport of Asgard, posing as traders from Tanith to seek information. Reginald Mathes posed as the ship's trader and sold the last of the goods they'd brought with them from Joyeuse and some of the trade items they'd picked up cheap on Tanith and Marduk. Meanwhile, Historian Selner and his assistants had been dispatched to the Odin Central Public Library, which was the largest surviving library from the days of the Federation, to locate worlds in this sector that had remained "undiscovered" since the Fall of the Federation or were ripe for looting.

From what they were able to overhear in the local taverns, the Confederacy was very unhappy with Marduk's territorial claims but unsure how to respond beyond verbal belligerence. Odin had typically traded within about a three-hundred hour sphere around their system, which Marduk's sovereignty claim didn't come close to infringing upon. Nonetheless, the Confederates were talking about forming trading partnerships and alliances—with both the civilized and semi-civilized worlds separating theirs and Marduk's spheres of influence—to create a no-man's zone between themselves and the nascent empire.

They were on Odin less than a hundred hours before they were contacted by an agent of the Confederate Colonial Office. Captain Morland was told, in no uncertain terms, that his presence was required immediately by the Special Deputy of Colonial Affairs.

Rather than kick up a fuss, Morland had accompanied the Junior Undersecretary along with his Second and Ship's Historian. Noticing that Ulrik Selner was chuffing on his pipe, with a result similar to that of a steam locomotive he'd observed—during a raid on Rimmon—puffing along a rail line. He whispered, "Don't worry, they're more interested in what we can tell them than who we are. My guess, is there hasn't been much recent traffic from the Marduk sector."

They took the nearest slideway, which had numeric, alphabetic and color-coded signs at each off-ramp, and followed the green trail that would lead them to Government Center. As the slideway took them through Asgard, the Historian remarked, "Look how alike the Confederate Citizens appear on the outside. They all wear the same gray and blue tunics, their faces are blank and their posture is rigid. It's as if they've adapted protective coloration to mingle with their fellows and stay unobserved."

Morland nodded. "If this is the most civilized world in the Old Federation, you can take me back to Gram!"

Vann Stenger broke out into laughter, which drew stares from everyone within hearing distance.

Morland noted one man with a silver sigil on his tunic whisper something into his pocket recorder. Probably taking notes, he decided; if Stenger were a Citizen he might go on report for the heinous crime of laughter. Who knew what the punishment for having fun on Odin might be?

11

"Why aren't we allowed to land on Odin?" Hereld Norwell, the *Pay Dirt's* Fourth Officer whined. "Captain Morland gets to make all the decisions. Why not you, Cap'n?"

All the ship's officers were seated at a table in the ship's Wardroom. Captain Javen DeBorder looked over at Wil Haversham, his First Officer, rolling his eyes. *Because we've struck out twice and, if we do it again,* he thought to himself, *we'll find ourselves stranded on some long-forgotten Neobarb world that makes Tanith look like paradise.*

"Mind your own affairs!" Haversham snapped at Norwell. Norwell was a chronic complainer and his Executive Officer didn't like him one little bit.

DeBorder held up his hand for peace, giving his Exec a frown. "The boy's got a legitimate question. We're here because Captain Morland ordered us to wait outside Odin's heliopause. They're involved in some delicate espionage on Odin and for this trip only the *Skull Splitter's* senior officers are going planetside. Captain Morland's the squadron senior officer and we have to do whatever he orders. Understood?"

Several heads nodded in unison, although no one looked happy about the current state of affairs.

"You all know we've had a run of bad luck with the *Pay Dirt.*" "Run" was short for saying two disastrous raids on Noebarb worlds that were supposed to be low-tech and pacified; unfortunately, their paid-for information had been wrong and they'd been chased off of Liothe, which had been falsely represented as a Level-6 world with steam-engine technology and primitive firearms. Instead they'd found themselves up against a Level-8 world with jet aircraft and solid-fuel rockets. They'd taken some bad hits before they could make an out-system microjump and escape. At least, the Liothians hadn't developed interstellar spaceflight or nuclear weapons.

They'd had them on the other planet they'd hit. Nergal, had supposedly been an abandoned Sword-World base planet, but unknown to DeBorder's informant, refugees from the Gram Wars of Instability had fled there bringing with them two well-armed ships. The *Pay Dirt* had just touched atmosphere and was headed down to Sarmash, the largest city on the continent of Cuthah, when they were ambushed by two ships from the backside of Negal's twin moons, Enlil and Ninlil. The *Pay Dirt* took serious damage to the hull and was almost breached, before narrowly escaping. Now, after two big failed trips, the ship's accounts were empty, and it had cost King Rodrik over two hundred million Sword-World stellars to get the ship repaired at the Rivington dockyards.

To say the *Pay Dirt* was in hock to the King of Tanith up to her gunwales, was an understatement. Their only hope was that some of the Captain Morland's famed luck would rub off on the *Pay Dirt.*

"What we don't need is any dissension over Captain Morland's orders."

"Right," the ship's Hyperspace Astrogator said with a chortle. "It's not like we've done so well on our own. By Nifflheim, if we don't earn some stellars quick, we're all going to end up stranded on some Neobarb world that will make Tanith look like Old Terra."

"Well, Cap'n, I don't see where parking outside the Valhalla System is adding any stellars to my purse," Hereld Norwell groused.

"You're still getting paid, so stop complaining," the Exec said, pausing as a mess-robot he'd summoned refilled his coffee cup.

That was advice DeBorder doubted his Fourth would follow. It wasn't entirely Norwell's fault; he didn't know any better, being raised on Balmung, the Lost Sword-World. When the System States refugees had left Abigor, not all of them had reached Excalibur. A few ships had been battle-damaged and were lost when their hyperspace drives failed or their life support systems crashed, others had navigation problems and ended up who-knows-where? One or two mavericks struck out on their own, not content with the Council's decision to stop at Excalibur and start their own colony.

The Captain who'd discovered Balmung had been one such maverick. He'd believed the Sword-Worlds were still too close to the Federation and had traveled another eight hundred hours beyond Excalibur to the very rim of the Sword-World Cluster. There they discovered a marginal high-gravity world that, due to worsening shipboard conditions, they were forced to colonize. The Balmung colonists had quickly lost their higher technology as the small party of colonists, less than six hundred survivors, attempted to wrest a living out of a world that was almost too far from its primary and had a 1.3 Gravity that made childbirth difficult.

Balmung had been rediscovered about eighty years ago by a Space Viking captain searching for new worlds. To his surprise, their discoverer had found that in their own way, the Balmungians had prospered despite the world's harsh conditions. In fact, they had managed to populate their marginal world almost beyond its carrying capacity. So it was no surprise that many of the younger colonists were eager to emigrate and because of their general hardiness and brute strength were often recruited by desperate captains as ground fighters.

Hereld Norwell was one of the rare few who actually reached the officer class; however, his manners often left something to be desired. On the other hand, he was a good man in a fight and would go down with the ship—a trait that could no longer be taken for granted in a run-of-the-mill Sword-Worlder.

"Let me explain," DeBorder continued. "After several centuries of raiding we're running short of prosperous worlds to sack. Many of the Neobarb worlds have either been raided one too many times in the past and are dirt poor, decivilizing to Level-1 or -2s. Or they've raised their technical level to the point where they have rocket-propelled nuclear missiles and their own spaceships. This development has been encouraged by Marduk and Odin's attempts to revive the former Federation in their own image. So, guess what?"

"What, Cap'n?" Norwell asked, intent on every word, as were the rest of his officers. Uncivilized he might be, but stupid he was not. One of these days, if Norwell lived long enough, the younger man might even make captain, which was why he was taking the effort to fill him in on the Old Federation political impasse.

"In another few decades there won't be any Neobarb worlds left to smash and grab. They'll all be part of some protectorate or empire or grand conglomeration. Space Vikings like us will be out of work and washed-up planetside."

"Then, what'll we do, Cap'n?"

"Good question, isn't it? And it happens to be one I can't answer. For now, we follow Captain Morland because he's got better answers than anyone else I've run into." He stopped to bang his fist against a bulkhead. "And we've got one Gehenna of a big mortgage to pay off."

III

The Colonial Office Building was one of the newer edifices in Asgard. It was shaped like a dumpy wedding cake and had all the charm of any structure built to house soulless bureaucrats and paper shufflers. A dedication plate, the brass already tarnished, claimed it was designed in the Classic Confederate Style.

After calling ahead, a contragravity lift took them to the 188th floor, where they were met by the Undersecretary of the Special Deputy of Colonial Affairs. The walls were painted institutional gray and stained with the perspiration of the many thousands of penitents before them who had walked these hallowed halls for reasons they neither understood nor dared object to. The Undersecretary took them to the Special Deputy's office and brought them inside, acting as if he were doing them a great favor.

The sad part, Morland thought, *he probably is.* Most petitioners probably spent the better part of a day waiting in the cramped outer office on uncushioned plastisteel chairs.

"Welcome, Captain Morland," said the nondescript man, wearing a dark-blue tunic, as he rose to his feet to press palms. He made a flick of his hand to dismiss his Undersecretary.

After the door had whooshed closed behind them, Morland said, "You must be Special Deputy Defarge."

The Deputy, sitting down, replied, "Yes, Captain, you can take a seat now. Who are your *friends?*"

Pointing to the Historian, Morland answered, "This is First Historian, Ulrik Selner, of the *Nebula.* The man seated next to him is my

Second Officer, Evard Vann Stenger."

The Deputy bit down at the Vann honorific, his left eye crinkling. From what Morland knew about the Odin Confederacy, they had abolished all titles as ostentatious relics of the failed past and called everyone Citizen. Their system was what Harkaman called managed socialism, which meant the wealth was managed by those who ruled the masses. Anyone who didn't like it conveniently disappeared. He suspected the Deputy was one of the managers and wanted to see if their operation-as-usual was going to continue under the threat of a new and emerging superpower.

"We recently received news that Tanith's League of Civilized Worlds has been disbanded due to undue pressure from the Mardukan Throne. Is this true, or just another rumor?"

Not knowing how much the Deputy knew and how much was window dressing, just to keep him guessing, Morland told the truth. He described how the Mardukan Diplomatic Service had used their navy and economic muscle to disband the League with very little warning to Tanith or its government.

"I would imagine that King Rodrik will not suffer this insult in silence?"

Obviously the Deputy was fishing, so Morland held out his hands in supplication. "What's the King to do? The Empire"—it was almost fun watching the bureaucrat flinch at the E-word—"has several times more warships than His Majesty. The Mardukan Empire has now declared all worlds within five hundred light years to be under their protection." He shook his head. "What's the universe come to?"

"They'll find out in a hurry, if they infringe upon the sovereignty of the Confederacy."

My, my. There's blood in those veins, after all, he mused.

Once the Deputy had determined there was little to be learned from his guests, and that he might possibly be giving away more than he was receiving, he dismissed them with a warning. "I understand you are traders from Tanith. But don't be misled. We are familiar with Space Vikings who fly under false colors and dispatch them accordingly. We are aware that the Trasks were Space Vikings themselves not so long ago. You are on a world that's been civilized for over fifteen hundred years. Therefore, be on your best behavior during your passage through Confederate Territory. My Undersecretary will give you a list of those worlds under our aegis as well as those we consider allies and trading partners. Do not attempt to strain our patience or our courtesy."

As they exited the building and stepped onto the moving slideway towards the spaceport, Vann Stenger said, "That was a bum's rush, if I ever saw one."

Morland nodded. "He was looking for something we weren't giving him. I suspect that we'll be shadowed by the Odin secret police for the rest of our stay. We got what we wanted with the list. Maybe it's time for us to space out."

Van Stenger nodded.

"Ulrik, has your crew finished their research?" Morland asked.

"Not yet, Captain. We've found a major Federation Archive and my men are sifting through it—a lot of it paper, most never computerized. I think we're going to have quite a list of planets for you. Many of these worlds were only lightly populated or young colonies and, thus were never accredited as Member Worlds of the Federation. They were forgotten after the System States war, especially during the Breakup of the Federation that followed. Interstellar trade has only revived just recently, and many of these worlds are still unknown."

"How many worlds are you talking about?"

Ulrik Selner paused to relight his pipe. "Some two thousand, possibly more. Most of them haven't been visited since Federation times."

"Those are the kind of worlds I've been looking for," Morland said. "We'll stay until your team's finished."

Selner nodded, muttering, "Some very good stuff. I could spend a decade searching through files in that Archive—"

"Don't make it too long," Morland added. "DeBorder's already getting antsy."

PART TWO

DEEP SPACE

I

Astrogator Reese Duggan twisted the big red handle and shoved it into the board, activating the *Skull Splitter's* hyperdrive engines. "Jumping, Captain."

The viewscreen changed from the brilliant star field of Odin to the dull gray of hyperspace. It was a surprisingly pedestrian sight for such a miraculous process. Without hyperdrive capability space travel was nearly impossible; the travel times between stars, even with the Abbot lift-and-drive, stretched anywhere from decades to centuries. Generation ships were the only other answer, but no one who began the journey would live long enough to see the trip through to its destination.

Traveling six hundred and thirty hours, at a light-year an hour in hyperspace, they would reach their target world in a little over twenty-five Galactic Standard days. Twenty-five days more before their first raid in what had become a very long voyage. Twenty-four hundred hours out of Tanith; they had been traveling for almost eight months since they left Joyeuse. He wondered if they should have gone to Hoth or Jagannath instead of Tanith, but immediately dismissed the thought from his mind. That sector of the Old Federation was closest to the Sword-Worlds and had been picked clean.

There were many worlds in that region, such as Susanoo and Neith and Xipototec, that were so poor they were good for nothing but chicken stealing. The more advanced worlds, like Cernunnos or Schacabac or Junrojin, that had something worth stealing and limited defensive weaponry were raided too often. There were a few worlds like Agni, that were very lucrative, if you could successfully raid them and survive the attempt—which meant that most didn't even try.

For the New Base Venture to be successful they would have to go a long way from the usual Space Vikings haunts, and far beyond the sector claimed by the Mardukan Empire. Marduk had the largest space navy in the Old Federation and no sane Space Viking courted it willingly.

Given Odin's interest in the quadrant directly between the Confederacy and Marduk, he decided to raid in a different direction, one that was outside Odin's usual trade area. He would then work his way back toward the edge of Mardukan territory, which would shorten their trip back to the Sword-Worlds.

While on Odin, the Ship's Historian and his staff had come up with a list of all the known worlds within two thousand light years of Odin. For any world more than five hundred light-years from the Confederacy, the information was typically centuries out-of-date, often predating the Interstellar Wars that occurred after the collapse of the Federation.

Astrogator Reese Duggan stood up and picked up his cup of coffee. "Six hundred and thirty hours to Sucellos, if I'm pronouncing it right. Your watch," he added as his relief took his seat.

Morland shrugged. "Your guess is as good as mine. The *Bestiary of Worlds* doesn't have a pronunciation guide."

The Astrogator laughed as exited the bridge. "You mean to say, Captain, that St. Harkaman didn't think of everything?"

Morland just shook his head; he was used to getting ribbed about his near-deification of the legendary Space Viking.

"What does it say about Sucellos, Captain?" Rovard Harvan asked.

In an attempt to encourage the younger officer to obtain a copy, Morland brought out his prized Hesh-Naza leather-bound edition. *The Bestiary of Old Federation Worlds* (usually called the *Beast* or the *Bestiary*) was a compilation of all the known Old Federation worlds, during Harkaman's lifetime, that were either visited by Otto Harkaman, or by Space Vikings encountered by Harkaman during his wide travel. Or any surviving written accounts by Space Vikings from the first Sword-World raids in the mid-Fourteenth Century to the time of his death. It contained the planetary coordinates, the Civilization Level (Civ-Level) of each world, system and planetary information as well as colorful descriptions and information on local weaponry and fighting prowess.

He read aloud the *Bestiary's* entry for Sucellos:

Horatio's System:

Discovered by Esteban Horatio in 783 A.E., a planetary scout working for the Federation Survey Division of the Colonial Office Bureau, in the scout ship the *Wanderer.*

Sun: F3V Star

Location: Coordinates are MVGF3-147D-6983320/44582-1347J

Distance from Terra: 1,655 light-years.

Planets: 8, including one Jovian super planet and one planetary body, Sucellos, within the habitable zone.

SUCELLOS:

Moons: None

Habitability: Sucellos has an iron core and is 7,213 miles in diameter. It's gravity is .93 Terran-Standard. Air content: Dry air contains roughly (by volume) 69.83% nitrogen, 27.41% oxygen, 0.21% Zeon.

0.043% carbon dioxide, and small amounts of other gases. Air also contains a variable amount of water vapor, on average around 1%. Due to high oxygen content colonists appear to be invigorated, but tire easily. Water/Land ratio 46/54. Little inclination. Polar areas less than 3%. The northern continent, Arverni, displays moderate climate with sufficient water fall for agriculture. The southern continent, Boii, is arid and inhabited only by very primitive life forms.

Colonization: According to the *Astrogators' Guide to the Worlds of the Federation* the colony rights to the planet were purchased by the Du-Pont Corporation due to survey findings showing large concentrations of petroleum. The first transport ship, *The Northern Star*, arrived in 786 bringing 8,462 colonists, most of them engineers and oil workers.

Planetary Population: 23,488,323 according to the Galactic Census of 1002 A.E.

Class III World: Due to the availability of petroleum, combustion engines are the primary fuel for automobiles and aircars. Primary export plastics and petroleum derivatives, as well as several rare earth minerals.

Notes:

#1: According to the diaries of Captain Surni Albann, when his ship, *The Rakehell*, raided Sucellos in 1589, the planet had still not recovered from the Interstellar Wars. There were still slag heaps in the major cities and significant building debris. They were able to locate fourteen buried bank vaults and found a sizeable amount of jewelry, gold and silver coins, as well as ingots to the value of 800,050,000 stellars.

Note: #2: I interviewed a former ship's officer off the Valiant, who claimed to have visited Sucellos 80 years later. He noted that the cities had either been reclaimed or torn down. There was evidence of increased prosperity among the inhabitants, but no fissionables and little rare metals. He described the Civ-Level as being at Level-4. They were able to loot several of the local towns, but the total value of their booty came to less than 600,000 stellars.

Recommendation: Not a recommend destination. Too far from Sword-Worlds' sphere of influence and Civ-Level is too low. It's unlikely to change for at least another hundred years. O.H.

Rovard Harvan snorted. "Sounds like a pigsty, to me, Cap'n. A waste of our time."

"That's what Captain DeBorder said when I told him our destination. He protested that Sucellos was unlikely to be good for anything but chicken thieving. I told him what I'm going to tell you: I picked Sucellos for the first raid because it was in the right quadrant, it's lightly developed and pastoral—or least it was two hundred years ago.

"I also told him that given the large number of inexperienced crewmen aboard both ships, I preferred that our first raid be an easy test." He paused to look the younger man directly in the eyes. "Space Viking legends like Kintour, Harkaman, and Sanchez all liked to start raiding voyages on chicken-stealing worlds when they had a green crew.

Harvan nodded. "That makes sense when you put it like that, Cap'n. When do we strike?"

11

The ship was noisy with the sounds of a happy celebrating crew, especially with a double ration of grog—in this case Sucellos high-proof vodka. The raid on Sucellos had come off with no casualties, at least among the *Skull Splitter's* crew. All the newcomers had performed well, most had kept their lunch down; it had also given both crews a chance to learn to work together on an easy job. The technological level of Sucellos was low and it hadn't taken much effort to run them out of what little there was in the way of loot.

Space Vikings typically wanted maximum value and minimum bulk in their loot. Gold and silver fit the bill perfectly, although jewels and rare metals like platinum were fine, too. Then came valuable furs and art objects, lastly manufactured goods. As for the feelings of the people of Sucellos about being raided, one either learned to not worry about such things, or didn't last long as a Space Viking.

There were only a few officers who knew of the incident, and they had followed Morland's orders to keep it quiet until he spoke to DeBorder. *And that's going to be right about now,* Morland thought, as the bridge paged him with a call from the *Pay Dirt.*

His pinnance had just returned to its berth on the *Skull Splitter* and knew it couldn't be anything else. He'd ordered the on-duty communications officer to put the call though directly to his quarters so he could handle things privately, although he knew it would be all over both ships shortly.

DeBorder, his face beet red, was practically screaming the moment he got on screen. "Who do you think you are? My crew's just about ready to fire on you, do you know that?"

"Javen, if you want our partnership to end, just say the word," he said, coolly.

DeBorder swore up a storm, then visibly began to force himself to calm down. "What do you mean by that?"

"It means that when you asked to team up with the *Skull Splitter*, you agreed that I would be lead captain. You also agreed that your crew would follow my rules, didn't you?"

"Well yes, but—"

"There are no buts. My rules are simple. No wanton destruction. No murder. No rape. Your two men were raping that girl. So I shot them dead.

"But, there should've been a trial," DeBorder sputtered. "We should select a jury, talk to witnesses, we—" he stopped.

"There was no need for a jury. And there were plenty of witnesses. An entire squad of men saw them, heard her screaming."

Lord Ladbrok had been the squad leader. He had taken the two rapists into custody and called him immediately. The testimony of all the men present had been the same. He hadn't even needed to talk to the obviously shaken girl, who couldn't have been more than sixteen or seventeen. It had given him no thrill to shoot the two men, but he had learned the hard way that the toughest jobs could not be delegated.

The two offenders had loudly demanded to see their captain, saying he wouldn't have any problem with what they had done to some Neobarb slut. They had stared in disbelief as he pulled his gun and shot each one in the head.

DeBorder was clearly rattled, shaking his head. "There's going to be trouble over this, David. I mean real trouble…I'm going to have to talk to the crew, try and calm them down…reason with them."

"Javen," he reproved, "you're the captain. You do not have to explain things to your crew. You give orders—they follow them." Of course, there was the real problem: DeBorder had allowed his crew to argue and question every decision. This had been going on long before he partnered up with the *Skull Splitter*. He wasn't a very strong leader, and most of them knew it.

He debated telling DeBorder that the only reason Lord Ladbrok and his men had been in the building was because some of DeBorder's crew had fired the warehouse Ladbrok was looting, forcing him and his squad to hastily evacuate to the other building. Since DeBorder was still fuming, he decided that it was a good time to change the subject. "I've selected the next target. I will have the bridge squirt the information over to you."

Once again DeBorder appeared to be reining in his emotions. "All right. Where are we going?"

"A world called Morrígu, about one hundred and eighty hours away. It was a major regional power before the Interstellar Wars. It should provide some profitable targets."

At least he hoped so, as DeBorder's screen blanked. A good raid would have everybody feeling better.

Morrígu was a big disappointment. The world had suffered tremendous damage from nuclear bombardment, maybe even a planet-buster, during the Interstellar Wars. Most of the cities and towns had been destroyed, including the spaceports and industrial areas. The remote areas that hadn't been attacked had decivilized to Civ-Level 2, a pre-mechanical civilization, barely above village peasant level. There hadn't been a town on Morrígu larger than twenty to thirty thousand souls. They had come away with about a million stellars in loot, less than a third of what they had gotten on Sucellos.

The Maddox System was one of those rare G class suns with more than one inhabitable planet. Morrígu was the third planet out from the sun, and Nemain the fourth planet. Morland had sent a pinnace, one of the four two-hundred foot auxiliary vessels that were part of the *Skull Splitter*, commanded by his Third to check out Nemain. It was unlisted in the *Bestiary*, but it was listed in the *Astrogator's Guide to the Worlds of the Federation*. It was described as having a limited amount of livable areas, with a correspondingly low population. The reports were correct: Nemain was heavily glaciated, cold and dry, as would be expected from a world at the edge of the system's habitable zone.

Morland had sent the pinnace there primarily to give Zandra Konigstrum, his Systems-and-Detection Officer, a little command experience, and to keep Ladbrok's ground squad away from any interaction with the *Pay Dirt*'s crew. They did not need another *incident*. He hadn't expected that any significant loot would be found, but, in fact, they had located a mining town and returned with a small amount of rare gems, including some striking sapphires.

Lord Ladbrok had been shaken by his first command on Sucellos. As if the normal violence of looting hadn't been enough, witnessing a rape and the subsequent execution of the rapists had proven to be a tough experience for the new recruit.

That wasn't unexpected. Being a Space Viking sounded exciting and romantic to many. It was the actual process of robbing civilians and destroying buildings that many found they couldn't stomach, especially when they realized killing people was a large part of the job. Otto Harkaman had said it best: "Space Vikings are professional robbers and murderers." Typically, a good percentage of the green hands dropped out after their first voyage, nor was it unusual for even a veteran or two to say they'd had enough after a particularly bloody raid.

He had found Ladbrok cradling his head in his hands in one of the *Skull Splitter*'s lounges late in the second shift. Morland had offered him another position aboard ship, one that didn't involve a ground command and fighting. Ladbrok had objected strenuously. "Captain, I just want to learn my job. I didn't foresee all the killing and gore." He shook himself as though waking from a bad dream. "I'm determined to do my job; I'll get over it, I promise."

"Not everyone does."

"I will. There's nothing left for me on Joyeuse. My family's holdings were destroyed during the revolt. I was the third son; no one expected anything from me. Now, I'd just be a burden...."

"It's your decision. Regardless of what you decide, you'll have a place on this ship."

"Thank you, Captain. I'll be okay."

Morland agreed to let him stay in his position. He would keep an eye on him for the time being. The successful raid on Nemain had helped.

There had been no incidents with the *Pay Dirt*'s crew. They had raided separate cities, not even attempting to cooperate. If his own crew was disappointed that Morrígu had not been more lucrative, he could only imagine how the *Pay Dirt*'s crew felt. DeBorder had been polite, but nothing more in their discussions before the raid and after. He was feeling increasing pressure to live up to his reputation, to deliver the big score.

There were more than a dozen people crowding into the Wardroom which at best seated eight comfortably. However, it was better to keep the discussion private. It wouldn't do any good to let the crew know how frustrated their officers were. Fortunately, the bartending-robot could hang from the ceiling, bat-style, out of the way in a corner until it was needed.

The pressure for some kind of success had only grown when the next two planets had proven to be total washouts. Morrígu was a garden world compared to Bastet and Ra, both of which had been almost totally destroyed by nuclear bombing, nothing but puddled cities with fur-wearing barbarians hunting animals in forests—Level-1s, both of them. He had called a meeting of his senior officers and historians to discuss what to do next. He had invited DeBorder and his officers, but only his First Will Haversham had showed up. The discussion had gone on for a while without any decision.

Morland shrugged. "Ra," he pointed out, "was one of the civilized worlds at the peak of the Federation in the Eighth Century Atomic Era. It must have been hit bad in the Interstellar Wars. We're in territory incognita here: there are no listings in the *Bestiary* for worlds in this sector. No Space Viking has come before us, at least, as far as any known recorded histories show."

"Some of those old-timers didn't know the meaning of too far," the Astrogator said.

"Which of the major worlds are the closest?" Tylor Ragnarsans asked, getting down to brass tacks.

Ship Historian Ulrik Selner noted that there were several civilized worlds within two to three hundred hours, according to the Odin Central Library Archives. He named them off: Osiris, Aton and Vishnu.

Vann Stenger's face scrunched up as he finished his drink. They were down to the cheap booze that was distilled from the vegetable scraps generated by the hydroponics lab. The Sucellos vodka had gone quickly. Vann was a connoisseur who preferred good whiskey. "Do we have any hope that they'd be any better than the last three worlds?"

"Forget Aton," Morland said. "No one's gone there since Prince Havilgar of Haulteclere led six ships against Aton over two hundred years ago. Only two ships returned. There hasn't been a Space Viking raid there since. Osiris is another Civ-Level 10 world that's managed to hang on to civilization. It would take far more than two ships to crack that nut. Vishnu?" He shrugged his shoulders. "They keep to themselves and have a credible navy."

"They can't all be highly civilized or destroyed," the Historian said. "There have to be worlds in between. Ones that we can sack and loot."

"What if there aren't any?" Gytha Valkanhayn, the Signals-and-Detection officer, argued. Gytha was a short, spirited woman with fox-like features, a well-endowed figure and golden hair. She was very attractive in a feral sort of way, but her aggressive manner was off-putting to many. "What do we do then, return to Tanith?" She grimaced, clearly preferring any alternative to returning to her empty house.

"There is no need to return anywhere for at least twenty-five hundred hours," Morland stated calmly, taking a small sip from his glass. Listening serenely while others griped because things weren't going well was one of the things he didn't like about being in command. They had a plan and he was going to stick to it until it became clear that it wasn't going to work. Visiting less than half a dozen worlds that didn't have what they wanted was hardly an indication of failure.

"We left on this venture well stocked with supplies because we were going to start a base; we're not even close to the end of those supplies."

Vann Stenger waved his hands in agitation, causing the Weapons officer to duck his head. "We're a lot farther from the Sword-Worlds than we planned. Even if the next world turns out to be just what we need, we're over four thousand hours away from Joyeuse. The King won't be happy we've taken so long to return."

So this is how my friends support me, Morland thought to himself.

Laz Rivera shook his head. He typically was the least talkative of the senior officers. He spent all of his spare time in his cabin painting, so Morland had not really gotten to know him. He had visited occasionally with Vann Stenger, who also painted as a hobby; Stenger claimed that he wasn't in Rivera's league, and never would be.

Morland knew that Rivera had been foisted on him as First Officer by King Alwyn as his way of asserting his control. As a fledgling captain, he'd been in no position to refuse the King's request. The question in the back of his mind was whether or not his First had orders to take command from him if he believed the expedition was approaching failure.

"Alwyn won't be happy no matter when we return," Rivera said. "so don't worry about it. He's never understood the distances involved in space travel. He'll be jumping like a Joyeuse rockjack if we can't generate a better return than we have so far!"

That was putting it mildly. They weren't even covering ship's expenses now, much less making a profit.

"Maybe we are going about this the wrong way," Lord Haversham suggested. Will Harversham, Executive Officer aboard the *Pay Dirt*, was a gentleman-adventurer who'd been on a dozen raids into the Federation. He was always impeccably dressed and tended to be very formal and reserved in his manner. Though he was older than Morland he looked younger because of his youthful face. "Perhaps the major worlds were the main targets during the Interstellar Wars. Those that could not defend themselves were raided continually until they were either destroyed or they decivilized to the point where they weren't worth looting. Those that could defend themselves remained civilized. Some of the less developed worlds might not have been attacked because they had little of value or were not a threat. Maybe we should take a look at some of the less important worlds."

"But the major worlds are the ones most likely to have an extensive industrial infrastructure," Selner argued.

Everyone started talking at once. Most of them were worried that they might not find anything better than another chicken-stealing world like Sucellos.

"Gentleman, quiet!" he ordered.

They quickly stopped their chattering, looking a little shocked. Morland rarely raised his voice.

Walter Ovard, Assistant Historian, looked thoughtful. "May I speak, Captain?"

Duggan nodded.

"Some of those so-called minor worlds may well have continued to prosper, even after the Federation's fall. They might prove to be worth visiting."

They all looked at him.

"That's a better strategy than jumping from one major world to another and finding nothing but damaged goods," Haversham added.

Morland ran it over in his mind, then turned to their hyperspace astrogator, asking, "What's the next closest world continuing outward?"

He accessed the wall screen and called up a star chart. "Horus, forty-two hours away," Reese Duggan replied.

"Gentlemen, that will be our next stop."

HORUS

I

Initial scouting showed Horus to be undamaged. Signals-and-detection were not picking up any other ships, off-planet energy or radiation signatures. At first, Morland feared the worst—another chicken-thieving raid. His hopes grew when the orbital detection survey began to pick up possible signs, including radio and electromagnetic waves, of an extensive civilization. After several orbits of Horus, along with detailed surveying by a couple of robot probes, the Ship Historian's consensus was that the planet appeared to be at about Civ-Level 6, an advanced steam age with locomotives, heavy machinery and telegraph communications—about where Old Terra was Second Century Pre-Atomic Era.

Wooden sailing vessels were the primary form of transportation. Which made sense given that there were eleven different island-continents, some of them separated from each other by no more than a few hundred miles. None of the continents were particularly large, all under a thousand miles in diameter, but three of them were located entirely in the temperate zones and were well-populated.

However, they weren't heading for any of those continents for the time being. After talking with Captain DeBorder about the morale of the *Pay Dirt*'s crew, he had made a suggestion which DeBorder enthusiastically embraced—shore leave. They were headed for the most isolated and least-populated continent named Bast. It had one large port city that the historical records had identified as Paulo. The city had a population of around three hundred thousand, possibly more. They would land a combat car outside the city and see how they were welcomed.

If things went well, they'd send down the rest of the crew.

Morland stressed to the *Skull Splitter's* crew that no looting would be tolerated. DeBorder had done the same, claiming that he wasn't worried about his men; his crew knew the difference between shore leave and work.

I sure hope so, Morland thought. He wasn't looking forward to dispatching any more of the *Pay Dirt's* thugs.

The city was surrounded by stone walls but large sections were crumbling from lack of maintenance and old age. There were large suburbs blooming out beyond the old city walls; he suspected many of the new structures were built using stones from the city walls. It was a typical pattern for a growing and peaceful city, but one that could backfire if an enemy fleet appeared on the horizon.

As the combat car came in for a landing, he watched from the *Skull Splitter*, which hovered five hundred feet above the city on contragravity. Horus' small orange sun gleamed weakly through what appeared to be, based on the lack of leaves on the trees and the harvested fields, a late fall sky.

The combat car contained Lord Ladbrok, Gytha Valkanhayn and their driver, Sergeant Xavier Burris. Ladbrok and the others had volunteered for first contact. Radio transmissions had given them some information about the local culture. On this island-continent the ruling class consisted of landed nobility in league with merchant oligarchs. Morland had agreed with Ladbrok that someone who had a title and the proper manners would have an inside track with the locals.

Gytha Valkanhayn had volunteered because of a bad case of cabin fever and from being one of the few women aboard ship for far too long. Morland thought that maybe a female face would make the inhabitants less suspicious. If things turned ugly, she was experienced in using the combat car's weapons.

The walls were manned by troops wearing steel-armored chest protectors and carrying guns. Single-shot guns from the way many of them were stuffing ramrods into them. Several outlandishly garbed men had gathered at a central position on the wall. A probe they sent down the day before had picked up the odd dress and Ladbrok had done his best to copy it. Morland thought he looked ridiculous, particularly wearing the round hat with long black and red feathers as well as the red-velvet padded doublet and billowy trousers.

"I wonder what they're thinking about the ship?" the Chief Engineer asked.

From five hundred feet, a two-thousand foot hyperspace warship filled the sky like the fist of god to those watching from below.

"A demon visitation," Ship First Historian Selner suggested.

"Especially when they see our device, a skull split by a hatchet," the Astrogator added.

Morland chuckled. "Maybe that's why they gave the old Space Viking ships such iconic and terrible names."

Ulrick Selner nodded. "The first Space Vikings who ventured into the Old Federation believed that they needed to overawe the Neobarbs and that, if they played it right, they could take whatever they wanted without any fighting. Corpses don't pay ransoms, nor do they make new things to steal. However, if the locals believe in sky gods maybe they'll give away their treasures as offerings. Conquerors, like Cortez and Pissarro, were doing that as long ago as Four Hundred Years Pre-Atomic."

Morland knew from experience that there was no guessing at how a world fallen into barbarism would interpret its origins. He had been on utterly destitute planets where the natives had retained an oral tradition of emigrating from another world; a few even remembered the world their forefathers came from was called Terra. On the other hand, some of the more civilized worlds he had visited, such as Agni or Junrojin, had lost all references to their past, or had completely forgotten that their ancestors arrived from a home world. They believed they were indigenous to their world, even down to spurious archaeological evidence.

Their explanations for the ruins of large cities on their worlds ranged from the pragmatic, that there had been a great war, to the ridiculous: On Junrojin they still believed that their ancestors had once been mighty warriors who had been cursed by the gods for trying to reach the clouds; therefore, the gods had taken all the ancients' powers and magic. It was worse on Abbadon, there they believed the Elder Race had lost a great battle with the Sky Lords and been punished by starfire: "Look at all the Great Cities turned to slag and debris! How else can you explain it?"

Lord Ladbrok was now in radio contact with the people on the wall. The car's communication screen was turned on but they could only pick up parts of the conversation. The natives were speaking Lingua Terra but with an accent that for Morland left a question mark after every word. After a while the combat car slowly moved away from the walls and headed back to the ship. He met them at the main airlock.

Ladbrok was quite cheerful. "They're very willing to let us visit. I think they're in awe of our ship. They couldn't stop staring at it."

"I'm not surprised; the *Skull Splitter* is larger than all the wooden ships in their harbor combined. Did you discuss what we could use for money?"

"I showed them some of our aluminum tokens; as Historian Selner suspected, they have not reached the stage where they can refine aluminum and they believe it to be another rare metal. They were quite taken with the tokens and found them an acceptable means of exchange."

"As I thought," the Historian said smugly. "Aluminum, like glass before it, was a precious commodity until late in the Second Century Pre-Atomic. Most of the early processes relied on displacing aluminum with more reactive metals, but the metal remained expensive and elusive. Aluminum wasn't available commercially until pioneering chemical engineers developed a smelting process based on electrolysis."

"They use both gold and silver as their primary currency," Ladbrok announced. "They want you to meet with their leaders, whom they refer to as the Twenty Four."

"Twenty-four families, or merchant oligarchs? Must be their ruling body," Selner said.

"I suspect so," Ladbock replied. They have given us two Galactic Standard hours for our 'Leader' to meet with their Twenty Four."

Morland and the Historian joined Ladbrok and Valkanhayn at the meeting. It was held in a large presence chamber that could have easily contained over a thousand people. At the moment there were less than fifty of the locals in the room, a third of them guards with elaborate pole arms that appeared more ceremonial than dangerous. The entire building was made of wood, but all the walls featured detailed and elegant carvings and colorful wall hangings.

First Historian Selner had been right: The Twenty Four were the representatives of the large merchant families that controlled the trade in Paulo, and probably throughout the rest of Bast, and made up the oligarchy that ruled the city. The outlandish and ostentatious clothes of their mercantile princes made their gold-braided Space Viking jackets seem plain.

The oligarchs appeared to have taken him as just another guard, as they addressed most of their comments to Ladbrok. Everyone present was male and wore a hat with feathers and as near as he could tell, the larger and longer the feathers, the more prominent the person. The man with the longest and most colorful feathers was called Sir Claudio Grundeen. He seemed eager to talk about trading possibilities.

Before the meeting, Morland had suggested to Ladbrok that the two hundred engineers and technicians the *Skull Splitter* carried to build their base world might be of great assistance to the Basts, as they called themselves, given the technical level of their civilization. He thought an ounce of gold per hour per man was acceptable; although, for the technical assistance they would be getting, the rate was cheap at one hundred times the price.

Lord Ladbrok and Sir Claudio were discussing that subject when, seeing he wasn't needed, Morland used his hand-phone to organize the crew's first wave of shore leave.

He was sitting with Rivera, Stenger, DeBorder and Haversham in an outdoor plaza at what had become their favorite bar in town. The bar served a very potent whiskey and excellent fried fish. The heat from nearby charcoal braziers compensated for the overcast fall weather. They all had an enjoyable few hundred hours of shore leave.

Morland had been able to spend a couple of days with his nephew Richard, joining an encampment that several families had setup in a heavily wooded area by a few lakes over two hundred miles from Paulo. There they swam, fished and hunted for small deer-like creatures. It had been a wonderful time. He was the only adult male relative in Richard's life since his father's death, and he wished that he could tear more time from his duties as captain to spend more time with the boy.

Zandra had joined them there and he had been pleased to see her smile and laugh for the first time since her husband's death. She had also commented to him that it was nice not to be under pressure while trying to restock supplies. The ship's systems officer was traditionally in charge of any resupply effort, particularly fresh food. Normally when raiding a world, resupply efforts were hasty and rushed. Shore leave made things much easier and less stressful.

It also helped that their time off was taking place at a port city. People quickly grew tired of carniculture meat and hydroponic vegetables during long voyages and hungered for something different. There was nothing more different from carniculture than fish; Space Viking ships always tried to pick up fresh fish whenever they stopped at a world. The Basts had a variety of fish and many different ways to cook it. He hadn't grown tired of it yet.

Shore leave had borne other fruit than fish. They were planning where to raid on Horus based on the information they had picked up from the Basts. The city of Nekhen, located on the continent called Atum, was the target. Atum was the most prosperous continent, but Nekhen was far from the largest city. It had become the banking center because it was centrally located and the most protected city, having been built on a hill at the end of a narrow and easily defended harbor. They never would have targeted Nekhen if they had not visited Paulo first.

The Basts benefited from their visit as well. The Sword-Worlders had shown them everything from improvements in the rigging and construction of their ships to how to rifle their muskets and cannon, as well as how to take cure of the scurvy that was the bane of primitive sailors. They had also traded some of the low-level loot they had picked up on Sucellos and Morrígu. It wouldn't have brought much on the Sword-Worlds but it was valuable here. The booze and food they had consumed had been free as a result. He hadn't inquired as to the costs of any of the other services his crew had sought.

The only disappointment had been that there was nothing but a small spaceport on Horus, not any bigger than those at the smaller regional centers of Joyeuse. There were only a few industrial facilities dating back to the Federation and those they examined had been stripped bare. He wanted a base he could rehabilitate rather than something he had to build completely from scratch.

Ladbrok arrived and promptly doffed his ridiculous looking hat. "The place we want is called the Golden Way. It's about a half-mile long mall of banks and stores surrounded by the houses of the bank owners, minor nobles and the richest merchants. The bank vaults there are supposed to be full of gold and silver."

Gytha grinned. "We've confirmed the description of the area from probes. There are squares at either end of the site large enough to land pinnaces. They can provide plenty of protection and be loaded quickly."

They quickly decided which pinnaces and ground commanders would lead the raid. The *Skull Splitter* and *Pay Dirt* would hover overhead to offer support if needed.

Morland noticed that Ladbrok had more he wanted to add. He gestured to him to speak. "There is some sort of harvest festival going on in Nekhen now. The climax of the festival occurs in three nights."

They all grinned at each other. Nothing like raiding people who were recovering from a night of drunken partying.

The Nekhen raid went as well as anyone could hope. They landed right at dawn, the morning after the festival ended, the area still strewn with the debris of the previous night's festivities. Combat cars, armed with missiles and machine guns, carrying anywhere from four to a dozen people depending on their size, and egg-shaped air-cavalry mounts, with a single occupant armed with a set of machine guns on the front, spilled from the ships to lead the way. Troop carriers, followed by a variety of cargo vehicles, their sides swinging wide open for easy loading, came last. Troops spilled from the carriers and cargo vehicles carrying lifters to load the vehicles and driving grapplers for heavier loot. All of the equipment was on contragravity, allowing it to travel almost anywhere.

Two pinnaces landed at either end of the Golden Way, providing plenty of firepower for defense and another place to load booty. The other pinnaces hovered just above the rooftops, firing at any resistance. The *Skull Splitter* and *Pay Dirt* floated higher still, ready to discourage anyone coming to help from outside the area.

There was plenty of gold, jewelry and other loot inside the shops along the Golden Way. Most of the local soldiers in the area were garrisoned in the forts along the harbor, well away from the mall. Resistance was sparse. Most people were still recovering from the previous night's party. They quickly learned that musket fire was worthless; their lead balls ricocheted off the shiny collapsium-plated sides of the Sword-Worlders' cars and lifters, hurting the attackers more than the combat cars. Collapsium, material that had been collapsed down until the atomic nuclei were touching, was incredibly dense and could easily stop their primitive weapons. All enemy fire was promptly met with a hail of deadly return fire.

Soon streams of cargo vehicles were traveling back and forth between the pinnaces and the stores and big warehouses. When they were full, they flew up to the *Skull Splitter* and *Pay Dirt.* Small squads looted the private homes and villas adjacent to the Golden Way. They also hit some of the warehouses along the harbor, taking the usual furs, tapestries, paintings and any hand-crafted goods that might prove valuable. Morland did his best to limit the amount of bulk goods going into the ships. He wanted to concentrate on compact materials of high value.

Until they had a base, they wouldn't know what they needed in the way of raw materials and primitive machinery.

Even the *Pay Dirt's* crew managed to restrain themselves from setting the Golden Way on fire while looting the mall. Civilian casualties, for once, were low due to the lack of armed resistance. Once all the bank vaults had been emptied and the jewelry shops stripped bare, Morland gave the order to lift off.

When they reached high planetary orbit, the captains and the executive officers met in the Wardroom. After doing a post mortem of the raid and determining that for the most part things went just as planned, DeBorder wanted to know why they weren't raiding some of the other continents. "We had a great base in Bast; the locals were turning cartwheels for those aluminum tokens. They were providing us valuable intel about the other continents. I don't understand why we're leaving. As far as I was concerned the fun was just beginning."

"I agree, we should raid some of the other continents," Rivera urged. "We took in forty-eight thousand pounds of gold alone. That's over a million stellars in just a few hours, not counting all the jewels, silver, rare metals, artwork and other rarities."

"We can always come back again," Morland replied. He could understand DeBorder's elation; this was probably the easiest score of his career. "We're not on a trade-and-raid voyage, we are here to find a permanent base world. This world doesn't have the industrial base we need. There are better worlds out there."

"I don't believe this. We finally find a planet we can milk for months and you want to leave!"

"Those are my orders."

"My crew will not be happy."

"Make them happy. We've got bigger fish to fry than Horus."

NISSABA

I

The next planet on their list, appeared even less civilized than Horus. The sun was a G5 sun with twelve planets, most of them the size of moons. One was a Jovian gas giant about the size of Saturn, without the rings, and then there was an earth-sized world smack dab in the middle of the habitable zone. It had a large moon, but it was fortunately located more than half a million miles from the planet.

Nissaba had five continents, but only the largest one seemed to be occupied. There was evidence of a civilization at the mountainous northwest corner of the equatorial continent, plus a number of small settlements in the central plains and a fairly extensive grouping along the entire east coast. There were indications that some of the other continents and islands were occupied, but only sparsely.

The historians put the Nissaban's cultural level at Civ-Level 3, equivalent to Fifth Century Pre-Atomic. "There is one large city," Ulrik Selner stated as he reviewed the information, "of an estimated half a million or so in the northeast, and a handful of towns, of around fifty to a hundred thousand people along the eastern region. The mountainous area in the northwest is not as highly populated, and what appears to be their major center holds less than a hundred and fifty thousand inhabitants. The central continental plains area is dotted with fortified castles surrounded by farmland. There are a few large towns at river junctions, but none with a population larger than fifty thousand people."

"Any spaceports, old Federation cities or industrial areas?" Morland asked.

"Yes," the Historian replied. Everyone stirred, hoping that at last they had found a planet they could turn into a base of operations. "There's a spaceport in the center of the big continent near the major river. It's surrounded by an Old Federation city."

His exec cleared his throat. "How big is the city?"

Selner had consulted with his staff before the meeting. The youngest one, Walter Ovard, spoke up. "Not big. It's unoccupied at present, unless you count the hundred or so itinerant sheepherders living out of old buildings with their flocks. I'd guess the population, when it was occupied, was about a hundred and forty thousand people. Nissaba was one of the late colonies, settled after the Big War. We're estimating the present population of the world at approximately sixty to eighty million."

"Any idea of who settled it?"

Ulrik Selner paused to stroke his graying beard. "According to the records I found on Odin, Nissaba was colonized by a group of Persians, fleeing from persecution on Terra. They were a mixed group, including a large number of Zoroastrians, some Muslims and a few Christians. Initially, in the Third Century Atomic Era, they settled on Hathor, which is nearby. However, during the System States War, they were persecuted and driven off-world. Due to war time propaganda, it wasn't unusual for small minority groups on many Federation worlds to be accused of supplying aid and comfort to the enemy. On some worlds it was true; the records show there was active espionage and sabotage by a number of dissident minority groups on behalf of the System States.

"In this case, there is no evidence either way. The Persian community on Hathor was never very large; less than half a million refugees fled from there to Nissaba. Evidence indicates the majority of the evacuees were tradesmen and servants with a thin crust of technocrats and wealthy merchants. Once they arrived on their new world, they thrived under its pleasant living conditions. Their main exports were glassware, exotic perfumes, silk gowns, alpaca wool, a very fine llama's wool, and Persian rugs. Unfortunately they didn't bring enough educated people to Nissaba to sustain a high-technology culture by themselves—a recipe for decivilization during the disorder that followed the Federation's collapse—when interstellar trade went into a massive decline.

"From all the planetary evidence we've collected so far, it appears the collapse on Nissaba was severe. Not in the usual sense—civil war, insurrection and rebellion—but in regards to a loss of education and technology, leading to a return to a much more primitive and pastoral lifestyle. It appears they are slowly working their way back up from a Civ-Level 2 to a Level-4. Right now they're stuck in a feudal stage, at about Civ-Level 3."

"While our survey scouts and historical staff continue their examination of the planet," Morland announced, "I'm going to take a team down to examine the spaceport. Given the technological level of this planet, is there anyone in the area of the spaceport who could possibly communicate our presence to any of the coastal population centers in less than a few weeks?"

"No," reported one of the signals-and-detection officers.

When his officers objected to their captain going to the surface due to unknown dangers, Morland agreed that he would take a combat car, instead of an aircar, and do all his reconnaissance above the city.

The spaceport was in surprisingly good condition; the only damage the city showed from the sky had been caused by the passage of time.

He estimated that, with the equipment they had brought in their ship, they could have it cleaned up in a few thousand hours. The industrial areas, however, were in much worse shape. Many of them were in ruins and had probably been stripped of useful machinery during the planet's descent into barbarism. There were only a handful of buildings that appeared unscathed by vandals. He had just authorized a ground expedition to search for signs of fissionables when he received an urgent message to return to the *Skull Splitter.*

11

As Morland approached the bridge he tried to dampen his anger. *Things were going too well,* he thought, *I guess it was about time for another screw-up by DeBorder or his crew. I'd have been better off with that rummy and his wreck of a ship back on Tanith!*

"Have you raised DeBorder?" he asked as he entered the bridge.

"No Captain," Laz Rivera replied. "It seems they have to wake him. And Haversham as well."

A pinnace had left the *Pay Dirt* several hours before. It was now located in the middle of the continental plains; based on the energy discharge the *Skull Splitter's* energy detectors had picked up, the pinnace's crew was engaged in raiding one of the castles. He and DeBorder had agreed to hold off on any attacks until his examination of the port area was complete. The plan was to study the planet in greater detail so they could target their raids at those castles holding the greatest concentration of wealth. They would save the city for last.

Gytha Valkanhayn spoke up. "Message coming in sir."

A sleepy and disheveled looking DeBorder peered out of the screen. He gulped at what appeared to be a cup of coffee and shook his head. "This raid wasn't authorized, David. I don't know why they left."

"Who is it, DeBorder?" Morland asked.

Haversham appeared on screen. Unlike DeBorder he was immaculately groomed and dressed.

Figures, Morland thought.

"Hereld Norwell is in command of the pinnace," Haversham stated. "Without orders, I might add."

There was an explosive snort behind him. Morland didn't bother turning around; he knew where it came from. Norwell had been the one who had been knocked down by Gytha Valkanhayn when he wouldn't take no for an answer to his unwanted advances. He had also been friends with the two men Morland had executed for rape on Sucellos. According to Haversham he had nursed a grudge ever since, and had been trying to stir up trouble among the *Pay Dirt*'s crew. Why DeBorder tolerated troublemakers like Norwell, he didn't understand?

Haversham turned away from the screen; when he looked back, he said. "They aren't responding to our calls."

DeBorder stood up. "Will, leave them a message to get their tails back here as fast as possible! Call me when they arrive."

DeBorder came back on-screen, his face a grim mask, saying, "I'll handle this Captain." Then he left.

Morland stared at Haversham through the viewscreen. "Make sure there are some armed men with him when he confronts Norwell."

Haversham nodded.

Morland turned back to the bridge crew. "Continue sending probes down for information. Concentrate on the eastern coast of the inhabited continent. What's the spaceport called, Selner?"

The Historian responded, "The continent was named Eresh by original Federation discovery team and the survey team that followed titled the spaceport Uruk. It was common for survey and scouting teams to name continents, bodies of water and sometimes even islands after names from whatever pantheon of gods the original survey craft used to name the planet. When the colonists arrived they often broke with that tradition; in this case, Uruk was renamed Samandar, after the Persian word for phoenix."

"It sounds like they were trying for a rebirth; too bad the city's in about the same shape as Persia is back on Terra," said one wag. The entire Middle East had been nuked into a sea of glass and slag during World War III; there hadn't been anything left to incinerate in World War IV.

Ulrik Selner shook his head. "The people here were attempting to pay homage to the great cultures of the Achaemenid Empire."

"Okay, that's all I needed to know," Morland replied, to hold off an elaborate explanation. Selner could go on for hours, and during hyperspace downtime Morland enjoyed hearing him ramble about various historical events and personages—but not now.

He turned to the Chief Engineer. "While we're waiting, Chief, send some of your engineers down to examine the industrial area next to the spaceport." He hoped a detailed examination would turn up more than what he had seen during his quick tour, but he wasn't optimistic.

By the next day, all of the major and most of the minor industrial districts they could identify in Samandar had been inspected. There were some potentially useful bits and pieces, but most of the buildings had been thoroughly stripped down to their underlying steel girders, if not destroyed.

Meanwhile Fourth Officer Norwell of the *Pay Dirt* had returned and was under arrest. He had raided two castles with three squads of ground troopers.

Morland rode over to the *Pay Dirt* in one of the pinnaces to preside over the court martial, bringing a squad of his own troops along with him. The trial was held in the large assembly hall near the center of the ship. He was pleased to find out that the majority of Norwell's men were embarrassed when they found out that they had acted without orders.

Hereld himself was unrepentant. "I brought back gold and silver worth a quarter million stellars while everyone else was just sitting around *studying things*. What's to study? We're Space Vikings! Hit 'em fast, hit 'em hard and get out of there! That's how it should be done."

"How much did they make?" Captain DeBorder asked.

"Just about like *he* said. Around a quarter million," someone replied.

"Not bad for a quick grab-and-run," one the junior officers blurted.

"Nial, shut your mouth or you can join Norwell in the brig!" DeBorder shouted.

"And it cost six troopers' lives and a dozen more casualties," Morland said, gesturing to one the ground fighters who was limping badly from a sword slash.

"Space Vikings expect casualties," Norwell sneered. "This isn't a job for someone who wants to play it safe," making it clear he included Morland in that group.

Morland knew it was a waste of time to try and reach Norwell, whose punishment would be grounding for life on Nissaba, for disobeying orders and dereliction of duty, on the next dirt-side visit. However, this was an opportunity to educate the rest of the *Pay Dirt's* junior officers. "Let's see, with six people dead—assuming no one else dies—after death benefits are paid, officers will get less than a thousand stellars and the crew barely more than a hundred each from this raid. If we continue with this strategy, there'll be nobody left to return home and nothing to bring back."

Norwell's reply was a string of curses.

After he was judged guilty and stripped of his rank, DeBorder ordered, "Throw him in the brig. I hope you like Nissaba, Hereld; you're going to spend the rest of your life there."

"He should be returned to one of the castles he raided," Morland stated.

"Enough! I'm captain of this ship, not you," DeBorder said, with more steel in his voice than Morland had ever heard before. "Norwell's going to regret this breach of discipline. Oh, yes that son-of-a-

Khooghra will rue the day!"

Morland had to agree. The *Pay Day's* ship discipline was DeBorder's bailiwick, not his. On the inside, he was secretly pleased to see his fellow captain finally growing a pair.

Discussion with the ground fighters revealed that the Nissabans were armed with single-shot hackbuts, swords and laboriously loaded matchlock cannon. Moreover, the two castles they'd raided were constructed of stone blocks and contained many levels with narrow, twisting corridors. And, like anyone attacked in their home, the Nissabans had fought courageously and desperately—with the advantage of knowing their ground.

One of the most embarrassed troopers, a Corporal Torran, noted, "Both treasure vaults were well below ground, sirs. If we had used heavy weapons, the castle would have collapsed right on top of the vaults. I was afraid to even use grenades in the corridors for fear some of the bracing would fail and the roof would cave in on us."

Afterwards, Morland joined DeBorder and Haversham in a conference room, a jug of rotgut whiskey from Horus to share between them.

"You were right, David," DeBorder said, his shirt open and his feet stretched out on a spare chair, cigarette in hand. "We can't expect to fight our way down through every castle and do it profitably." He gulped down what was left of his glass, belched and refilled it. "Damn, that Horus brew's got some blow-back!"

Morland also had his feet stretched out, though as usual he was drinking much more slowly than DeBorder. "We have identified several areas where there appears to be wars or skirmishes going on. I think we should land in one of those areas and try and make friends. People fighting wars, especially on the losing end, are often desperate. If we gain some local allies, they'll provide us with intelligence so we'll know where to concentrate our efforts in looting the planet."

"Like on Horus," DeBorder said, nodding.

Haversham leaned forward attentively. "If it turns out the only valuables are in the basements of their castles, maybe we can get our new friends to do the hard fighting if we cut them in for a share."

III

Once again Lord Ladbrok and Gytha Valkanhayn were slowly approaching a castle wall with Sergeant Xavier Burris as their driver. The aircar traveled slowly, causing the prominent white flag it carried on top to flap listlessly in the still air. The castle overlooked a small town, and Morland watched as the aircar landed just outside the town walls. It was late in the afternoon but the air temperature felt like early summer to him as he sat on the bridge, alternating his attention between the castle and town gates, where the aircar was preparing to land.

There was a contragravity probe hovering just above the castle and using the telescopic-screen Morland could see everything going on within the castle courtyard and outlying walls as if he personally were flying over it. Unlike on Horus, the Nissabans wore more practical garments and were on military alert. As soon as the *Skull Splitter* had appeared in the sky, the castle swarmed with troops and the parapets were quickly manned with hackbutters, pikemen and halberdiers. Some of the artillery men were loading their guns and lighting their matches. One waved his broom-like cannon swab at the sky.

Morland turned to the lift-and-drive officer, saying, "Let's drop down to about two hundred feet above the town. I want to keep a close eye on that parley.

"Aye aye, sir."

The *Skull Splitter* quickly lost altitude and within moments they were hovering over the small town. The buildings were mostly stone and timber construction with whitewashed walls. The roofs were mainly verdant copper or tin, although some of the lesser outbuildings had thatch roofing. There was one large stone building near the center of town, close to the palace, that had four open walls under its roof. He suspected that was the town fire temple.

The aircar was now within speaking distance of the castle wall without any shots being fired. Through the telescopic-screen, he could see that Ladbrok was speaking with a large, broad-shouldered man who was standing on the parapets above the town gates. He wore a high-combed helmet, similar to a Fourth Century Pre-Atomic burgonet, and his air of command indicated he was the castle's general-equivalent.

The soldier was wearing an elaborate metal breastplate that showed the nicks and dents of frequent use. The probe's pickups magnified his voice so it was as clear as if he were speaking right next to him in the bridge. He was obviously speaking Lingua Terra but with an atrocious local accent that was even worse than the one they'd encountered on Horus. Morland suspected by the man's halting speech that Lingua Terra was a trade dialect rather than the language in everyday use. He was having problems following the conversation, and Ladbrok was apparently having trouble as well, because he kept repeating himself and asking the soldier the same questions over and over.

After a few minutes of back-and-forth everyone seemed to be more relaxed and the large bearded man turned and said something to someone out of sight. There was a loud squeal and the big timber and iron-reinforced gates began to open by an elaborate pulley system. Once the gates were fully open, Ladbrok and his party entered the town. Three people came forward to greet them, while a few hundred residents crowded the staging area between the town gates and the town proper.

The oldest of the three was a man in a flame-red robe, with long white hair and a thick white beard. There were pictograph markings on the robe and he was carrying a golden staff. He deferred to the other two, but his manner screamed senior advisor. The other man appeared to be in his mid-forties and was wearing a gold cap with wings on his head. *That's got to be the man-in-charge*, thought Morland, probably the local equivalent of duke or prince.

He wasn't armored but carried two long-barreled pistols in his belt. His clothing seemed to be of a higher quality than anyone else's and he wore a large gold chain around his neck.

The woman was in her late twenties and wore a simple gown with a collar ruff; her raven-colored tresses were in some sort of French braid. She was strikingly beautiful. From the obvious deference everyone gave them, including Ladbrok, he assumed they were the duke and duchess.

Conversations continued between the "duke" and Ladbrok, with the duchess occasionally weighing in. Finally Valkanhayn said something in an approximation of the degraded Lingua Terra they were speaking to each other, and everyone laughed.

"Well I guess we're all friends now," one of the crewmen at the monitors said.

"I'd sure like to be friendly with that woman," someone else said to general agreement.

"Captain," the communication screen buzzed, and Ladbrok said, "they'd like to meet with you. "I believe they're going to be just the Trojan Horse we're looking for."

He hoped so. Probes had shown armies massing on what might be their southern border, and there was another very large group, of between four to five thousand heavily armed soldiers, coming from much farther south. There had been a large force marching away from the castle to the south during the past two days. He took an individual air-cavalry mount down to the town gates.

The small courtyard inside the town behind the town gates was packed with people milling about. They quickly moved back into a circle to give him room to land when he zoomed down over their heads. You didn't have to be a sophisticated city dweller to understand that the 15mm machine gun mounted at the fore of the air-cavalry mount could do serious harm. He landed and popped open the side door, and a mechanical stairway shot out from the vehicle to rest on the hard-packed earth. It was an impressive display of engineering to people at their Civ-Level, and many of them were gasping and oohing and ahhing.

He stepped down, making a grand entrance. This was the part of command he did not enjoy.

"Your Majesty," Ladbrok said, "I would like to introduce Prince David Morland of Joyeuse, Captain of the *Skull Splitter*, our space-traveling ship."

He threw Ladbrok a sharp look for giving him a title he didn't own or rate, and received a canny smile in return. Then he hastily turned his attention back to the people he was being introduced to. The man with the winged crown on his head was the Shah Parviz. The old man was a high priest—he called himself the Magis Zarir—while the soldier was Argbod Omid. The beautiful woman was addressed as the Shaheen Janna, which probably meant princess. His own title as Prince translated as Sanjar.

Morland was captivated by Janna's eyes; they were like pools of deep amber, and he felt as if he could drown himself in them. It took all of his willpower to tear his eyes off her delicately featured face. He hadn't been so taken with a woman since his school days. She noticed his attempt to look away, smiled sweetly and blushed.

He felt his heart thump.

This is no time to get involved with one of the locals, no matter how beautiful. We have a raid to pull off, then we may be leaving, he told himself. *A princess, yet!*

Morland forced his attention off the Princess and back to the problems the Satrap was having with its neighbors. Morland had difficulty understanding them as the discussion continued.

Historian Selner, who was listening to their pidgin Lingua Terra over the ship com system, told him—through the transmitter in his mastoid implant—that he had some Farsi language programs. *"Later when we get back to the ship, I'll hypnotize you and use hypno-instruction to help you learn the language. That will also help you understand their pidgin Terran."*

Most planets, even the worst of the Civ-Lev 1 and 2 barbarian worlds, spoke some form of Lingua Terra, no matter how debased. However, every once in a while, a Space Viking ship would land on an unexplored world where the inhabitants had brought their native tongue—from one of the forgotten nations on Old Terra—to their new planet. Nissaba was one of them. It was for those unlikely exceptions that any well-outfitted Space Viking ship kept a library of Terran-based language programs.

Fortunately Ladbrok was making progress in communicating with the locals through their degraded Terran, although he often had to ask them to speak more slowly or repeat themselves. At last, they were beginning to get some useful information. Signals-and-detection had been correct that the armies to the south were enemies, and that the Satrap of Jannat was under attack from a neighboring satrap, but he couldn't quite grasp who was who or why they were being attacked.

Valkanhayn was having the same problem. During a break, while refreshments were delivered, Gytha leaned over and whispered into his ear, "It sounds like our friends are fighting Eeny, Meeny, Miny and Moe."

It took another couple of hours of conversation, but he finally put some names to their enemies, one satrap was called Sardis, the other

Taxlla. The western mountains were called the Mountains of Istakhr and were ruled by one overlord, the king of kings, Padishah Kourosh III in the city of New Persepolis. The Padishah was more a title than power, as many of the provincial shahs refused to do his bidding.

They had sent an envoy to Persepolis to ask for the Kourosh's help, but the Padishah was too busy preparing his kingdom for an imminent invasion by the Muslims, who were invading Greater Veda from New Iran on the other side of the continent. He wondered if the large force they had seen were the invaders; if so, the little Satrap of Zarani was in a mess of trouble.

The rulers of Zarani, the town and satrap of the same name, were all younger than they looked. In his experience, this was not an unusual situation on Neobarb worlds that did not have access to modern medicines and conveniences. People aged quickly. The beautiful princess was actually the prince's sister. The prince's wife, it turned out, had died some years ago in childbirth. "My sister has acted as mother to my children as well as her own since then," the shah said.

The Shaheen Janna had been married but her husband had died over a year ago in first battle of the war with the Satrap of Sardis. Tears welled in her eyes when her brother mentioned his death. Morland was touched, he wanted to take her in his arms and tell her everything was going to be all right...but he restrained himself with some difficulty.

What's wrong with me? Has she put me under some kind of a spell? He had been on worlds where witches and *brujas* were both feared and respected, but most of them were out-and-out fakes or frauds. They either used the power of suggestion and subtle hypnosis, or they had hidden receivers and transmitters. Janna had done no such thing. He might be bewitched, but it wasn't her fault—it was his heart's.

He forced himself to listen to the conversation and try to make sense out of it. The shah let them know he was eager for an alliance, especially when he heard the descriptions of some of their weapons. He kept asking for fires, which Morland assumed meant guns or cannon. They assured him they had more than enough fires to deal with his neighboring satraps, Mehrak, Taxlla and Sardis, or even the emperor, or Padishah, if need be. Hearing that, the king and princess broke out into huge smiles, and the priest lifted his arms in supplication and praised their god, Ahriman.

They were quite eager to tell them about the gold and other valuables their enemies had hidden in their castles once they discovered that loot was what the Space Vikings were interested in. When it came to describing where the valuables were located, the language barrier reared its head again. Taxlla was clearly the enemy to the east, while Sardis was to the south, but where was Mehruk? Then they described another place where there were apparently a lot of valuables and all three of the Space Vikings looked at each in puzzlement.

"What?" asked Valkanhayn quizzically.

Checking with *Pay Dirt*, which had remained in high orbit, Morland found that the two invading armies were still several days away from the borders of the shah's lands. He conveyed that information to the shah and he in turn thanked them for the news, as if it were a good thing. Well, maybe knowing where your enemies were—when you didn't have telescopes and aircars—was something to be thankful for. He knew he was grateful for signals-and-detection every time they entered a new star system; one never knew what might by lying in wait—a Confederacy cruiser or a Mardukan warship? Or even another Space Viking…?

Finally, frustrated because of the language problem and his yearning for this woman he didn't even know, Morland returned to the ship to organize the attack. Lord Ladbrok and Valkanhayn remained behind at the castle to continue their language lessons.

IV

The Wardroom was buzzing the next morning as the senior officers came it. Every officer of the night shift seemed to still be there and they were clearly excited. After getting coffee from a serving-robot Morland asked what was going on.

"There's been a communications breakthrough!" the young watch officer exclaimed excitedly. "Gytha wants to tell you about it herself!"

Morland grinned to himself. The watch officer was a fine astrogator and would probably be an excellent senior officer one day, but she was still at that stage of life where everything was an exclamation point. He had placed her in charge of the night shift in hopes that the experience would calm her down a bit, but it didn't seem to be having any effect. Valkanhayn, who was good friends with her, told him it would take more than a few shifts to mature her. "She's smart, but high-strung. Give her a few heart-stopping emergencies and she'll get some perspective—if she lives long enough."

He had ordered breakfast from the Wardroom menu and was waiting for the robot-server to bring it to the mess table when they got Gytha Valkanhayn on the viewscreen. It was about noon planetside.

Valkanhayn appeared as excited as the watch officer when the screen cleared. "We're making progress, Captain, we had it all wrong!" she exclaimed. "This war isn't over territory, it's a religious war. The satrapies are mostly Zoroastrians, an old Terran religion having to do with the duality of good and evil—or Ahriman and Angra Mainyu, light and darkness. Opposing them are the Muslims who see the Zoroastrians as infidels to convert to Allah—or kill, although many are taken captive and end up in the Eastern slave markets."

To Morland, Muslims and Christians were all the same, religious fanatics who would kill disbelievers at the first opportunity. He had studied Old Terra's Crusades, Inquisitions and Jihads, finding little to distinguish them from each one another—all had killed unbelievers with great fervor. Fortunately, the founders of the Sword-Worlds had not brought Terra's religions with them when they fled the Federation. They had, for the most part, lost faith in religion after the Big War. There were no temples of any kind on Joyeuse or Excalibur, or any of the other Space Viking home worlds.

It was one of the reason Gilgameshers were so hated; their polyglot of a religion contained just about everything the Space Vikings despised.

"I don't know anything about Zoroastrians, but I have heard of Muslims and their Holy Wars. What brought about this one?"

"A decade ago one of the high ayatollahs in Mashhad, the Muslim's Holy City, had a vision at the Imâm Ridha Mosque. Apparently, they brought the Imâm Ridha's (the martyred and eighth Imâm of the Twelver Shiites) remains from Terra—I have no idea what they went through to find them in that nuclear wasteland, or even if they are Ridha's true bones. However, they have built a great building in tribute, a shrine that's filled with goldware and precious gems—even the roof is gold plated!"

"That's the kind of information we've been looking for!" Morland exclaimed.

"The Ayatollah Mustaffa's vision was that the Prophet's Word would be spread from sea to sea," Gytha explained. "He called for a Holy War, or *Jihad*, about fifteen Galactic Standard years ago, or twenty-two by the local calendar. His vision managed to energize the entire nation of New Iran, the East Coast civilization, and it took them over ten years to conquer their Zoroastrian neighbors, seeing as they were outnumbered three to one. But, they did it in detail; the eastern fire worshipers didn't realize how serious they were about their Holy War, since such a thing is anathema to them. When they did, it was too late.

"More recently the army of the Jihad has made its way through the midlands, taking any castles in their way by siege craft. Apparently, they have rifled cannon and enough of them to knock one of those stone castles down to its dungeon in less than a week. Rifling cannon is a recent innovation, probably based on the rifled Jezails the Iranians use as their principal missile weapon. The Zoroastrians are still using smoothbore hackbuts and primitive guns, not much advanced over bombards, which puts them at a great disadvantage. Ideal for us, because they're desperate and badly in need of our help."

"Good detection and scholarship, Gytha."

"It's not all my doing, sir. Ulrik came up with a lot of this. This is the first ship I've been on that's had its own History department, but I'm beginning to see the advantages."

"Have the Muslims conquered the Vahistan midlands?"

"No," Valkanhayn said, "they left most of the castles untouched since the local Vahistas (or what we would call dukes) are robustly independent and refuse to surrender, even when their castles are demolished. Which is one of the reasons they've been able to maintain their independence from the much larger civilizations on both coasts for so long."

"Are the Vahistas Zoroastrians or Muslims?" he asked.

"Zoroastrians, like most of the inhabitants of Nissaba are—or were until this bloody jihad began. On the east coast territories, the Warriors of God, as they call themselves, have converted, killed or enslaved almost half of the population. I know it doesn't pay to get emotionally involved in our job, Captain, but these fanatics are a scourge upon humanity! I'd like to drop a hellbuster right on their capital, and another one on the Imâm Ridha Mosque."

"Bloody business, indeed," Morland said. "For people who claim not to get any pleasure from murder, these zealots sure do a lot of it."

"It gets worse, Captain. The Warriors of God, as they call themselves, have reached the West Coast satraps of Greater Veda, which is where we are right now. This is the Vedic homeland of the Zoroastrians, or *Persis* as they sometimes call themselves, or Persians as the Federation knew them. The jihad's mission is to conquer all the satraps of Greater Veda so they can purify it of infidels, which sounds like a recipe for full scale genocide to me."

Morland nodded in agreement. "From what I've seen so far, I like these Zoroastrians. They're a pleasant people and haven't tried to shove their religious beliefs down our throat. They certainly don't need any cleansing by this gang of slave-dealing cutthroats."

"I agree, Captain. It may turn out that we can help them while we help ourselves. From what we've uncovered so far, the Warriors of God have camped their forces in the southernmost Satrap, Zarani, which they conquered last year and have been using as their base of operations, mostly reconnoitering and spying—so far. They brought with them an army of some fifteen thousand: five thousand are elite Holy Warriors who fight as cataphracts with bow and sword from armored horses; in addition, they have eight thousand infantry, two-thirds spearmen and one-third riflemen armed with Jezails. The rest are light cavalry and auxiliaries, some two-thousand armored Vahistan men-at-arms.

"No matter how you cut it, sir, that's a big force in these mountains, or even in the whole of Greater Veda. I doubt that the Satrap of Zarani has more than eight hundred men-at-arms and fifteen hundred infantry, mostly spearmen and hackbutters. Some of those are peasant levy and not worth much in a real dustup. They're a small satrap."

"Now that I've heard the bad news," Morland replied, "what's in it for us?

"Treasure, the accumulated treasure of the Jihad's journey across the continent; the loot from over fifty sacked castles and towns. They're carrying it with them in their baggage train."

Morland smiled. "How much?"

Valkanhayn shrugged her shoulders. "The locals only say it's a Big Treasure; from what the *Pay Dirt* got from raiding those two Vahista castles—what, a million stellars. So, as a conservative estimate—say half a million stellars per castle—the loot from fifty some castles would give us a minimum of two hundred and fifty million stellars. And that's not counting the gold the Muslims brought with them in their paychests, the loot of close to a hundred sacked towns and villages. The whole shebang could add up to five or six hundred million stellars—not bad for a Level-3 planet! And that's just from one army. No telling how much is in New Iran, or at the Great Mosque."

Morland broke out in a smile. "This kind of motherlode is why you don't write off a world as worthless until you've studied it thoroughly."

"I agree, Captain, but you have to admit we got lucky with Nissaba."

"I do, Gytha. But we've had our share of duds, too.

"But what about Sardis?" he asked. "Who is that Satrap fighting for? After all, they're Zoroastrians, too."

"Shah Zahhak is a depraved animal," Valkanhayn said with feeling, "at least according to what Janna's told me. Personal emotions aside, the Shah of Sardis is very ambitious, and he is not overly worried about how much blood he gets on his hands—as long as he gets what he wants. When Shaheen Janna's husband was killed in a battle against the Shah of Taxlla, over some border dispute, Shah Zahhak proposed marriage, hoping to add Zarani to his realm when her brother died. She has a violent hatred of Zahhak and refused to even consider his proposal."

"So, he's using the invasion as an excuse to get even, or take that which he could not win by pressing his hand in marriage."

"Exactly," Gytha said. "The worst part is that he's been making deals with the Muslims. In return for some of their Jezail rifles, he's given them maps and other information about the Vedic satraps. What he doesn't know is that the Muslims been playing him like a violin. They've got an army of more than five thousand coming up behind the Sardi troops. Zahhak would have a stroke if he knew that while his army was attempting to invest Zarani, the Muslim's will be taking his own Satrap."

"Cross and double-cross," Morland said. "Let's see what kind of monkey wrench we can throw into both of their plans."

"I like the way you think, Captain," Valkanhayn said with a smile. "By the way, that dark-haired beauty, Janna, keeps asking questions about you. It sounds to me like you've made a conquest in Veda of your own."

He quickly shut down the viewscreen so she couldn't see the flush her words brought to his face.

V

"Valkanhayn, is the Shah in agreement with our plan to attack his enemies?"

"Captain, the Shah wants you to tell him yourself, as a fellow royal or Sanjar—as he calls you. I think he's tired of talking with underlings, although he didn't put it that way. In fact, he was rather nice about it."

"Okay, it's time I went dirtside anyway. Thanks for having them ship up those oranges and peaches. As for that pomegranate wine—that would make a nice trade item—it's delicious. It's nice to have fresh fruit in the mess once in a while; I'm so damn tired of hydroponics and vat chicken...."

Besides, it would give him another chance to be with Janna, not that anything could ever come of it. An hour later he was getting out of his aircar in the castle courtyard. A yellow sun was shining bright and the castle flag, a golden falcon on red field, was flapping in the brisk wind. It felt good to be on solid ground again. His boots clanged as he walked over the cobblestones to meet with the shah, and his army commander and castellan, Argbod Omid. He was relieved to see Squad Commander Ladbrok was with them, but disappointed that the Shahreen wasn't there.

This is ridiculous, he told himself, *Janna's just another woman I can't have—that's why she's so desirable. She's beautiful in an exotic way and it was easy to imagine what might be resting hidden underneath the billowy dress and embroidered vest—*

It didn't help that the few women aboard the ship were either related or off-limits. Nothing was worse for a ship's morale than a captain involved in a shipboard romance with a subordinate. *We're four thousand light-years from home and it's up to me to see that this expedition succeeds and we all return safely. Get over it!*

They held the war council in one of the keep's third floor chambers in an ornate room that several hundred years ago had probably served as the shah's official presence room. Now it was used for meetings of state and councils of war. Shah Parviz was there along with Magis Zarir, who was in full regalia, wearing his flame-red robe with his white beard braided with gold wire. On his head, the Magis wore a black dunce cap with red tassels at the top. Argbod Omid, the Shah's military advisor, was there with two of his generals. Also in attendance was the Shah's chancellor, Kouros, a tall, elderly man he hadn't seen before.

He couldn't help but smile when the Royal Princess made an appearance. By the fact that no one complained or made note of her arrival, it appeared she had a vital role in running the Satrap. For some reason that pleased him. Maybe because that was how he envisioned his own future mate, a strong-willed woman who could run a ship's crew as well as raise a family.

After a night with the hypno-tapes, Morland had a better understanding of the local idiom. Although he wouldn't have wanted to run the meeting in Farsi, he didn't think he'd have any problem understanding or talking in the local pidgin Terran.

When everyone was assembled at a large circular wooden table, the Shah nodded at Morland, saying, "I will defer to Sanjar Morland to open this council of war. He has vital information on the disposition of our enemies' troops."

"Thank you, Your Majesty. Your problems are two-fold: on one hand, you have an invasion force in the south from Sardis."

Lord Ladbrok, his ground force commander, turned the field-projector on the north wall—which prior to the council had been stripped of tapestries and wall hangings—and projected an overhead view of the Sardis army, already lining up on the border. It was obvious there were close to four or five thousand troops, probably twice what the Zaranis could field.

He pulled out the ceremonial sword he used when dealing with Level-3 indigenes and used the point to show the location of the enemy's van. "They are within five miles of the border and will be starting their siege of Assur castle before this Council is dismissed."

He pulled aside his sword and Ladbrok projected the next image—the border castle of Assur towering over the western side of the pass leading to the Sardis Valley.

"Have you heard any words regarding the Muslims' powerful and accurate new guns?"

The Shah and the Argbod nodded their heads, both with worried expressions. "Yes," the Shah replied. "We have heard that their guns shoot with great accuracy and from farther away. It is said they can destroy the strongest stone walls within a week."

"The reason is that their new cannons are rifled to insure their accuracy."

Both men looked baffled.

Before they could ask, Morland said, "Rifling is a way of putting grooves inside a cannon's barrel, which greatly improves the gun's accuracy and range. We will teach your gunsmiths and founders the secret of rifling, but not in time for this battle. So we will send one of our pinnaces, or small flying sky ships, to help guard the pass of Assur."

All the Zarani nodded, smiles breaking out on all but the most stern.

What he didn't tell them was that the pinnace would have orders to bomb the Sardis' positions and then strafe the survivors with their 40mm auto-cannons and machine guns. He wanted their army broken, if not completely destroyed, leaving the survivors in total shock.

The next was a series of projections showing the Holy Warriors of Allah and the Army of the Jihad.

Gasps of shock and horror went out when the Zarani realized both the size and enormity of the forces they faced. Magis Zarir dropped to his knees, his hand upraised in supplication, and began praying in *Parsi.*

Morland made wide a smile. "The Army of the Jihad is not your problem anymore. The wing that is preparing to besiege your satrap will be bombed by our sky ships into oblivion. When we're through with them they will no longer be a threat to anyone. However, for our next operation, we are going to need some of your men-at-arms to draw the rest of the Holy Warriors away from their encampment in Jannet."

"But why?" the Argbod asked. "Five hundred men against two hands of thousands! Why don't you use your star weapons on them?"

"First we need to draw them away from their baggage train. We want to raid their encampment without using our weapons, which might destroy part of the treasure we're seeking."

"But what will happened to our men-at-arms?"

"They will be decoys to draw off the main force. After they have left their camp, this is what we will do to your enemies."

"What is that?" the Shah asked.

"Show them, Lord Ladbrok."

Ladrok projected a scene from a raid on another planet of nearly the same Civ-Level. The wall showed a score of heavily armed Space Vikings against hundreds of armored cavalry not much different than the cataphracti of the Holy Warriors. The emplaced machine guns and full-auto rifles tore the men-at-arms into pieces, tossing off their horses or driving them into each other in a mad scramble to escape the butchery. The screams of dying men and wounded horses filled the air, and Morland could almost smell the cordite as well as the stench of the charnel house. A final shot showed the entire battlefield strewn with thousands of corpses and wheeling birds of prey feasting on their remains.

All the Zarani were in complete shock, until the Shah began clapping and stomping his feet. Soon the room was full of applauding and shouting men.

Several of the guards came running into the council room, swords drawn. They were quickly dismissed by the Shah, then they got down to business going over the details of the upcoming operations.

VI

Captain Morland watched as DeBorder's scowling face came to life on the bridge's viewscreen.

"I was wondering," DeBorder said, "if the *Pay Dirt's* still being punished for that unauthorized raid. Your men have been on shore leave, while we've been orbiting this mudball for the past eighty hours."

"It hasn't been all fun, nor has my crew gone dirtside. Some of my officers and I have been negotiating with one of the local kings, or shahs as they call themselves. We've stumbled on quite a nice windfall; let me tell you all about it." He went into detail describing the local religious war and their new ally, the Satrap of Zarani, and the gold caches he'd told them about.

"Okay, I jumped to conclusions again. I apologize. So just what is it that you want my command to do?"

"First, while we're drawing off the Holy Warriors with the Zarani men-at-arms from their base camp in Jannat Town, I want your men to drop down and pry open Jannat castle, then sweep the interior for hidden treasure right down to the dungeons. I don't care about enemy casualties; the more of these religious fanatics you can kill the better. Most importantly, I don't want you to leave a single centistellar behind."

"Those are the kind of orders I like. If that place holds half the treasure your new friends claim, it will be my pleasure! For half a billion stellars, I'd storm Marduk by myself."

"Well, in comparison, this will be a cakewalk. Here's the timetable for tomorrow morning's operations." He had Valkanhayn do a direct data dump from the *Skull Splitter's* computer to the *Pay Dirt's*. Afterwards, they discussed logistics and how they would handle the locals.

"And, that's not even half of the riches on the planet," Morland continued. "According to the Shah, New Iran keeps most of its gold and securities in the old Federation-era bank vaults in New Tehran. Plus, there's another treasure trove at some shrine to a dead prophet, somebody named Imâm Reza. Once we bag this bunch, we'll hit the east coast."

"Hey, I'm drooling all over myself here," DeBorder sputtered. "You've got Hellmut's own luck, at finding treasure worlds! At this rate, I might even be able to pay back King Rodrik what I owe him."

The next morning they gathered again at the castle wall on a warm sunny day. The Zarani troops were being loaded onto the troop vehicles, although there was resistance from some, who were afraid of the "steel birds," as they called them. There were priests, wearing their flame-red robes, riding with every vehicle to try to keep them calm. Nor were the destriers sanguine about the prospect of flying in one of those metal birds.

However, the priests couldn't do much about the horses, who were immune to spiritual help, and didn't like climbing into strange contraptions. The historians had gone into near ecstasy over the fact that there were actual Terran-Clydesdale horses on Nissaba. By some genetic quirk, the Clydesdales had only prospered on a few worlds.

Perhaps, Morland thought, *if the historians like the horses so well, they can help muck out the troop vehicles after the horses disembark.*

It was decided that Lord Ladbrok and Valkanhayn would ride with the Shah to command the attack against the forces besieging Castle Assur on the Zarani border. Meanwhile, he would lead the forces, with Argbod Omid, for the attack on the Holy Warriors camp at Castle Jannat. The Zarani troops would do the ground fighting while the combat cars and air-cavalry mounts would provide air support. The Shah had asked them not to kill everyone; some of their enemies were mercenaries who could be expected to switch sides if they were losing. This consideration did not extend to the Holy Warriors or the Imâms and priests of Allah.

The area was alive with the sounds of more than just troop loading. There was a horde of the *Skull Splitter*'s engineers and technicians scattered thoughout the castle and the town. They were doing everything from teaching gunsmiths how to put rifling grooves into gun barrels, to demonstrating new techniques in metallurgy and welding. Twice he had to have the Shah intervene when one of his crew inadvertently violated some local religious taboo.

He had thought he was getting more of a handle on the local accent until Shaween Janna said something he couldn't understand that threw everyone into an uproar. The Prince and the general were yelling at her, and so were some of the other officers who hadn't entered the ships yet. Janna spoke again, stamping her foot, and he got it—she wanted to go along.

Joining the royal party, Morland tried to convince the Shah that Janna would be safe aboard the combat car. Valkanhayn added her words to his. Finally, after extracting a promise from the Princess that she would not leave the ship during the fighting, the Shah relented. He turned to his son, a young man of about twelve or so whose name Morland had not yet grasped, gave some final instructions, and boarded a troop vehicle.

"Princess," Morland said, gesturing to her to accompany him aboard the aircar.

"Thank you, Prince David," she said, more or less managing to pronounce his name correctly. She stood next to him as the combat car went on contragravity and rose, her face rapturous with delight. He ordered the driver to travel slowly, no use having her lose her breakfast.

"Are you enjoying the view, Princess?" he asked.

She clutched his arm, as she turned and exclaimed, "We're *flying* like a bird! It's everything I dreamed it would be as a little girl."

By the end of the day most of the other Nissabans they encountered were equally amazed by how far and how quickly they had traveled aboard the metal birds. The expedition set down well away from Castle Jannet and the Zarani disembarked. He was impressed with the army's discipline as the general and some of the priests rode out to address them about the coming action. Though clearly nervous they didn't seem close to panicking, considering the superior force they'd soon be facing.

"If they're all as good as this bunch, I can see why it cost Norwell so many men to take those two castles," said the driver of the combat car. Morland turned and scowled at the speaker but the Princess didn't seem to have noticed anything, her eyes were still wide and trying to drink in all the views she could. Abashed, the man turned back to his screen.

Tylor Ragnarsans's voice came over the communication-screen. "Enemy cavalry approaching over the next hill, Captain." The combat cars and air-cavalry mounts were hanging back behind the hill so they wouldn't be spotted. Ragnarsans was half a mile overhead in a pinnace, watching the battlefield through his telescopic-screen. Vann Stenger was commanding the pinnaces and air-cavalry mounts assisting Argod Omid. Laz Rivera was in command of the *Skull Splitter*.

"Wait until the Holy Warriors are fully committed to their advance against the Zarini forward elements, then commence firing," he ordered.

"Aye aye, Captain," Ragnarsans replied.

Hearing that, Morland grinned. Tylor Ragnarsans, his Third Officer, was an intense, almost anxious man during downtime between raids. Once a raid began however he was calm and relaxed.

In a few minutes General Omid had his troops in formation and advancing toward Jannat Town. There were about three hundred infantry and maybe five hundred cavalry. As they advanced over the hill he saw that the Holy Warriors had ten times that amount in just cavalry. Their van consisted of Holy Warriors with sleeves of mercenaries, wearing a variety of colors, on both sides. The Muslim Jihadists were dressed in green and red with banners portraying a green crescent and star on a white field.

When the Holy Warriors spotted the Space Viking combat cars and air-cavalry mounts rising over the hill, the Muslim advance dissolved, some units continuing to advance while others stopped to gape in amazement. As the air units opened fire with machine guns on the front ranks, spewing death and destruction, even those Muslim units that weren't engaged tried to wheel and flee. The Zarani cavalry units who were still moving forward slammed into the vanguard of the disordered Holy Warriors who hadn't turned tail and run.

The air-cavalry single mounts dropped down from above, firing their machine guns, while the combat cars peppered the enemy cavalry with their 40mm cannons. Within seconds the remaining van was falling back against the center, which was dissolving, with some units retiring and others advancing, turning the battlefield into complete chaos.

The slaughter was overwhelming. To Morland, it was like shooting ducks in a barrel; the battlefield was so crowded it was impossible to miss. Horses driven mad by cannon and machine gun fire, threw off their riders and trampled them underfoot, while battle-crazed Holy Warriors shot at the enemy and each other.

He ordered his crew to concentrate fire on the troops wearing green and red. Most of the mercenary cavalry were throwing down their pistols and lances, arms reaching for the sky. At this point the surviving Holy Warriors began fleeing back to their stronghold. When they encountered their own infantry, advancing behind them, they smashed into their formations, running them over, intent only on getting away as fast as possible. The cavalry was in full rout and the air-cavalry were thinning the ranks as fast as they could fire.

Their combat car caught the infantry in a cross-fire with half a dozen air-cavalry mounts, just as it was preparing to hold off the advancing Zarani cavalry with their spears. Suddenly, what was left of the Muslim army dissolved, everyone trying to get away as fast as possible—riding and stepping over each other, anyone or anything in the way.

Then the main body of the Zarani cavalry arrived. Until then, the Muslim troopers had been too scared to try and surrender. When they saw enemies that were on the ground with them, rather than hovering impossibly in the air, spears and rifles were thrown to the ground as thousands of men tried to surrender. The cavalry acted as if they were blind to their enemy's surrender and drove into the weaponless troopers like a hatchet through a wedge of cheese.

Ragnarsans cried out, "You'd better do something, Captain, or they're gonna massacre every one of those wogs."

He turned to his officer, saying, "Let them. It will be one less problem for the Zarani to deal with later. These are not soldiers, but god-anointed—in their own minds—Soldiers of Allah. Well, I say, if he gives a fig, let their god come down and save them!"

His Third just shook his head, muttering, "This raiding can be bloody business...."

The battle was completely over by the time the infantry came up. The only action left for them was cutting the throats of the wounded, killing the few surviving prisoners and stealing their purses and Jezails.

This was a war of complete extermination.

"We won, we won!" Janna was positively jumping up and down with delight and flung her arms around him. He couldn't understand more than a few words of what she was saying due to her excitement so he just grinned and hugged her back.

In the distance, hovering over the Castle Jannath, was the *Pay Dirt*. Explosions rocked the ground and smoke billowed out of the castle windows. He hoped they didn't screw up and bury the treasure under thousands of tons of stones and timber.

"Ask Lord Ladbrok how things are going on his end," he directed Ragnarsans. The pinnace and air-cavalry mounts were still firing into small bands of fugitives trying to escape the carnage. Those with any composure left were trying to surrender. Many simply clung to the ground crying or wailing to Allah.

"Ladbrok says they've broken the back of the Sardis army and they're in full rout. He wants to know if he should follow them and massacre them all or fall back?"

"Tell him to keep going until he's destroyed about half their force, then he's to fall back. I want to give Shah Zahhak a good example of what a superior force can do."

"Why don't we fly this wonderful war bird to his castle and drop some of those lovely 'bombs' on Zahhak's head?" Janna asked.

Morland thought she might have seen enough blood spilled for one day, but then her people had a long history with the Shahs of Sardis—none of it good.

"We will let him sue for peace, or we will dismantle his castle—"

"Like that one," she said excitedly, pointing to Castle Jannet which was still smoking.

"Yes. Once he learns of this castle's fate, I doubt Zahhak will cause anymore problems. Besides, if he's still alive, your brother can make him pay reparations."

"Reparations…? Please explain, Sanjar."

"That's when the losing shah has to pay the winner gold to pay for any damages he or his soldiers have caused to Zarani."

"I like that, and so will my brother."

He smiled. *It's nice to be able help your friends, especially when they're pretty girls.*

"Look, what are those?"

"Those are contragravity hand-lifters and skids….I mean flying wagons. They will carry the treasure from Castle Jannat up to the *Pay Dirt*—the big airship with the gold-bag design inside a red circle. It looks like the fighting is just about done for the day."

Ragnarsans landed the combat car near the castle where Captain DeBorder and several of his officers were standing by. They all bowed to the Princess as she exited the vehicle. One of them directed her toward a group of prisoners. She questioned them and turned to him. "They are mercenaries from Mehruk. They didn't like fighting for the Muslims—"

Several of the Mehruk mercenaries spat on the ground at the mention of their former employers.

Morland held up his hand. "Let the Shaheen speak!"

They all bowed and nodded their heads.

"They say they will swear oaths of service to the Sky Gods, if they are needed in the battle against the unbelievers."

Morland had a thought in the back of his mind that they might prove useful later on. "Tell them I will speak to your father about their plight."

They all nodded and left when one of the *Pay Dirt's* crewman took them to a holding pen. The mercenaries were being gathered up into several groups according to nationality.

He watched with DeBorder as a steady stream of contragravity skids made their way up to the *Pay Dirt* and back down into the bowels of the castle."

"Looks like you lifted the lid on that place."

"That we did. Had to use some explosives to remove the roof, but we were very careful."

"You did good. We ought to take enough off this planet to help pay off King Alwyn and some of our investors."

"My crewmen who hit those Vahitstan castles were a big help," he said sheepishly. "Indirectly."

Morland nodded. "But let's not tell *them* that."

They both laughed.

They left the Zarani Army to guard the mercenaries and hunt down any of the Muslims who might have escaped.

It was DeBorder's idea to put a bounty of ten of the aluminum tokens for every Muslim's head that was brought back to the castle.

"Aren't you worried that some of the more unscrupulous might just lop off any old head just for the reward?" Morland asked.

"It'll only stay up for a Standard week. By then, there won't be a living Muslim or strange face in the entire Istakhr Mountain range." DeBorder gave out a deep belly laugh.

Morland just grinned. "This isn't supposed to be this much fun…."

"Sure it is, when you're killing vermin or the kind of scum that think they have some sort of celestial pipeline to their personal almighty. Some people, like rabid dogs, just need killing—or else the plague spreads. Nothing else works."

"You're right. They're mad; you can't talk to them, you can't argue them into a sensible state of mind. This religious fervor is like a disease. The only thing that ends it is a bullet to the head."

"True, nothing else works."

"How many casualties did you take storming the castle?" he asked.

"None dead," DeBorder replied. "A few wounded, falls mainly."

"Good! We only had three wounded ourselves. The Shah's men fared a bit worse, but nothing like they would have if they'd fought the Muslims by themselves."

DeBorder nodded. "They'd all be dead. But what about the Muslims on the east coast?"

"I was thinking of taking the *Skull Splitter* over there and sacking New Tehran myself, but I'm impressed by how well you and your crew handled this castle. I'll have my signals-and-detection staff send over all the data we've gathered so far. That'll give me a chance to set things up here."

DeBorder gave him a lascivious wink. "I saw the way you and that Princess were looking at each other."

Morland threw back his hand. "Well, I'm interested, but I don't know if it's going to go anywhere. After all, we're not going to be here much longer."

"What! After that haul, I thought we might spend a couple of months recuperating and relaxing."

"It's a nice place for some R&R, but it's too primitive for our New Base Venture."

"Cap'n, you are one single-minded son-of-a-bitch. And that's all I'll say on the subject."

VII

Morland woke up wondering where he was for a moment. Then he recognized the arching marble ceiling and the walls covered with rich tapestries, friezes and wall-hangings showing the revelations of Zoroaster. The hand-made and elaborately carved wooden furniture and silk sheets of his bed told him he was inside the palace in New Persepolis. The warm but empty spot next to him indicated the Princess had just recently left. He heard scratching at the door and realized what had caused him to wake. It would have been nice to have gotten some more sleep, but today was another busy day.

The servant girls entered the room with breakfast, flat bread and dolmas with *Aab Talebi*, cantaloupe juice. He told them to leave it on the table and they quickly departed. As he ate he thought back on the last few weeks. This had been the most enjoyable Space Viking raid Morland had ever led. Though not as lucrative as Agni three years ago (Great Gehenna, had it really been three years?) but a lot less costly. He had only lost a few men; some to lucky shots from castle walls in New Persepolis, and others who had sent their air-cavalry mounts too enthusiastically down into narrow castle courtyards and crashed as a result. This world's guns and cannon had barely scratched their ships.

Shah Parviz of Zarani was now Padishah Parviz I of all Persepolis, while the former Padishah was lying in an unmarked grave outside the capital city. The new Padishah had bestowed Morland with the title of Jah-Angir, or Conqueror of the World, and in addition offered to crown him Padishah, or emperor, of the east coast, which was more than generous since the satraps at that end of the continent were not only much larger but also had correspondingly larger populations.

Had Janna given her spirit as willingly as she had given her heart he might have taken Parviz up on his offer. They had spent almost every hour of the last few weeks together. Their affair had started as part of the celebration after the conquest of Sardis and had raged like a summer wildfire. Morland loved her like no other woman he'd ever known, but she was as stubborn as Muslim mullah. She had sworn her love to him, but refused to make it binding until he accepted her faith.

Of all the things Janna might have asked of him, she had asked the one thing he could never give. To willingly embrace the Zoroastrian faith was impossible; religion was nothing more than a miserable fraud, designed to allow parasitic priests to live off their believers. He would have cut off his arm for her, but not this—

When he'd told her a few days ago that they would be leaving soon, they'd had a terrible row. He'd all but ordered her to marry him; she had steadfastly held to her guns: convert or we remain friends and lovers. They had made up, but even though she knew he was leaving, she remained happy, putting on a good show. On the inside, he knew she was as miserable as he was.

As he finished his cantaloupe juice, Morland remembered he had a meeting with the Padishah in about fifteen minutes. He washed up, got dressed and hiked over to the Padishah's wing of the palace, which was the size of the town of Zarani, including the castle.

Inside his private audience room, Padishah Parviz was dressed informally in trousers and a long tunic with some beautiful gold-thread embroidery showing the Imperial Crest, a gold falcon, with a crown, on a red field. The Padishah rose up out of his high-backed chair to greet Morland with a hug.

"It is a shame my sister is so stubborn," Pavriz said, shaking his head. "I apologize for her lack of courtesy, my friend. She should be thrilled to join Our house with yours."

Morland shrugged. "What can we do?"

"Nothing, it appears; she is a woman and her ways are beyond our comprehension. Again, I encourage you to become Padishah of the Borazjan. You could use this as your base for your off-world operations, as well."

Despite the esteem the locals professed for them, Nissaba was not what he desired as a base world. The people were far too technologically backward and their population was collectively less than a hundred million, especially after the east coast bloodletting in the former New Iran where millions died as the Zorastorians paid the Muslims back with their own blood-vengeance.

"It would be too painful for me to stay. I love your sister, and I know she returns my ardor, but...."

"Say no more. I have attempted to sway her mind but to no result. She has always been stubborn and strong willed. Despite my new elevation, I do not share her fervor for our gods. If they were so powerful and so concerned about their people's welfare, why did they let the Muslims kill and enslave so many of our people?"

Morland shook his head.

"I know, I'm not looking for you to provide an answer. The answer lies in my own heart. The gods are a lie, a convenient fabrication to keep the people pacified."

"You misinterpret my intentions. I'm not here to disparage your beliefs: I just have none of my own."

"I know that, David. I just think my sister is mad for spurning the best man she will ever know for gods, who—if they even exist—are indifferent to man's fate. What will you do now?"

"Press on, Parviz. The King who financed our expedition into the Old Federation worlds did so that we might found a base world of operations for future raids and even trade. I believe we will become good trading partners, once we find a home base…I would have liked it to be here, but—"

"Say no more. What will be, will be. You will always be welcome on Nissaba, especially in New Persepolis. Let me know what you think are our best trade goods and I will see that you fill your ship upon your next visit."

"Thank you, my friend—"

"NO!—brother. You are like a brother to me. You have saved our lives, lifted Us to undreamed-of heights; only a brother would do such."

They embraced again.

"I feel the same and I promise I will be back. Now that *I* have a brother to visit."

The Padishah nodded, wiping his eyes with his silk sleeve. "Your words touch my heart. But, now, it is my turn to beg for a favor. I would like for you to take my oldest son, Navid. He is twelve years old, almost a man. I want you to train him on your ship and give him a starman's education. He is the future of this world."

Morland clasped hands with Parviz. "You have my word, I will educate and raise Navid as if he were my own son."

"You have my humble thanks."

"I also plan to leave several technicians and one engineer."

Parviz reared back in shock. "A gift beyond my wildest imaginings!"

"They will help you *industrialize* Nissaba in my absence. These are willing recruits; often crewmen and technicians, or artisans as you might call them, sometimes grow tired of travel between stars or the fighting and death that accompanies our arrivals on new worlds. There are also a couple of our warriors who wish to disembark and make lives on your world."

"Excellent. They shall know Our favor. This will be good for the both of us."

Morland nodded as they clasped hands in accord.

Javen DeBorder did not want to leave Nissaba. His ship was filled with loot, and now he wanted to hit the Vahistan castles in the midlands. Many of the *Skull Splitter's* crewmen didn't want to leave, either; they thought Nissaba would make a fine base. It had a spaceport that was in decent shape and they had already made friends with some of the locals. Others wanted to make Nissaba their base because that would mean that exploring new planets had come to an end and they could return to the Sword-Worlds. Space exploration, raiding and looting had lost its charm for them. They'd been gone well over a year; they had a little money in their pockets and they wanted to go home to spend it.

Morland turned them all down. While their return on investment was good so far, he thought they had to do much better before returning to Joyeuse. For his new base world, he wanted to find a planet with more of its industrial infrastructure intact. One with fissionable ores would be ideal, since you couldn't build an industrialized base without nuclear power. The biggest installations needed their own power plants, and nuclear power plants were the most powerful and reliable. The smaller installations could run on power cartridges, which converted nuclear material directly to electricity—either way, no fissionables, no base.

Nor had he forgotten King Rodrik of Tanith's comments about how his planet's population was so small that Marduk wasn't interested in trading with it. Morland wanted a more populated world than Horus or Nissaba as home of their New Base Venture. He was convinced that the Mardukan Empire was not going to go away, and was probably a harbinger of the future. The Neobarbarian age was coming to an end and the age of empire was coming. When the Mardukan Empire reached him, he wanted to meet it on the best terms possible. He didn't think a planet of seventy to a hundred million people without nuclear power was going to be able to do that.

Morland had just finished putting on one of the ceremonial red robes he'd been given when the Princess entered the room. "Don't forget that my brother wants to hold a ceremony honoring you before you leave."

He smiled. "I have a gift for you."

"A gift? You mean a gift beyond saving my life and the life of my family? Beyond elevating my brother Parviz to Padishah and breaking the power of the Muslims, those who would have killed or enslaved us? What kind of gift could be better than that?"

He smiled again, as he had worked very hard on this gift. He had the Chief Historian working for a week to put this package together. It was a study cube containing all the knowledge needed to elevate Nissaba from Civ-Level 3 to Level 8. He'd had the entire engineering team design a format that was virtually indestructible but useful. He turned and took the study cube out of his robe's pocket and gave it to her.

"What is this?"

"In this cube is the knowledge of a thousand great minds, the accumulated wisdom of centuries. It contains both books and moving pictures to illustrate how Nissaba can raise her education and culture to civilization. With this, and the people I'm leaving behind, your world will have a chance to join the rest of the civilized worlds."

She looked at him in astonishment, and, for the first time, with a hint of awe. One of the things he had liked about her was that she had not regarded the Space Vikings as gods, as many of the other Nissabans did. She had treated him as a normal man, and indeed, hadn't spared him her sharp tongue when she objected to anything he did.

He turned it on and showed her some of the programs.

"How will this affect our people?" she cried. "Is this some sort of magic?"

"No magic," he said. "We have discovered that when a person can see, as well as hear and read, they believe. There is no reason why your people cannot raise themselves to be great. With this knowledge cube, they will have their opportunity."

For the first time since he had met her she began to cry. "This is as great a gift as those you have already given me. Thank you, David." She fell into his arms.

How long they stood there he did not know. They were at last interrupted by a cough. The Padishah's son, Navid, was standing in the door.

"Sorry to disturb you Aunt Janna," he said, although the smile on his face indicated something other than sorrow. "But father sent me to fetch you. He'd like to start the ceremony now. All of the other guests are here."

"We better not keep the Padishah waiting, then," Morland said.

Princess Janna smiled and ordered one of her retainers to put the cube in her quarters. "Lead the way, Navid," she said, gesturing to her nephew.

Encircling her with his arm they strode out the door.

ESHMUN

"So how much longer are we going to keep searching for a base world?" Will Haversham asked.

They had been having one of those relaxed gatherings, as much a cocktail hour as a staff meeting, aboard the *Skull Splitter.* They were using their Abbot lift-and-drive in normal space, four hours from their jump site, and they still hadn't pinned down their next target world. Except for the heavy drinkers, Nissaban pomegranate-wine appeared to be the drink of choice. No one was smoking out of respect for Morland. Then DeBorder had dropped the question everyone had been thinking about. "Captain, don't you think it's time to return to Joyeuse?"

Morland looked quickly at Vann Stenger, who had already asked him the same thing a day before. His Second shrugged, indicating that he hadn't discussed it with DeBorder.

"We have room left in the storage holds, why not keep going?" he replied. They had left Joyeuse almost two years ago. Some of the crew were anxious to go home; others were ready to get started on the second part of the venture. They felt that Nissaba had enough good qualities to make a base. Just about everyone on both crews felt that Morland was being too finicky about the new base world search, rejecting every planet they encountered.

After Nissaba they had jumped to Dazbog. Dazbog was more advanced than Horus, but with less population. Much of the land was a vast desert, the biggest he had ever seen. There was also an exceptionally large mountain range. Tylor Ragnarsans, originally a geologist, had been very excited about it and spent as much time as he could studying the land masses. What population existed was located on two continents with a major city on each one. They hadn't tried to make friends and had sacked both of the cities, making about a third of what they had made on Nissaba. Dazbog had one minor spaceport, with no intact industrial facilities worth speaking of. It had been easy to go on.

Ammon proved that even minor planets, by Old Federation standards, could be destroyed in wars. However the war had started, whether by an external attack or between existing factions or nations, it had ended with the almost total destruction of the planet.

The planet they had just left, Eshmun, had been different. Though not well populated, its people were the most advanced they had encountered since they left Odin. Their technological level was at about the First Century Pre-Atomic. They were just beginning to use electricity and radio.

Unfortunately their tactic of landing and making friends had not worked this time. They had been attacked almost immediately when they landed at a city their maps called New Kembla. The city's weapons had damaged the aircar, forcing it to land.

However, neither Lord Ladbrok or Valkanhayn, who were in the aircar hoping to continue their string of successful first contacts, had been injured. They had counterattacked and captured New Kembla, but a warning had already gone out by radio. The entire planet was armed and lying in wait for them.

With their two ships and vastly superior weaponry, they could have defeated anyone they chose to fight. However, that would have meant using their ship's heavy weapons, resulting in massive destruction to Eshmun's fledgling industrial base, and the possibility of serious casualties among the Space Vikings. In the end, Morland decided to leave, taking just the loot from New Kembla which was worth a little less than fifty million stellars.

The crew had been ready to fight. There were two spaceports on the planet, along with some industrial areas. They hadn't surveyed either of them since they were all within populated areas. With the planet warned and ready for them, he didn't feel like fighting a war just to examine old spaceports.

The staff meeting had been called to review their supplies while they were leaving Eshmun's system. However, the main topic had quickly turned from inventory levels into the old argument of whether to continue raiding, or instead return to the Swords-Worlds. Before Morland could make his point everyone was weighing in, often with contradictory views. Most of the senior officers of both ships were there, along with the Ship's Services officers of both ships.

He wasn't particularly impressed with Boris Prather of the *Pay Dirt.* Porter was one of those types often found in Ship's Services. Once inventory dropped below one hundred percent Prather was always badgering to return to a civilized world and restock until his shelves were full.

"We have almost a billion and a half stellars worth of loot. That's a good haul," DeBorder argued. "We should stop exploring and establish our base at Nissaba, or return to Joyeuse."

Surprisingly to Morland, Will Haversham disagreed and wanted to keep searching, as did Stenger, Ragnarsans and Valkanhayn. Besides DeBorder, Rivera thought they should return to Nissaba and establish their base there. The Second Officer of the *Pay Dirt,* Joris Kirbey, was one of those who wanted to return home, which for him was Tanith. Prather wanted go to any civilized world.

His older sister Zandra had already told him privately she was ready to return to Joyeuse, but she didn't say anything publicly. The Chief Astrogator of the *Pay Dirt* wasn't present: he was a taciturn older man who wasn't interested in anything but navigation.

The Fourth Officer of the *Pay Dirt* wasn't present either. The position had been vacant since DeBorder had arrested Hereld Norwell. He had since been released from the brig and demoted—against Morland's advice, since he'd wanted Norwell exiled on Nissaba—and was now just a ground squad leader. Norwell had carried out his duties well on Dazbog and Eshmun, but DeBorder was still unhappy with him, and he hadn't promoted anyone to take his place.

"We have plenty of supplies left," Morland said, "and we have room in the storage holds for more loot." He nodded to the Historians, who hadn't said anything so far. "I think our Historians may have some suggestions for us." He had asked First Historian, Ulrik Selner, in light of what they had discovered so far, to come up with some likely possibilities for planets that could be turned into a base.

Selner stood up a little uncertainly. He'd certainly heard the Wardroom comments that the academics hadn't contributed anything to the expedition, since most of the worlds they suggested had been destroyed or decivilized. Once Will Haversham's suggestion of visiting only minor worlds had proved successful, many had openly questioned the historians usefulness for the expedition.

Although Morland had assured them he valued their input, they were all feeling a little self conscious.

"We have three target worlds," Historian Selner said. "All these worlds were heavily industrialized at one point in the Federation's history. They also suffered through long depressions and were no longer major worlds at the time that Odin's histories ended, around the time the Interstellar Wars began."

He paused for a moment, and Morland gestured to him to go on. "The first world, Ashur, was one of the first ones settled in its sector and had a peak population of about four hundred fifty million people.

That declined during the Troubles, but Ashur's population was still over three hundred million when Odin lost contact with her."

"How far away is it?" someone asked.

"Ashur is roughly five hundred hours away," he said, giving the location.

Morland frowned. That was in the opposite direction of the Sword-Worlds and Tanith, where he had intended to trade their loot for the machinery and help he needed to construct a base. "Let's hear about the next two."

Selner turned to another historian. "Namtar, our next choice, was also heavily industrialized but fell into an economic depression as other planets around it developed their own industries. Namtar's population was about three hundred million when the records stopped just before the System States War. Namtar was a member of the System States Alliance." She noted the location. "It's about six hundred hours from here," she added, smiling, to show that Namtar was clearly her choice.

That at least was the right direction, thought Morland, although it was almost too close to the edge of Marduk's claimed area. "And the last one?"

Walter Ovard said, "The third planet has a similar background to the other two described. The only difference is that it was one of the headquarters for the Federation Force during the System States War."

"The Big War," Morland added when he saw some blank looks on some of his officers' faces. Most Sword-Worlders referred to the conflict that drove their ancestors out of the Federation as the Big War.

"The planet's about three hundred and fifty hours away," the historian concluded, pointing out the location.

Morland stood up. "This third planet is the closest and it's in the right direction. What's its name?"

"Poictesme."

POICTESME

I

"We are detecting residual nuclear radiation, Captain," reported Gytha Valkanhayn, the Signals-and-Detection Officer.

Almost instantly the crew changed from a relaxed group to an active one. They had just taken their final microjump and were a little over a light second away from Poictesme. They had not detected anything on their initial microjump into the system, nor on the jump previous to this one.

"Another nuclear-bombed hell-hole?" DeBorder asked, his face a study in disappointment on the viewscreen feed from the *Pay Dirt.*

"I'm picking up an odd reading," said the crewmember currently on radiation detection. "Come over here and take a look, Chief."

Gytha Valkanhayn joined him with two other signals-and-detection crewmen.

Laz Rivera followed behind. His Executive Officer made a suggestion that Morland didn't hear, then they examined a few more instruments.

"Captain," Rivera stated, "in my opinion, what we are reading is radiation leakage from a ship or ships. The radiation we're monitoring is not coming from the planetary surface. If the world had been nuked, the reading would be more diffused with sporadic hot-spots of radiation."

They had another eight hours of travel, using their Abbot lift-and-drive for normal space, before they made orbit.

"Continue all scans," Morland said. For the next few hours, signals-and-detection continued scanning for any information they could pick up. It was a tri-star system—the Gartner Tri-System according to *The Bestiary*—and there were lots of moons and planets. Only Poictesme showed signs of life, with faint radio signals.

Morland sat restlessly in the command chair during the entire time. This was one of those moments when he almost wished he had taken up smoking so that he could relax by puffing on his pipe the way Captain Allison had done on the *Prince of Thieves*. The last thing a well-trained crew, like the *Skull Splitter's*, needed was their Captain looking over their shoulders during routine work so he did his best to appear relaxed. Finally he left the bridge for his quarters.

They were two hours out of Poictesme when he heard the recall buzzer and returned to the bridge.

"They're ships," Ragnarsans, who had come on duty, said. "Based on the other readings I don't think any of them are operable. It looks like the leavings of a big space battle."

"How long ago?" Morland asked.

Ragnarsans shook his head and turned and looked at Rivera.

His executive officer had probably visited more worlds than all of them combined and had seen just about every condition that could exist. "I can't tell yet. They appear to be abandoned hulks. I'll wager my share of the Poictesme loot they're not recent, though."

"Reduce speed. We will approach slowly and cautiously."

After several more hours it became clear that there had been a major battle. Wrecked ships littered the outer orbit of Poictesme.

"Their weapons were not nearly as powerful as ours," Ragnarsans observed.

Morland nodded. In current battles, it was rare for a ship to be damaged enough that it could no longer fight to move or remained intact. The weapons used by the Sword-World ships, or by any civilized world like Marduk or Aton, were so powerful that once they plowed deep inside a ship they would blow it to Em-See-Squared.

"Their missile-warheads weren't as powerful," stated his History officer, who was on the bridge, "and ships after the Collapse were not as well-armored as ours are today. They didn't use collapsium shielding on their master bulkheads, either, which meant a nuke that pierced the hull could fry the entire ship's crew. They were built more like freighters are now."

Space Viking ships were built larger and more powerful than most warships because they had to fight their way down onto a planet and carry a large cargo of loot upon leaving. Morland had noticed that Mardukan ships, which used to be smaller than Space Viking ships, were now being built to the same standards.

"Captain, we are detecting nuclear radiation from the planet," Valkanhayn said.

Morland's heart sank. Another wasted trip?

"It seems fairly isolated," said Rivera, looking at his instruments.

When the *Skull Splitter* reached orbit it became clear that only one area on the planet had been hit with nuclear missiles. "According to our world maps it's the capital city, Storisende," Selner said. "Former capital city," he corrected, as the amount of devastation became apparent.

Poictesme had one large continent and several smaller ones. The large continent had been home to most of the population. As they moved further inland they noticed a city to the east. "More nuclear radiation detected," the signals-and-detection officer reported. "This is different...Captain, I think it's from a power plant."

"Any chance they've detected us?"

The crew examined their instruments, but no one could find any evidence of radar or any other detection device.

Gytha reported back, "No sign of alarm, sir."

"This planet requires more examination," Morland stated. "Continue scanning."

Poictesme had a number of paradoxes when examined up close. There was undoubtedly a functioning power plant in a city that records identified as Litchfield. Though the city was clearly occupied, from orbit most of it appeared abandoned and in ruins. There was also a section of the city that appeared well maintained, but the buildings were different from the older part. They were not anywhere as tall and were closer together.

There was no sign of contragravity, or that anyone in Litchfield knew they were overhead in orbit. The rest of the continent, though populated, appeared even more primitive. They detected electric discharges from a few cities, while others showed none. The other continents were even less populated and didn't give off any sign of nuclear or electrical energy, nor did they detect any radio waves.

When they gathered later in the Wardroom, Walter Ovard said, "Like a lot of Neobarb planets, Poictesme has a broad Civ-Level range, from early post-atomic down to over a century or two Pre-Atomic. Signals reports that initial examination by probes of several industrial areas is very promising. A surprising number of buildings and structures appear intact from this height."

"But there's no spaceport," Valkanhayn said.

"I don't know," DeBorder said by screen from the *Pay Dirt.* "My signals officer is reporting a possible spaceport area in that city in the middle of the continent."

"Litchfield," Ovard supplied.

"It's too small to be a true spaceport," Rivera said.

The gathering was interrupted by an urgent call from the bridge.

"Third called in to say he's made a big discovery!" the communications officer on duty exclaimed.

Tylor Ragnarsans had taken an aircar down to take a look at a desolate island that appeared to have an exceptionally large extinct volcano. Ragnarsans's hobby was geology and he practiced it every chance he could.

"Patch him through," Morland replied.

"Captain," Ragnarsans said. "This is incredible—there's a spaceport inside this extinct volcano!"

They looked around at each other in surprise.

"We didn't detect anything until we were almost right over the mouth. The floor is over three miles wide with a spaceport and what appears to be a variety of installations, some of which appear to be machines shops and fabricators, around the port itself. I can see a number of caverns, maybe volcanic flumes, which must lead off into the walls and underlying strata."

"Have you detected any life forms?" he asked.

"No. Any inhabitants are either in hiding or long gone. I suspect the latter, since the area is partly in ruin. We are detecting some radiation, but very little. Probably minor leakage from an old power plant. I'm going down to see what's there."

His report was astonishing. Not just a spaceport, but one with a variety of industrial installations, many of them intact, and quarters capable of holding over ten thousand people.

"Captain, I think we found our base."

The spaceport had been called Barathrum, which was also the name of the island. The island looked as if a large asteroid or small moon had slammed into Poictesme, then, after broiling in lava for a few millenniums, had been regurgitated by an underground volcano. There were sheets of basalt jutting out of the ground as well as spires of blackened rock and lava. The surface was still cracked and split by old fault lines and ash cones jutted out of the ground. What little there was of green plant life was mostly lichen and moss. A few twisted and stunted trees pushed their way out of the inhospitable rock.

The spaceport had been built during the System States War by the Federation to help defend the world against possible space attack. There were signs that it had been used for at least a century or two after the war ended. All things considered, it was in good shape and it didn't look like it would take much work to clean it up.

They landed both ships in the volcanic spaceyard and gave them a thorough overhaul. Neither ship needed much work: the *Skull Splitter* had taken a few hits while sacking New Kembla on Eshmun, but the collapsium armor had limited the damage and it was easily repaired. *Pay Dirt* had a few dings, but nothing serious except for an Abbot drive unit that needed overhauling.

While Barathrum had far exceeded what Morland had been looking for in a spaceport, it had very little to recommend itself in terms of habitability. Consequently, he decided to make contact with Litchfield, the largest surviving city in the middle of the continent. Following up on past successes, he sent Lord Ladbrok and Valkanhayn to make the initial contact.

11

"Your Worshipful, we have a report that an aircar has been spotted heading for the center of town."

"Good," Lord-High Mayor Morgan Fitch said. "It's taken them long enough. I understand we're dealing with Space Vikings." While ships arriving on Poictesme were rare occurrences, maybe one or two ships made landfall every ten to twenty Galactic Standard years. They had learned about the Space Viking raids several centuries ago from a Gilgamesh freighter. Poictesme melon-brandy was still a trade commodity of great value, as well as the detritus from the industrial sites of the Third Federation Force.

"Yes, Your Worshipful," Sylvester Zareff answered. As Arch-Archivist, it was his responsibility to keep the records as well as interpret the Merlin Oracles. "It was written in the Testament that we would be receiving visitors at about this time, give or take a century or two. They would either be barbarian looters or agents of the next configuration; a Third Federation, an alliance of worlds, a union of civilized planets or even an Imperial ambassador. The Oracle was unclear on this point; however, we are to give them our complete cooperation—thus it was spoken and recorded.

The Mayor nodded. "It's not as if we could fight them off. The Oracle left us little in the way of weapons to defend ourselves."

"It was all foreseen, Lord Mayor. The Oracle knows all, sees all and is all powerful."

Just more cant, thought the Lord Mayor, who'd found the legends of the Oracle to be somewhat suspect. However, the Voters believed, which meant—if he wanted to continue with his privileged position and life—that he *believed*, as well. He knew what happened to those who scoffed about the Oracle before other ears. They were shunned, and if they persisted, left naked in the wilderness to the mercies of wild animals.

"Now, remind me, Zareff, are we supposed to refrain from mentioning the Oracle or provide them with illumination?"

"Your memory is betraying your age, Lord Mayor. It is our place to provide the newcomers with whatever aid they request, even so far as rebuilding the space docks and sun-fire devices, thus it was spoken and recorded. No information as to the Oracle or his acolytes is to be provided. As the Oracle has proclaimed, hints and clues are disseminated where they will be found by the others. They will tell them much, but give them little."

The Lord Mayor shook his head. *I think they're all insane, but the Voters believe and so must I. At least, on the outside.*

III

They landed their aircar in what was once a thriving open mall, near the center of Litchfield. The area had appeared deserted from above, but they quickly saw evidence of people peeking from behind the crumbling walls and even a few looking down from abandoned towers. "What do you think, Gytha?" Ladbrok asked.

"No one's made any hostile moves, but after New Kembla I wish we had a squad of ground fighters backing us up."

Ladbrok laughed. "The problem with being on point is, even if you have troops in reserve, they'll probably be too few and too late. Let's give them twenty minutes and, if we don't make first contact by then, we'll leave. Times like these are why we get all the glory."

She shook her head.

"Besides, most Terro-human males will not hesitate to kill another male, but a female—especially an attractive one like yourself—calls forth all sorts of atavistic instincts. *I'm* the one who's taking the real risks."

Gytha punched him on the arm, which elicited an ouch from Ladbrok and a couple of laughs from behind a nearby building.

"See, we're making progress already."

A few minutes later, a tall man wearing a white tunic and followed by two guards, dressed in what had once been Federation era body-armor and helmets, came out to greet them. He gave his status rather than his name; he was Registrar of the Fifth Ward. "Follow me. I've been instructed to bring you before the Lord-High Mayor."

His Lingua-Terra was impeccable so they followed.

From the inside, the mall was not as tumbledown as its exterior led one to believe. Many of the buildings had been carefully restored and now they housed shops or professional offices. This was a civilization which might have fallen to its knees, but was making a valiant attempt to get back up on two feet.

Ladbrok knew that the Captain would be impressed; if this world wasn't what Morland was looking for, he was leading them on a wild-goose chase.

The Registrar—whatever that meant—brought them to the largest and best maintained building in the mall, which a couple of hundred years ago had probably been a bank or civic building. Already, Ladbrok was wondering if the old vault was sealed and full of treasure; true, there were always lots of worthless bonds, banknotes, stocks and paper currency, but also jewels and gold coins and even ingots. His mouth was beginning to water. *I'm like an old space dog,* he decided, *too old to change and too satisfied to bother trying.*

They followed the Registrar through what appeared once to be a courtroom or presence chamber, then through some hallways into a spacious audience room. The Lord-High Mayor was seated in a high-back chair on a dais at the rear of the room. He was wearing a tall black tophat and dressed in black robes. Ladbrok had seen kings with lesser jewels around their neck. The chain-links were large and appeared to be solid gold.

As they approached the dais, the Registrar whispered to Ladbrok, "Do not look the Lord-High Mayor directly in the eye. He is to be addressed as The Right Worshipful."

Ladbrok nodded his thanks. It was always helpful to be apprised of the correct forms of address before one made a serious *faux pas.*

When they were within a body-length of the dais, Ladbrok fell to one knee, saying, "Right Worshipful, I am Lord Ladbrok of the Duchy of Vinehold on the planet Joyeuse. My companion is Dame Gytha Valkanhayn."

Playing her part to perfection, she made a quick curtsy.

"It is my pleasure to announce the arrival of Prince David Morland of the Sword-Worlds and his crew."

"Am I to understand that I am in the presence of the infamous and demonic Space Vikings?"

Ladbrok, without looking directly into the Mayor's eyes, replied, "Yes, Right Worshipful. However, I fear our reputation has been greatly exaggerated."

At this, the Lord Mayor lifted his head back and laughed. "I would not be surprised!" he finished, once he'd regained his composure.

The Mayor appeared to have made a decision because he suddenly waved his hands about, scattering his retainers. "The rest of you leave, now! I want to speak to my visitors in private."

When the room had emptied, the Lord Mayor took off his tophat, revealing a bald head with a fringe of white hair at the sides. "I so tire of this routine, surrounded day and night by nothing but flunkies. It's a change to be around a new and more sophisticated couple. So, what are you here for—really? If it's gold and treasure, you're going to have to work for it. Anything that wasn't bolted down was lifted long ago during the Interstellar Wars. The only things left are our trade goods like our melon-brandy and the junk left behind by the Old Federation Third Force."

Ladbrok felt as if a fresh wind had blown its way through the chamber, and decided that candor might be the best policy. And, if that didn't work, a few thermonuclear bombs might do the job.

"We're here searching for a new base of operations. Pickings in our former sector of the Federation have been getting scarce lately and every year there's more competition for fewer and fewer worlds."

The Lord Mayor nodded. "We used to be part of one of the major trade routes, but that was long ago; so I suppose we are off the beaten track so to speak." He pointed his hand skyward. "Which hasn't always helped us in the past."

"We saw the broken and blasted ships coming in. Was that from the Big War, or later?"

"Much later. Peace broke out before the Third Force was finished mobilizing. No, that battle happened during the Tenth or Eleventh Century Atomic-Era. I guess it was part of what most people call the Interstellar Wars. We were doing too well, trading with many of our neighboring worlds, and that attracted the wrong kind of attention. The ships came from Osiris and, after defeating our Navy, they looted and despoiled our world. Almost a thousand years later and we're still recovering...if you can call it that."

Ladbrok nodded. It was a story he'd heard far too many times. And would hear again and again. "I'm familiar with your tale. However, in this case, it might have a happy ending. Prince Morland is an honorable man and more interested in building something lasting, rather than tearing things down."

"Admirable and rare qualities in a leader during these dissolute times."

"Yes, I've come to admire him, myself." *Much to my surprise,* Ladbrok thought. "He has brought the tools and equipment to turn the right planet into an industrial powerhouse. And, with the facilities we've observed from orbit and through low altitude reconnaissance, Poictesme might well be that world."

The Mayor smiled. "I'm very pleased to hear that. Help is needed here and long overdue. My given name is Duggan Fitch, and I welcome you to Poictesme. I very much look forward to meeting your Prince.

Litchfield, I fear, is probably the height of civilization on our world; however, we do retain some of the old wisdom and teachings. I believe we have much to offer. As Lord-High Mayor of Litchfield, I'm the highest ranking official on the planet and I will do what I can to ensure your stay is profitable to all parties. Now, how would you like to sample some of our melon-brandy?"

"That's the best offer I've had today," Ladbrok said, smiling. Even Gytha Valkanhayn was beginning to relax.

"Let's go into my office, where we can find some good libation and comfortable seats."

IV

Eschewing the barren island of Barathrum, several hundred of the crew moved to Litchfield. The inhabitants of Litchfield proved reasonably easy to deal with. The Lord-High Mayor was the man in charge, although he was subject to re-election every other year. However, it looked like his constituency were backing his decision to welcome the Space Vikings with open arms.

They were welcomed with equal enthusiasm by the supervisor of the local nuclear power plant. Over seventy, operating mainly by rote rather than by knowledge and with just two remaining functioning robots, he was very aware that the plant was running on prayers and baling wire. Sword-World technicians promptly took over the plant, transferring some robots from the ship while salvaging and repairing the others.

The rest of the population treated them with a little more reserve. Litchfield had originally been built by a contra gravity-using society, so the buildings were tall and spread apart, with walking paths between them. It was not an easy city to live in for people who no longer possessed contragravity vehicles. A jumble of smaller, crowded buildings with roads linking them together had been built on the northern edge of the Litchfield over the last few centuries.

Not wanting to cause any dissention, the Space Vikings moved into a deserted and unused part of Litchfield on the west side of town. There they found a semi-habitable large building called the Airlines Building and started repairing it to make it livable. Mayor Fitch had aided them in this, stating that something called the Abandoned Property Act allowed them to take possession of any vacant buildings.

Transportation between different parts of the continent was primarily by railroad. Morland had seen rail trains like this on other Neobarbarian planets, and had read that railroads had existed on Terra in the Pre-Atomic era. The trains were powered by an oil byproduct. There were also roads that led away from the railroad stops. The roads consisted of well-traveled hard surfaces to dirt tracks that seemed impassable to the Space Vikings. Oil-powered wheeled vehicles traveled along these roads.

This was all amusing to the Space Vikings, who were the products of a civilization that hadn't used wheeled vehicles for over sixteen centuries, as all travel was done by contragravity.

Litchfield's population was about one hundred thousand people, although it clearly had been much larger in the past. It was primarily a manufacturing and agricultural center, since its location in the center of the continent gave it a dominant position in trade.

Litchfield was located in the middle of a large fertile valley, with additional fertile land to the north, but several mountain ranges separated it from the other parts of the continent. The area in the northwest of the continent around Storisende was uninhabited due to lingering radiation. The southwest part of the continent seemed to consist of a number of low fertile valleys with scattered small towns. A vast area of scrub desert the locals called the Badlands started on the other side of a range of mountains east of Litchfield. Beyond the Badlands were a large number of small to medium sized towns. Although the network of railroads seemed to link the continent together, each section operated under its own government. That might have been because of the natural terrain that separated parts of the continent or due to the general breakdown after the Osiris attack.

Morland put Lord Ladbrok in charge of making contact with each little town and finding out more about the planet.

The area around Litchfield—indeed the whole continent—was full of crumbling military or industrial installations that mostly dated from the Big War. A few of the industrial areas were restorable, but the majority were beyond repair due to old age. As near as they could tell, the attack on the capital city appeared to have started Poictesme's decline into decivilization. Without the educated minds and know-how that had resided in the capital city, the rest of the world had been unable to maintain an advanced technological civilization.

The people of Litchfield, in particular, spoke of a time in the past when Merlin had led them to prosperity and happiness. Morland assumed Merlin was the name of some former leader who had morphed over time into a religious icon.

The greatest discovery had come by happenstance, when the former power plant supervisor overheard one of the Space Viking engineers wishing that more of the world's industrial infrastructure was intact. He had asked them why they hadn't checked out Koshchei.

Koshchei turned out to be the next planet out-system from Poictesme. It was one of those rare stellar bodies that had formed at such a high temperature that it was almost all heavy elements, primarily iron ore. It was littered with industrial installations, almost all of them intact.

V

"There's evidence of previous attacks on Koshchei, but they were not nuclear," reported his Second Officer, Evard Vann Stenger, who had recently returned from a survey of the dead world. "Maybe just different local factions fighting one another, or raids by nearby worlds? The historical records at Litchfield have huge gaps and there's very little written or recorded information about the period directly after the Big War."

"Not at all unusual," the Ship's Historian said, nodding. "You'll find this on many former Federation Member Worlds after the Interstellar Wars, even those not directly involved in the fighting. Most of the inhabitants of these struggling worlds were more interested in surviving, than record keeping. What little has survived the ravages of time, is usually jumbled and highly inaccurate."

They were gathered in a large office at the top of the old Airlines Building. There hadn't been enough time to furnish the entire office, so some of the officers were sitting on overturned crates and boxes because there weren't enough chairs. It was another one of those late afternoon meetings that had stretched effortlessly into cocktail hour. Since almost everyone was enthralled with the local brandy, there were plenty of reasons for cocktails.

"I don't know whether it was an internal struggle on Poictesme or the same attackers that wiped out Storisende," Vann Stenger concluded.

"We have been going through the library archives," Ship's Historian Selner said, topping off his glass, "and there's very little information from that period."

"For every one of the old tapes or discs that we can read, two or three fall apart when we pick them up," Walter Ovard, his assistant, lamented. "And even the ones we can read are patchy, with parts of them illegible."

"Some of it doesn't appear to be time-related damage," Historian Selner added. "It looks to me as if some of the tapes were purposely wiped."

"But why?" Morland asked.

"I don't know, Captain," Selner said. "Maybe someone slipped up during the attack and erased some of the tapes to cover up their mistakes. Or, it was deliberate sabotage or any number of things…."

Morland shook his head. "We may never know what happened and, whatever it was, it's probably not relevant now."

The historians frowned, and Morland quickly assured them that he valued their efforts.

DeBorder, Haversham, and Giffard Zhorgay entered the room and immediately headed for the melon-brandy pitcher. Zhorgay was the *Skull Splitter*'s chief engineer. He had supervised everything from ship construction to a variety of industrial processes on several of the Sword-Worlds.

Vann Stenger hastily brought the others up to speed. "We only stopped at a couple of places before we headed back. We picked out ones that sounded interesting according to the old map we had: Iron Mountain, Gold City, Port Glad—"

"Gold City!" DeBorder interrupted. "Now there's a name to fire the imagination—"

"Not much there, I'm afraid," Vann interrupted. "Just an old gold mine and related industrial buildings with a few residential units. All the storage rooms and bins had been picked over pretty well."

"Looted?"

"No, it looked more like the place was carefully stripped before the planet was abandoned," Vann Stenger said thoughtfully. "Koshchei is a lifeless world, abandoned to the ghosts of its long ago dead occupants. The place gave me the willies. Hell, as far as we know, no one's been there since the Big War, like those dead warships—the abandoned jetsam and flotsam of a forgotten battle. Still, it's one of the areas we should check out to see if there's anything still worth mining."

"I was hoping for more gold ingots to fill the remaining holds on the *Pay Dirt*," DeBorder said.

Morland smiled, thinking, *he'll never change, the old reprobate.* Javen DeBorder was a Space Viking through and through; if he wasn't raiding, traveling or celebrating, he got edgy. They had been on Poictesme over three Galactic Standard months and, while DeBorder had done a fine job helping with the thousand and one things necessary to establish a viable base, he was clearly getting restless—not that Morland blamed him. DeBorder already had accumulated enough plunder in his holds that the captain's share would make a substantial down payment on his loan from King Rodrik. He'd have to come up with something to keep DeBorder busy—and soon.

"Actually in Port Gladstone we found a power cartridge plant that required minimal work to make it operable," Vann Stenger said. "We stripped a nearby power plant and used some of the radioactives for new power unit cartridges. Filled up the pinnace with them."

"That was smart; they'll sell for a good price on Tanith," Morland said. Power unit cartridges weren't as exciting as gold, silver or rare metals but there was always a market for them.

"What about fissionables?" he asked. Fissionables were the one thing that were in short supply on Poictesme. According to local records, the main source of uranium on the planet was a mine adjacent to Storisende that had been destroyed in the nuclear attack. They'd found another small mine that was nearly played out, and he had people working on that. There was very little enriched uranium left in the storage rooms at the Litchfield plant. If they found the right equipment they could convert the Litchfield plant to a breeder reactor, but that would take time.

Vann Stenger shook his head. "Nothing at the port. We found some small amounts in other areas but nothing to get too excited about." He paused to fill his glass with melon-brandy. "However, we did find one thing I thought was exciting."

He grinned as all eyes turned to him. "There's a ship under construction at Port Gladstone, and it's over a third complete. The construction plans are still readable."

Now that is exciting, Morland thought. They hadn't brought a shipwrights' crew along with the intention of constructing a ship, but any Space Viking base that wanted to attract return visitors needed to be able to perform heavy repairs to damaged ships. It was just a small step from there to ship construction itself. They were going to have to do more exploring on Koshchei.

"Do you think the ship is salvageable?"

Vann Stenger nodded. "I asked myself the same thing and had my engineering staff do some checking. First of all, remember that Koshchei is a dead world with no atmosphere and no oxygen to corrode metal. Plus, most of the construction facilities and factories were either underground or built inside large domes so there's minimal radiation, light and cosmic wave damage."

Morland smiled. "So, what you're telling me is that it's not going to take much to get some of these facilities back into operation."

"Right," Vann Stenger said. "There's some residual human damage, probably dating back to when Koshchei was abandoned, but most of the fabrication places and factories had automated cleaners and robotic repair units. I'd say that with the right workers we could have that spaceship fabrication shop up and running in six to eight months. We'll have to bring in some equipment, of course, and make some new machines, but overall we can have ourselves a working spaceyard before the year is over."

VI

Morland sat at the end of the command room, facing the door. Vann Stenger sat to his right and Tylor Ragnarsans to his left, nervously smoking. He didn't have to ask if they were armed; he knew they were. A message had just been sent to Rivera, explaining his plans and asking him to meet them there. Although he had been planning for this moment ever since they had left Joyeuse, he was still uncertain about what was going to happen. A lot would depend on Laz Rivera's reaction to the news.

He had just finished a very fruitful meeting with Javen DeBorder. DeBorder had left in high spirits, eager to return to the *Pay Dirt* and finish loading his share of the Poictesme loot for a trip back to Tanith. After the most lucrative series of raids of his career, DeBorder was looking forward to paying off most of the interest and about half the principal on the loan he had received from King Rodrik to buy the *Pay Dirt.* While most of the *Skull Splitter*'s crew would remain on Poictesme to continue work on the base, some would return home aboard the *Pay Dirt* to Tanith or go with DeBorder from there to the Sword-Worlds, or wherever their homes were.

When Morland had initially sounded DeBorder out about changing his plans to include a visit to Joyeuse, he hadn't been the least bit interested. It added a couple of thousand hours of travel time to the journey and he had no plans to visit the Sword-Worlds, especially Joyeuse since his birth world was Excalibur. Offering him a quarter of Morland's share of the spoils had changed his mind.

After DeBorder left, he had sent word to Rivera that he wasn't returning to Joyeuse, as planned.

Laz Rivera entered the room alone, which was a relief even though he couldn't see if there was anyone waiting in the hall. He tried to read his First's face, but it was a complete mask. He'd gotten to know him pretty well over the two years, but there was still a lot he didn't know about him.

"That was not a routine message you sent me, Captain. Did you mean it?"

"Every word," he answered.

Rivera noticeably relaxed. "Good. If you had intended to deny King Alwyn his rightful share of the loot, I would have been faced with a difficult choice."

Morland felt a wave of relief wash over him. He had always known that Rivera was King Alwyn's hand-picked man, but nevertheless he had served Morland faithfully throughout the voyage—to the extent of backing some of his unpopular decisions to keep looking for a base world when everyone else wanted to stay on Nissaba. Sword-World law required that the investors in any raiding voyage receive their rightful return, and custom decreed that the Captain of the raiding ship himself hand over that return in person. But Morland had no intention of placing himself in Alwyn's power again; therefore, he was glad there would not be any repercussions from Rivera over his refusal to return to Joyeuse.

"I informed DeBorder that you will be returning with him to present King Alwyn and the investors their shares of our profits. He said he would be happy to have you serve as one of his officers, or you can make the trip as a passenger if you so wish."

Rivera licked his lips, his expression puzzled. "Are you ordering me to return to Joyeuse?"

Now it was Morland's turn to be puzzled. "Don't you want to go back?"

"No. Not any more than you do."

Tylor Ragnarsans looked astonished. "But, King Alwyn is your friend."

Grimacing, Rivera shook his head. "Not mine. Alwyn doesn't have friends. He only has business associates, whom he supports as long as they further his own ambitions. All I ever was to him was a leash around your throat, one to remind you that he had your parents in thrall."

As they spoke further it became obvious that his exec feared the King's irrational temper as much as Morland did.

"I could return and hope for continued support from our unpredictable and volatile king," Rivera said. "Or I could retire to Excalibur or Tanith, find a woman, settle down and paint, living off my savings. But I'm not ready to do that."

"I'm glad to hear that." Morland agreed that it would be a waste for someone as organized and talented as Rivera to retire. Plus, like himself and everyone else who was staying on Poictesme, he saw greater potential for himself in the Old Federation than in the Sword-Worlds.

Rivera did express one concern. "What about your family?

"I will take care of that in my own way," Morland replied stonily.

VII

The officers of both ships were having a final drink together before the *Pay Dirt* departed. She would go straight to Joyeuse, a three thousand, four hundred hour journey. On the way back to Poictesme, she would stop first at Tanith so DeBorder could make his payment on his loan to King Rodrik. At both stops they would recruit engineers, technicians and the other specialists necessary to make Poictesme a fully functioning base. It was eight hundred light-years from Poictesme to Tanith, and another two thousand five hundred light-years from there to Joyeuse. With negotiating, recruiting and shore leave, Morland figured the round trip would take almost a year and a half.

"I don't know how much ship-building material you can get on Joyeuse," Morland said, "since their shipyards have been half-shut down for decades. If necessary, you can try Morglay or Excalibur. Maybe even Tanith; now that the League's gone belly-up, King Rodrik may be retrenching."

"I don't know," DeBorder replied, "a lot of Tanith's income comes from ship repairs and laying new keels for Base World barons whose own worlds aren't up to making their own ships anymore."

"Well, be that as it may," he concluded, "even more important than the equipment, are good mechanics, engineers and line workers. And, any industrial teachers or engineering professors you can find will be worth their weight in gold on Poictesme."

DeBorder nodded. "This place was a Gehenna of a find; my hat's off to you, David. My guess is in ten years Poictesme will be the busiest and most important Space Viking base world since Tanith. When the other captains learn of our haul, we'll see some ships—that's as sure as sunrise."

He had provided DeBorder a detailed list of equipment the base could use. Hopefully, King Alwyn and the other investors would provide it. If they didn't, Javen would just have to purchase what he could from his share of their haul. DeBorder knew that he'd be reimbursed for his half. Though they seemed to find new installations of useful equipment on Koshchei every other day, he didn't want to depend on serendipity. In Morland's mind there was no such thing as a base too fully stocked.

His reverie was interrupted by DeBorder's rising to his feet and lifting his glass. "To the best raiding voyage I've ever had. And to my partner, David Morland, who led the way."

"Hear, hear."

"Cheers." Everyone else in the room rose and chimed in.

"And," Javen added, "to even better luck on future raids." He downed his glass, strode over to Morland, and pulled him up, giving him a bear hug. "David, I'll see you as soon as our business is finished."

Surprised by the show of emotion, Morland returned the embrace. DeBorder shook hands with the other officers and left the room.

"I didn't think I'd ever say this, but I'll miss him," Valkanhayn laughed.

"Me, too," Ragnarsans said. The others weighed in, filling their glasses for another toast.

Draining his glass, Morland said, "All right, people, enough partying for now. We have a base to run."

Morland was surprised by the wave of sadness that momentarily overcame him when Javen DeBorder's ship left. They had come a long way from the days when their partnership had nearly broken-up after their arrival on Sucellos. Most of DeBorder's testiness had brought about by the stress of his situation. He'd been desperate to both prove himself a successful Space Viking and pay off his loan from King Rodrik. This desperation and anxiety had led to excessive drinking, further exacerbating the problem. He had also coddled his crew and ceded too much of his authority to them.

With each successful raid DeBorder had become more relaxed and confident; he had even begun to display the quirky sense of humor that had caused him to name his ship *Pay Dirt.* It was a measure of how relaxed DeBorder was that the bottle of brandy they had opened for their final toast before he left the *Skull Splitter* remained over half full. Morland still believed that DeBorder was too lax with his crew, but he had to admit that ship discipline about the *Pay Dirt* had come a long way since departing Tanith.

He was even sadder about his departing sister, Zandra, who was determined to return to Joyeuse. He couldn't blame her; she was not as convinced as he was that their family was safe under the auspices of King Alwyn. He would miss her and her son Richard, but no one was more disconsolate about their leave-taking than Navid, Parviz's son. The two boys had become fast friends and fellow cabin boys. They had been inseparable since the ship's departure from Nissaba.

They had loaded all of the manufactured goods, rare metals, jewels, trade goods and the better part of the silver and gold onto the *Pay Dirt.* Morland had retained his own share in gold ingots, his crewmen's shares and enough specie to provide for their rule on Poictesme and facilitate further trading on other worlds.

The *Pay Dirt* had left two of its pinnaces behind in order to carry more of their plunder and trade goods. It would also make the return journey back to Poictesme more comfortable for the new personnel they recruited. Morland intended to send the *Pay Dirt's* pinnaces out to explore nearby worlds. He had put Walter Ovard, the Assistant Historian, in charge of that effort. Walter seemed to have a good feel for where profit could be found in any level of civilization. His job was to scout nearby worlds and report back to Poictesme. The other academics continued to scour the information found in Litchfield and other old libraries for anything that might prove useful in their search.

Poictesme was becoming a home away from home to most of them. Yorick Ladbrok had done an outstanding job, making friends with most of the local leaders across the planet. He had been aided in this by Mayor Fitch, who due to his export business knew most of the civic leaders personally or through correspondence.

His other officers had taken up special duties of their own. Vann Stenger was running things on Koshchei. Although Stenger was primarily concerned with continuing the construction of the partially completed ship, the search for all of the many installations necessary to manufacture the components needed for ship construction had resulted in a continuing series of discoveries. One of them was a field full of hundreds of interplanetary ships. They had repaired several and had them shuttling back and forth between Poictesme and Koshchei with cargos either for trade locally or for the base at Barathrum. Giffard Zhorgay, the Chief Engineer, had been put in charge of the new ship's construction.

His Third, Tylor Ragnarsans, was running Barathrum spaceport where the *Skull Splitter* was being serviced. Morland had joked with him that he volunteered for that duty just so he could easily study the remnants of the giant volcano, but he had done a great job putting everything back in order. He was just a handful of items away from having a spaceport as functional as any in the Sword-Worlds.

Laz Rivera was in charge of cleaning up the section of Litchfield that they had taken over as their living and command quarters. Morland wanted to have the refurbished buildings and storage facilities ready in time for the new personnel DeBorder would bring back. The massive old Airlines Building's warehouse space was the perfect place to store their spoils, while its offices functioned as their main headquarters. Rivera was refurbishing several nearby towers as living quarters for the new arrivals. He was also setting up perimeter defenses—missile and anti-missile stations and defensive bunkers—all around Litchfield to ensure their base remained secure from either internal or external threats.

Gytha Valkanhayn spent most of her time shuttling Ladbrok around. He had first become aware of their relationship on Nissaba; although Vann had joked that he was amazed Morland had noticed anything other than Princess Janna—just the mention of her name felt like a stab to the heart.

The voluble Ladbrok and the reserved Valkanhayn were an odd couple, and not just because she was the taller of the two and four years older. Morland had become aware that underneath her reserved exterior was someone just as driven as DeBorder to be a success.

Given the time before the *Pay Dirt* was due back, he intended to make one or two raiding trips. He needed fissionables, which had proved to be in short supply on Poictesme, Koshchei and all the other worlds of the Gartner Tri-System. If he couldn't find them on the worlds he raided, he would head for the nearest civilized world to trade for them.

VISHNU

The front room was a small one, and the secretary's desk took up almost half of it. It was clearly a room that was used to expecting visitors. Morland tried to relax and not show his frustration. Vishnu had not lived up to his expectations of what a civilized world should be like. He had come to Vishnu to trade some of their loot, mostly liquors, tapestries and Persian rugs, that they hadn't had room to load aboard the *Pay Dirt*.

Vishnu, at two hundred and fifty light-years away, was the nearest civilized world to Poictesme that was also outside Marduk's sphere of influence as well as Odin's Confederacy of Worlds. Aton was equidistant, but Aton still held a grudge against Space Vikings; not even ships from Tanith were welcome.

It would be a year and a half at the earliest before the *Pay Dirt* returned. Poictesme was still a long way from being a functional base and there were still items he needed that he didn't want to wait that long for. So he had raided his way to Vishnu.

The *Skull Splitter* had first stopped at Sekhet, a world identified in Poictesme's records as barely industrialized at the start of the Interstellar Wars, when they had lost all contact with the outside worlds. The records had been correct. Sekhet was a Civ-Level 3 world good only for chicken stealing, but he had chosen it to provide some easy training for the new recruits they had picked up on Poictesme.

Takama and Ammut had proved to be better targets, being slightly more civilized and populated. They had accumulated cargo worth around fifty million stellars by the time they had orbited Gwydion. After listening in on their local radio chatter for a few days, they had been able to target their raids precisely. When they left, they were loaded with gold, silver, and jewels, along with the normal odds and ends picked up on any raid. Unfortunately, Gwydion was at a pre-atomic Civ-Level and they hadn't been able to take away any fissionables. Still, he estimated their plunder at almost three hundred and fifty million stellars. It was the most lucrative raids he had commanded since Nissaba. And now no one on Vishnu seemed interested in buying their spoils.

It wasn't that the Vishnuians were squeamish about where the *Skull Splitter's* cargo had come from, there was something else going on.

He'd had Lord Ladbrok and Valkanhayn making the rounds of all of the major trading houses, and later most of the minor ones. No one on Vishnu appeared even remotely interested in trading with them. It wasn't because they were Space Vikings; indeed, the Vishnuians acted as if they were some sort of exotic myth come to life. The comment they had all heard repeatedly was: "We haven't had Space Vikings visit for generations."

Generations turned out to be a common theme on Vishnu. Every trading company seemed to have been trading with the same planets, for the same products, with the same families, doing things the same way, for generations. They didn't trade anywhere beyond two hundred hours from Vishnu, nor were they interested in changing or adding new customers.

After several weeks of visiting every firm on the planet, the rest of his officers, even Vann Stenger who was noted for his patience, had retired to a nearby bar to soak up their frustrations. Morland had continued to visit every interstellar trading house in the capital city of New Durban, whatever their size.

Now he was in the waiting room of a company which did not look any bigger than that of a local-area freight forwarder on Joyeuse. He had a ship full of cargo and no one to trade with. The last thing he wanted to do was make the almost three month voyage to Tanith, much less go all the way back to the Sword-Worlds. If they couldn't work out some arrangement here soon, they'd have to go back to raiding and work their way to Baldur. Baldur was one of the richest worlds in the Old Federation and held some of the oldest trading houses; besides, they'd trade with anyone, even Satan himself. Baldur was about a thousand light-years from Vishnu so they could probably hit another dozen worlds and probably fill their cargo holds before arriving there.

His musings were interrupted by the return of the attractive receptionist who had been eagerly talking to him until she had stepped away. She appeared star-struck to have finally met one the Space Viking of news reports and Tri-D shows; he was beginning to think that she might be the only success he was going to have on this planet.

She quickly ushered him into a small office. The man who rose to greet him was a stocky individual of medium height with olive skin and very short black hair, who appeared to be about the same age as Morland. He introduced himself as Vin Qual. "I'm happy to meet a real Space Viking at long last," he said after Morland introduced himself.

"I hope your secretary didn't oversell me," Morland said.

"Oh, it's not just Nadira," he said. "I just returned from lunch with several colleagues from some of the other trading firms in town. You and your crew were the main topic of conversation."

"That interest doesn't extend to doing business with me, I've noticed." He smiled to remove some of the sting from his words.

"To the contrary, you will find I am quite interested depending on what you have to sell."

"Really," Morland said, brightening, "I'm happy to hear that."

"My father started this company just one generation ago."

There's that generations comment again, Morland thought. It must have something to do with the way they looked at the world.

"We have only a couple of small off-world contracts. I would be happy to increase that number. What do you have to sell?"

He handed him a list of the booty they had picked up or brought from Poictesme. Qual reviewed it carefully.

"What are you looking to buy?" Qual asked.

He handed him a second list. "A variety of machinery," Morland stated, discussing some of the items on the list, "as well as plutonium and power units."

After reviewing the list Qual said "I can obtain all of the machinery you are looking for. But I'm afraid I can't sell you any plutonium or power units."

Surprised, he asked, "Why not?"

"Fissionables are in short supply on Vishnu. The government tightly controls the supply and resale of them. They are not going to allow any to be sold to someone without any connections, like you."

Morland was concerned since fissionables were the one thing they were really short of on Poictesme. "Isn't there a black market?"

"Yes, but that's one of the few things the government is efficient at policing. If someone without any connections tries the black market, they'll almost certainly be caught. I wouldn't advise it; the penalties are quite severe. And," raising his hand to forestall the question before Morland could ask it, "I assure you I don't have those kinds of connections. That's why my firm is a small one."

He thought for a moment and asked "I need fissionables badly. Do you have any suggestions?"

Now it was Qual's turn to think for a while. "As I understand it, you Space Vikings raid and trade among many worlds, traveling long distances. You should find a nearby world that has a plentiful supply of fissionables."

Morland choked back a laugh. Finding a world with radioactives that could be plundered had been number one on their list since the *Skull Splitter* had left Poictesme. Most worlds at a Civ-Level that could process uranium and thorium were usually able to protect themselves quite well, which made them dangerous and expensive places to raid—especially with a single ship.

Still, he'd had no choice but to take Qual's suggestion to heart. After arranging for the disposal of his miscellaneous goods, selling enough of their valuables to procure the machinery and other items he wanted, and arranging for the loading of the cargo on the *Skull Splitter*, he spent several hours at a major library that Qual suggested might have the information he needed. After all, he had some time to kill until Nadira got off work.

RHIAMMON

The warning klaxons continued to ring as Morland hurried to the bridge. "Ship detected, status unknown," repeated Valkanhayn over the intercom.

He wondered who it could be? They were outside that part of the Old Federation typically raided by Space Vikings, although it was possible there could be others like him, striking out into the more unknown and remote areas. Rhiannon, which they were orbiting, was an almost uninhabited world. It had suffered heavy nuclear bombing during the Interstellar Wars of seven to nine centuries ago, or maybe earlier since records showed it had been a member of the System States Alliance.

They were at Rhiannon because a library on Vishnu had identified it as having a great deal of easily accessible uranium. It was the only reason anyone would have settled this cold world at the edge of a red-dwarf sun's habitable area. The few people they observed on the telescopic screens and probes were dressed in furs and living in caves or the ruins of former towns. At the glacier edges small bands of dirtsiders were observed herding animals that looked like reindeer. They even observed several small herds of mammoths, which had been recreated, according to what he'd read, by Terran geneticists.

After orbiting the planet several times, signals-and-detection had discovered an old industrial complex undamaged by bombing. It consisted of a large uranium mine accompanied by a dozen breeder reactors, automatic isotope separators, packing plants and storerooms full of unrefined ore.

The reactors were intact but contained nothing but spent fuel. They had repaired or replaced all the robots, emptied out and repacked the breeder reactors with fuel from the ship and started the entire complex backup. Knowing it would be several months before there would be a significant amount of plutonium to harvest, they had left to raid other likely worlds. They had just returned two days ago and were only midway through loading the plutonium onto the *Skull Splitter*.

The ship-detection buzzer going off got Morland jumping out of his bunk so quickly that he almost sprained his foot. He dressed quickly, hopping about on one leg.

As he entered the bridge, with Vann Stenger following behind rubbing his eyes, Morland asked, "What's up, Gytha?"

He tried his best to look casual as he took his seat. A crew member handed them both a cup of coffee, which they had restocked at Vishnu. He made a mental note: *Find a world with high-quality coffee beans at a reasonable price and make it a trading partner.*

"The bogie is a little over twelve hours away at its present speed," Valkanhayn said, giving its location and velocity.

He gulped at his coffee, trying to wake up. "Cautious," he said, commenting on the newcomers slow speed. "This clearly isn't someplace they've been before."

"Run all the detection records," Morland ordered. Before leaving the system to go raiding, they had left several sensors and probes so they'd know if there were any surprises waiting upon their return.

"Already done, Captain," Valkanhayn replied. "They arrived in the outer system almost a day ago and took at least several microjumps. That's why we're estimating they're about twelve hours away."

Considering that all their attention was focused on Rhiannon rather than scanning the heavens for unexpected ships, it was a tribute to his crew's alertness that they had detected the ship so quickly.

"Very cautious," Vann Stenger interjected, gulping his cup down and refilling it. "They could be more Space Vikings."

"Have they detected us?"

Valkanhayn shook her head, "I'm sure they haven't. We haven't used any active detection and we've not detected any sensors or radar from them."

"Get the remaining pinnaces ready. I want to get as much plutonium loaded as possible before that ship arrives."

Two of the pinnaces were down on the surface now loading plutonium and as much uranium ore as they could carry. One of the advantages of this mine was that it had a very high grade of uranium ore. Laz Rivera was on the planet supervising the work.

Morland sat there for moment thinking. Tylor Ragnarsans was in sick bay hooked-up to a Robomedic, recovering from a broken leg and several broken ribs sustained when he was a little too close to an exploding shell on Mara, the most recent world they'd raided. Eleven other crewmembers had been closer to the explosion and were not so lucky.

After first leaving Rhiannon they had traveled to several other worlds that were supposed to have fissionables. On Nepthys, civilization was at about Civ-Level 6, the Second Century Pre-Atomic level equivalent, with the world divided into numerous nations. There were no fissionable mines or plants still operating, but they had made a series of raids on a few major cities. Since the locals lacked radio capability, each raid was pulled off with complete surprise. They had carried away a large amount of gold, gems, and manufactured goods, worth at least a hundred million stellars.

Kalkin, which came next, was more primitive, at Civ-Level 5. Though not as lucrative as Nepthys, Kalkin was a well populated world, and they found a little silver, gold and some high quality furs. They estimated the lot at a little over half of what they obtained on Nepthys. But no fissionables.

Moloch, another former member of the System States Alliance, had seen nearly as much destruction as Rhiannon in the Interstellar Wars. The fissionable sites and large cities had all been destroyed; it was good for nothing but scraps. They had stopped at three other worlds and found they had been hit even worse, and were not worth raiding at all. He was beginning to wonder whether fighting over fissionables had been one of the major activities of the Interstellar Wars.

Mara had been atypical; a Civ-Level 8 world, with atomic power. They had detected several nuclear manufacturing sites and a number of atomic power plants. Mara had no off-planet detection and the *Skull Splitter* had surprised them at first, taking all the plutonium and power units at the first plant. By the time they reached the next site the Marians were ready for them, with jet fighters, bombers and nuclear armed missiles. They suffered more casualties on Mara than on all of the other raids combined since they left Joyeuse. The *Skull Splitter* had also been damaged, although not severely. Still, they had used up a lot of missiles defending themselves, and Morland was nervous about fighting in a ship-to-ship action when this ship was less than fully armed.

As much as he wanted Vann Stenger with him for what he feared might be coming, he needed him on the planet more. "Vann, you go with the remaining two pinnaces and take all the lifters with you. I want as much plutonium as you can fit into the ships." Taking in Stenger's bedraggled appearance, he continued, "You can complete your nap on the way down."

Vann Stenger grinned as he ran his hand through his sleep-flattened hair and left, after refilling his half-empty cup of coffee.

Gytha Valkanhayn had joined the crew on Tanith as signals-and detection-officer and had been on several Space Viking ships before this but only as a junior officer. He had given her several small commands during the past raids and even though she had carried them off flawlessly, she was untried in a major crisis. Still, he reflected honestly, he had no more experience than she did when his moment of truth had come on Agni, and she was older than he'd been then. He would have to count on her coming through when the action got heavy.

"Gytha, go get some sleep," he ordered. "I'll wake you in about six hours."

"I'm fine, Captain. Why don't you go rest?" Valkanhayn was near the end of her normal shift.

"I just got up," he said. "I got enough sleep."

"Are you sure?"

"Don't worry, Chief," he smiled, deliberately using her formal title, which he rarely did for any of his crew. "I won't let you miss any action."

After she left the bridge he checked all the battle stations. Everything was uniformly red-lighted and ready to go. He ran everyone through a series of drills and found no problems. The crew executed them well, not surprisingly, since he'd been running them through every battle drill he could think of ever since they joined the ship. He had been determined, after the near-destruction of the *Nebula* during Count Benedik's Rebellion on Joyeuse, that his next crew would be as battle-trained as he could possibly make them.

When the next shift came on after lunch he did the same thing with similar results. He settled back in the command chair and closed his eyes until Valkanhayn shook him awake, handing him a cup of hot coffee.

"They've finally detected us, Captain," Valkanhayn said.

Gulping at his coffee, he winced. It was too hot for anything but sipping. "How far away are they?"

"A little over four hours at their present speed," she replied. "They've radioed us using all frequencies. They're the Mardukan ship, *Challenger.*"

Morland sat up and came to full awareness. "They say anything else?"

"No, sir."

"Size of ship?"

"She's a two-thousand foot warship, same as we are."

"Recheck our position," he ordered.

"I have, Captain," the interrogator stated. "We are at least eight hundred light-years outside of Marduk's five-hundred light-year zone."

"The pinnaces?"

"One just returned," Valkanhayn said. "The other three are still loading and will not be finished for several hours. Shall I recall them, sir?"

At this distance the *Challenger* would quickly pick up any message they sent. *Best to determine her intentions first,* he thought. "Not yet. Call the *Challenger.*"

The viewscreen cleared revealing a slender man with piercing blue eyes and a short reddish-blonde beard. "This is Captain Vandarvant of the Mardukan Empire ship *Challenger.* Identify yourself!"

"Sword-World ship, *Skull Splitter,* David Morland commanding,"

After a short delay due to the distance, "You are in Mardukan territory Space Viking. Stand down and prepare to be boarded."

"Captain Vandarvant," he replied stiffly, "We are at least eight hundred light-years outside of Marduk's five hundred light-year zone. Furthermore, we are not raiding anyone; we are carrying out mining operations on a nearly unoccupied world."

The delay before Vandarvant's reply was probably not any longer than normal, it just seemed that way. "I'm not interested in excuses.

Stand down your ship and surrender immediately or prepare to be destroyed!" He made a slashing motion with his hand and with that the screen feed cut off.

After a moment of shocked silence, the bridge crew exploded into action. A dozen commands went out nearly at once and background chatter increased rapidly as the crew took their battle stations.

"Gytha, send the following uncoded message to Vann," Morland ordered. "Mardukan ship *Challenger* approaching. Attack expected in three hours. Complete loading operations with extreme vigor and return to *Skull Splitter* within that time frame."

Valkanhayn looked at him strangely but followed the order. He could count on Vann to recognize the hidden code and disregard the message. He hoped Rivera, who was much more of a by the book officer, wouldn't ruin the plan by calling him and debating the order.

A few minutes later Duggan reported "Captain, the *Challenger* has increased speed!"

"Expected arrival time?"

"About thirty minutes, sir."

"Good, compute their trajectory."

By increasing their velocity the *Challenger* would arrive much sooner but their higher speed would also limit their ability to get into orbit and engage the *Skull Splitter*. He carefully explained his plan to Valkanhayn and Duggan, who were tense and excited like the rest of bridge crew. And, by Gehenna, like himself; although he tried his best not to let his emotions show.

It was all he could do not to leap out of the chair and pace around the bridge. It calmed the crew that the Captain appeared to have a plan. Unfortunately, it didn't quiet his butterflies.

The *Challenger* came on until, "They've reached maximum firing range," announced Valkanhayn.

"Launch offensive spread. Change to position two."

"They're firing," someone yelled.

He heard Reginald Mathes, Weapons officer, ordering the launch of counter-missiles. At its high speed, the *Challenger* could not turn fast enough to stay with them. He felt a slight jolt as the *Skull Splitter* sped away and saw lights blinking on the board. A few missiles had gotten through.

Valkanhayn yelled out the *Challenger's* new vector. Morland hastily checked his charts. "All right, hairpin to position five," he ordered. "Give them everything we've got!"

Once again they managed to cross *Challenger's* path in a better firing position. *Challenger*, with limited maneuverability due to its high speed, was going too fast to avoid *Skull Splitter's* missiles, while their missiles had to chase after the *Skull Splitter* and were easier to pick off.

"Status?"

"We've damaged her, sir" replied Valkanhayn. "But we're down to less than ten percent of our defensive missiles."

"Son-of-a-bitch! Offense?"

She looked hastily. "About seventy percent."

Duggan checked his screens. "*Challenger's* made orbit. They are turning to engage us again."

There was little damage to the *Skull Splitter*. The only thing that worried him was the shortage of defensive missiles. "Here she comes," someone yelled. There were no advantages in firing positions this time as both ships spewed missiles at each other. Then they passed close enough to pound each other with their short range guns.

"Hellburner incoming!!" someone screamed. One of the screens tracked the Hellburner missile as it approached, firing its own counter-missiles as it came, picking off the *Skull Splitter's* defensive missiles one by one. If the Hellburner struck the ship it was powerful enough to destroy it despite the collapsium outer skin.

"Offense, target Hellburner!" cried Valkanhayn. All offensive systems fired in its direction. The Hellburner came on for a few seconds more until it exploded, momentarily shutting down all screens in a blaze of kaleidoscopic color.

"Good call, Gytha. Where is she?"

"Part way around the planet," Duggan replied. "Instruments show heavy damage to enemy craft." He paused to look at other screens. "She's hurt a lot worse than we are."

The screens showed numerous wedge shaped holes in the *Challenger*, leaking air and water vapor from where missiles had struck. Their screens would show the same thing on the *Skull Splitter*, just not as many. Without collapsium plating and shielded bulkheads, both ships would have been vaporized long ago. "Can she still maneuver and fight?"

"Not as fast as we can."

"Defensive missiles?" he questioned Mathes.

"Less than five percent remaining," Weapons stated.

"Call *Challenger*," he said. "Captain Vandarvant, our instruments show heavy damage to your ship."

True, he thought.

"Your Hellburner is gone, while ours remains."

Also true.

"We are more maneuverable and have greater fire power."

True, if you ignored the fact the Skull Splitter *had few defensive missiles left.*

"We are not in Mardukan territory and we are not seeking a fight," he replied. "If you break off your attack and let us load our ships, we will not attack you again and will withdraw from this system."

There was no immediate response.

"Captain, they are breaking orbit and heading away!" the Astrogator cried out, as pandemonium broke out upon the bridge.

Morland let out a deep breath and grinned as the crew slapped hands, hugged, danced or celebrated in whatever fashion they desired.

Captain Vandarvant's face suddenly appeared on the viewscreen. His voice announced in stentorian tones: "Space Vikings, you are in Mardukan space. If you return you will be destroyed. No surrender will be accepted."

The screen went black and a moment later Astrogator Reese Duggan announced. "They've jumped,"

"Send a message to the surface that all is well. Tell everyone to return to mother when all the pinnaces are full," Morland ordered.

"Congratulations, sir," Valkanhayn said, coming over to him while everyone else busied themselves checking the status of the ship. "Brilliant maneuvering."

"Thanks, but I hate counting on luck," Morland said quietly.

"That wasn't luck, Captain. That was sheer genius! Did you see his face? It was as red as a supernova."

Morland nodded.

"I think there's something wrong with Vandarvant. He did everything but drool when you refused his demands."

Actually, Vandarvant reminded him a lot of Fergus Byrne, the now deceased former Third Officer aboard the *Nebula.* Byrne had been a baron from Jagannath, a Space Viking base world, who had thought everyone without a title was beneath him and had had a flash point just above absolute zero. It seemed to him that Captain Vandarvant was another of that ilk.

"I hope we don't run into him again," Morland said, as Gytha turned away. *Two space battles and I've nearly gotten my ship destroyed each time,* he thought, thinking of their closc call during Benedik's Rebellion. *If the* Challenger *hadn't been in such a hurry things could easily have been different. I have got to come up with something that will give us a greater edge. Something beyond a skilled crew and luck.*

PART THREE

POICTESME 2

I

The area around the old Airlines Building in Litchfield was crowded, and getting more so by the minute. Morland could see people spilling out of that old shopping mall they'd fixed up as well. Radio broadcasters had been set up to repeat the speech to the old mall as well as to all of Poictesme, or at least everyone who had a receiver. It was a good thing that they'd landed the *Faerie Queene* before the ceremony started. There wasn't room to land her now without crushing hundreds of onlookers.

There had been a lot of dispute over what to name the new ship. Some had suggested a name and blazonry reflecting swords, arguing that Poictesme was now in effect a new Sword-World. He had disagreed, stating that the name should reflect Poictesme. There had been discussion over naming it after an important figure of Poictesme's past. Serious consideration had been given to Genji Gartner, the explorer who had discovered Poictesme.

They had also discussed naming it after Kurt Fawzi, the man history had credited with sparking the revival of Poictesme after the System States War. Fawzi had been Mayor of Litchfield and chief executive of the company that had led the way in pulling Poictesme out of a long depression after the war. He had later been elected planetary President. Morland had disappointed Lord-High Mayor Morgan Fitch, who claimed to trace his ancestry to both Gartner and Fawzi, by choosing neither.

Instead he'd taken a local historian's suggestion and named the ship after one of the novels that Genji Gartner had used for his original inspiration in naming the planets of the Gartner Tri-System. The local library had a copy and he had found it a bizarre, if entertaining read. *Faerie Queene* it was. The blazonry was a woman with wings and arms outstretched with three suns making a belt across her waist.

Evard Vann Stenger was going to command her, with Tylor Ragnarsans as Executive Officer. His first thought had been to offer command of the *Faerie Queene* to his First Officer, Laz Rivera. To his surprise, Rivera stated that he would prefer to continue as First aboard the *Skull Splitter.* After that, there had been many long discussions well into the evening hours over personnel, who should be promoted to what position and who should go on which ship. And, while it was true that some of the Poictesmes had so far proved to be good students, he had wanted experienced and loyal Space Vikings in every important position, and he and Vann had fought good-naturedly over who should get whom.

He had hoped to avoid some of the discussion by using new recruits from the Sword-Worlds. However, the *Pay Dirt* was over two months overdue and with her any personnel that DeBorder had managed to recruit on Tanith and Joyeuse. Despite his anxieties over the *Pay Dirt* and whether or not Vann's crew was experienced enough, he'd had no choice but to move ahead.

The battle with the *Challenger* on Rhiannon had shown him that the Mardukan Empire intended to be a lot more aggressive about acquiring new territory than their official pronouncements had indicated. Poictesme was too close to Marduk's five-hundred hour boundary, at only eight hundred hours away, to be comfortable. He had two rotating pinnaces keeping watch at the farthest edge of the Gartner Tri-

System's heliosphere to avoid any surprises.

Since his trading visit to Vishnu had gone so well, Morland wanted to have another base closer to that world. He already had most of the available pinnaces out exploring for possibilities for additional bases. He had directed the explorers to search the area outside of Vishnu's usual trading zone to Poictesme. They were also examining planets for future raiding targets.

A jab in the side from Stenger's elbow brought him back to reality. Lord-High Mayor Fitch's long speech sounded as if it was just about to wrap-up. He was up next. Fitch's speech had been long because it was much more about the Lord Mayor's ambition to reunite the world under one government and reinstitute the office of planetary president—with Fitch himself as the obvious choice for the position—than it was about naming a new ship.

Then he noticed an aide moving discreetly toward him. "Sir, a ship has been detected. It emerged over twenty-five light-minutes from the planet. Another jump has put it ten light-minutes away."

All the officers nearby froze. They had all been concerned after the battle with the *Challenger* that the Empire would send more ships to locate and punish them. Morland had concluded that the Empire would have no way of knowing where they were located and, in fact, would expect them to return to the Sword-Worlds or a Space Viking base planet for repairs.

However, as the Ship's Historian kept reminding him, Poictesme had at one time, during the Federation times, been part of a major connecting space passenger line, the Terra-Baldur-Marduk Spacelines, between Terra and Marduk.

He thought furiously. The *Faerie Queene* was fully loaded and ready to go. The climax of the naming ceremony was to be the officers entering the ship and the ship lifting off. "The ceremony will go on as planned. Gytha, call the *Skull Splitter* and have them start warming up and loading all the available ship's crew." The *Skull Splitter* was currently at Barathrum spaceyard undergoing repairs from the battle with the *Challenger*. "Also, tell the pinnaces to hold position and not to approach the incoming ship but call us immediately if it jumps closer."

When Mayor Fitch finished his introduction, Morland rose to his feet and strode to the podium. He had not intended to make a long speech; now he was going to be even more concise.

"Mayor Fitch, Litchfield residents, assembled guests, people of Poictesme. Thank you for welcoming us to your planet. We hope this is the beginning of many happy years of working together to further civilization on this great world. As a symbol of that collaboration, I hereby name this ship, *Faerie Queene*."

As the crowd cheered he stepped down and shook hands with Stenger and Ragnarsans. Gytha stood next to him clapping. "The ship took another microjump; it's now three light-minutes away."

He tried not to look worried. He was now convinced that it had to be an Imperial ship or someone equally unfamiliar with the system. The *Pay Dirt*, having been to Poictesme before, wouldn't have taken so many microjumps.

The aircar was back from the ship and they piled into it—all the while trying to look nonchalant. There was another cheer from the crowd as the *Faerie Queene* rose into the air. He chuckled grimly. Vann must have just boarded when he gave the order to lift off; he must still be on an elevator making his way to the bridge.

The aircar took off for Barathrum. It would take over an hour at full speed to get there.

Valkanhayn was yelling into one of the viewscreens at someone he didn't recognize. "I don't care whether we have any food aboard! Get the entire crew on as fast as possible or I'll bag your—"

Just then the aircar passed the sonic barrier and he couldn't hear the rest of her words.

"Captain," said Laz Rivera. "Pinnace One just reported in. The ship has jumped to within six light-seconds." He nodded confirmation. A minute later Rivera spoke again. "Captain, message coming directly from the ship."

The aircar screen flickered and Javen DeBorder's smiling face stared out at them.

When everyone had calmed down, Morland learned that the *Pay Dirt* had taken so many jumps because Javen's old Astrogator had retired and his new Astrogator was unusually cautious. That didn't matter to him at the moment. What mattered was that Javen was saying, "Hello, everyone. It's great to be back."

With a wide grin he continued. "Captain, I want to report my private mission was a complete success." The viewscreen feed widened and there were his father and mother, along with his sister, Zandra Konigstrum.

"Thank-you," he said, closing his eyes in silent meditation.

11

Morland heard most of the story in the hours it took the *Pay Dirt* to reach orbit and descend to the spaceport. Per his instructions, DeBorder had stopped at Joyeuse first. Zandra had been dropped off—ostensibly to recruit new personnel—but in reality to pick up his parents who had secretly made their way to the city of Roland under false names.

Rivera had been correct about his assumptions in regards to King Alwyn. To begin with, the King was upset that it took so long for the ship to return. Next, the King had complained bitterly that his return on investment was insufficient. It was obvious to DeBorder that he was most unhappy that the *Skull Splitter* had not returned, because he had no control over the *Pay Dirt.*

DeBorder shook his head. "You'd think the expedition had been a total failure, the way the King bitched about it. Now, I understand why you and Rivera didn't want to return to Joyeuse. Still, I noticed Alwyn didn't turn down his share of the profits. I believe the only thing that might have pleased him was if I'd come back with your head in a basket!"

They all laughed.

"Seriously, Cap'n, he's holding a big grudge against you. People in Longinus and Ogier speak well of you and think of you as a home-world hero. No one seemed surprised at our success; they all expected it. Good old-fashioned jealousy may be what's fueling Alwyn's hatred. Still, if you want my advice, forgot about ever returning to Joyeuse—at least while Alwyn's still alive."

Morland nodded in agreement. The King had only reluctantly given him command of the *Skull Splitter*. Instead of being thankful for his help during the Rebellion, he'd picked up that Alwyn resented both needing help and getting it.

"What's going on politically?" he asked.

"From everything we heard in the taverns and the Longinus Ports of Call, King Alwyn's control of Joyeuse has grown more tenuous," DeBorder said. "We heard rumors of protests and revolts that had been crushed. Any news of dissention is immediately suppressed by the king's agents."

"This may be a case of Alwyn's ambitions exceeding his grasp," Rivera mused.

Lord Wallace confirmed the unrest based on his discussions with his family. Morland had been surprised that Nevil Wallace had returned to Poictesme, but he said his father had ordered him back to the base world for more experience. Apparently Wallace was still the worthless scion, as far as his family was concerned, although he appeared cheerily oblivious to that fact. He was the only one of the gentleman adventurers to return from Joyeuse.

"At first, King Alwyn refused to invest any more stellars in the New Base Venture, saying it wasn't worth it," DeBorder reported, "although he agreed to let us use the dockyards for free to service the *Pay Dirt*. Later he relented, but only after I told him about the ship under construction on Koshchei. Only then was he willing to send some of the equipment you requested."

"What did he send?" Morland asked.

"Mostly equipment for ship construction," DeBorder chuckled, "but a lot of it is second-hand and well used."

Rivera shook his head. "Captain, I don't understand why you expected anything more out of that tightwad."

"Actually, it was to deflect the King's interest away from our real mission," Morland answered, "getting more trained engineers, mechanics and teachers."

"It worked, but wait until you hear this," DeBorder interjected, "Alwyn's final orders are that you are to construct several ships and return at once to Joyeuse. He's so unsettled about the political instability on Joyeuse that he wants to build up his navy at *our* expense."

Rivera scoffed at that demand. "Those two deathtraps that he calls the Joyeuse Navy couldn't stop a Space Viking chicken-thief attack. Notice how quickly they deserted him at the Battle of Longinus. Besides, any ships we build at Poictesme—or anywhere else for that matter—are clearly ours under Sword-World law. By our Letter of Marque, the King is not even entitled to any proceeds or shares from the plunder those ships obtain, much less the ships themselves."

DeBorder also noted that recruiting had been easy despite King Alwyn's attempts to discourage people from emigrating. "There's so much unrest, to say nothing of rising unemployment, we had people begging us to take them with us. I could have filled a dozen ships the *Pay Dirt's* size."

"Then, what took you so long?" Morland asked.

"That's a whole other story," DeBorder said, as he filled them in. Along with the *Pay Dirt's* astrogator, the ship's services and stores officer Fedvil Porter had also retired. Without thinking it through, and being distracted by Alwyn's belligerence, DeBorder had appointed Hereld Norwell in Porter's place.

Morland winced and Gytha nearly dropped her cup of coffee.

DeBorder shrugged. "Ever since I disciplined him, Hereld has been an exemplary crewman. He has so much potential…so I stupidly decided that he deserved a second chance! It turns out that what he was waiting for was another opportunity to strike it rich. Hereld and several of the services crewmen working under him accepted bribes, cramming thousands of people unmercifully into the lower decks where the pinnaces had been berthed."

Morland nodded. "That explains the horde of settlers disembarking from the *Pay Dirt.*"

"Right. The crowded conditions caused the transportees to riot shortly after we departed from Joyeuse. In addition, or because he was so busy seeking bribes, Hereld neglected to supervise the maintenance and refitting of the *Pay Dirt.* The air started to go foul shortly after we left Joyeuse. If we hadn't had such a short jump to Excalibur, we would have had to space half the passengers or face death ourselves."

"I've never heard of a ship being so overcrowded it fouled the air," Morland said.

"It wasn't the crowding," DeBorder replied. "The servicing of the ship wasn't done properly. Your sister detected it right after we landed at Excalibur."

Some of the officers present were still astonished that Morland's parents had managed to conceal their identity during their voyage. Only Vann Stenger had known Zandra was his sister, and even Vann hadn't known of Morland's plans to remove his parents from King Alwyn's reach. It helped that his nephew Richard, because of the closeness of their ages, had always called him by his first name rather than Uncle David.

"Someone had tinkered with the air system so that it wouldn't show any problems. I don't know whether it was a deliberate act of sabotage or if somebody simply wanted to avoid overhauling the system and fixed the detectors so he wouldn't have to do any work. I had the ship thoroughly overhauled on Excalibur, with Zandra, Will or myself supervising every second."

"Did Hereld do it?" Valkanhayn asked.

"No, but I wouldn't put it past him, and he did plenty of other things. I put him on a veridicator, so he couldn't lie his way out of the charges like he has before."

DeBorder was clearly disgusted with himself for promoting Hereld, especially after the debacle on Nissaba. "I should have exiled the Son-of-a- Khooghra on Nissaba...."

"What was his punishment?" Valkanhayn asked.

"I let him suck space along with the other guilty crewman," DeBorder said with finality. "Then I had all the passengers veridicated while we were approaching Excalibur. Many of them, it turned out, lied about their skills and education to get aboard. If they hadn't contributed to the riots or created any problems, I just tossed them off the ship once we landed on Excalibur.

"If they were guilty of the murders, robberies or rapes, I deep spaced them as well," he said grimly. "I used the stellars and jewelry we found in Hereld Norwell's and his cronies quarters to pay back the bribes and compensate the victims. I put what money was left in the Death Benefits account."

The others nodded. That was the traditional use for the funds of a crewman executed for disobeying orders. Morland believed DeBorder had finally learned the consequences for not having established his authority over his crew. It was clear those repercussions weighed heavily on him, just as it was clear DeBorder was determined not to repeat his error again.

"King Winston won't thank you for dumping all those unskilled people on him," Rivera commented.

DeBorder shook his head. "It's a small drop in a large bucket. We learned that because of its stability there's been so much immigration to Excalibur from the other Sword-Worlds over the last few decades that their population has risen to over a billion people."

That astonished everyone.

"A billion people!" Vann Stenger exclaimed. "Why, that's up there with the civilized worlds, like Marduk or Odin or Isis."

After leaving Excalibur, unsure that everything was working right with his air recyclers, DeBorder had broken-up his trip back into a series of short hops, stopping at Morglay and Curtana before leaving the Sword-Worlds.

"Did you stop at Abigor then?" Ragnarsans asked with a laugh.

DeBorder swore, moving his hand in the traditional gesture to ward off bad luck.

Morland chuckled. He never understood why so many of the Space Vikings were superstitious about the planet their ancestors had emigrated from. He had never been to Abigor, but had heard, in the Ashdod Ports of Call on Dagon, that it was at Civ-Level 3 and hardly worth a visit, unless you were truly desperate.

"No, we stopped at Aditya."

That made sense. Aditya was closer to the Sword-Worlds than Abigor. It was a Neobarbarian planet that Morglay had conquered and colonized centuries ago. During one of their many dynastic wars Morglay had abandoned it; as far as he knew, no one had been there for centuries.

Clearly enjoying his audience, DeBorder continued. "We detected radio waves and electricity, but nothing more than that. Although everything seemed fine with the air recyclers, I decided to go down into the atmosphere to freshen our air."

The audience nodded again. Even with the best filters, recycled air inevitably tasted a little stale, and most Space Vikings liked to renew it at every opportunity.

"They detected us as soon as we hit their atmosphere. The radio chatter turned hysterical, warning us to go away and leave the planet. Then we saw it."

DeBorder paused, milking the moment as he refilled his glass and drank. People laughed or swore at him good naturedly until he continued. "A ship. Sitting on its landing legs on the ground at the edge of a small city. It looked like any other Space Viking ship. We immediately went to battle stations and changed course as fast as possible."

He paused, dramatically.

"Then?" someone asked.

"Then, nothing!" DeBorder replied. "The ship didn't do anything. In fact, signals-and-detection couldn't detect a single kilowatt of energy from her. When we checked it through the telescopic-screen, it showed that brush had grown up over the landing legs. The ship had been sitting there for a long time—decades at least."

Now that was a mystery. It was rare for a ship to sit anywhere for very long; they were too valuable. Even heavily damaged ships were worth a small fortune as scrap.

Tylor Ragnarsans, with great interest, asked, "Do you think it's salvageable?"

DeBorder shrugged. "Whether the ship will fly again, who knows. We didn't stop and check it out. The natives were pretty stirred up and the city was in ruins—not even worth a quick snatch-and-grab. We hit another city and got a modest amount of loot. From Aditya, we went straight to Tanith, where I was able to repay half of my loan to King Trask." He ended by reporting that Rodrik now had fifteen children with another on the way, which caused chuckles from most present, and a big laugh from Gytha Valkanhayn, who knew the family well.

Then it was time for DeBorder to hear the story of the *Skull Splitter*'s raiding voyages and the space battle with the Captain Vandarvant and the *Challenger*.

"So now Marduk is unhappy with us," DeBorder said thoughtfully, after hearing about the fight.

"I'm sure that is putting it mildly," Morland replied. "There was something off with that Captain, too. What's he doing eight hundred light-years from Mardukan territory chasing honest Space Vikings?"

"Damn-it, Cap'n, you should have blown that ship to Em-See-Squared!"

He shook his head. "I didn't want to start a war with Marduk. A missing ship in our sector could bring us all kinds of trouble. Plus, we were low on defensive missiles and I didn't want to chance the *Skull Splitter* getting badly hulled."

"Still, something like this could bounce back on us," DeBorder said.

"You didn't hear anything on Tanith did you?"

"No," DeBorder replied. "But I've got a bad feeling about this. There was a lot of gossip at the Riff-Raff Tavern about Space Vikings staying away from the territory included in Marduk's new claims. There was also some bluster that a few ships were still raiding in Imperial territory, but I don't buy half of it. Most of that talk was under the table since there were plenty of independent traders and Gilgameshers on Tanith who'd happily sell that information to Marduk for a centistellar. In general, I will say that it's put a damper on Space Viking raids."

There were nods of agreement from the assembled officers.

"Have any Space Vikings visited Poictesme since we left?" DeBorder asked.

Morland shook his head. "No, we haven't even seen any Gilgameshers."

"Well, I thought a few independents looked interested when I told them about our new base. Maybe we'll start seeing some traffic soon."

"I sure hope so," Morland said.

"We'll probably have Gilgameshers out here once the word gets around," Rivera said. There were a variety of reactions to that statement, all of them negative.

Gilgamesh was the only civilized planet in the Old Federation known to have descended into barbarism, then pulled itself all the way back up to Civ-Level 10, which included contragravity and hyperdrive ships, all through its own efforts. The Gilgameshers were governed by a socialist theocracy and were the gypsies of the Old Federation, even so far as establishing settlements on the worlds they traded with.

They were traders only, as they had religious objections to violence; not that they weren't above protecting their own ships and settlements. Their religion had prohibitions against many things that were acceptable on most worlds, plus an incredible list of dietary, social and personal taboos. This, along with their distrust of anyone not of their religion, made them avoid any unnecessary contacts with outsiders. They were unpopular on most worlds, and especially hated by the Sword-Worlders, who—if any were in the vicinity—blamed them from everything from a broken air-recycler to selling information to the opposition.

There was lots of truth to the latter, as the Gilgameshers were avid rumor and gossip mongers. If an opportunity presented itself, they'd give aid and comfort to any Space Viking opponent. Unfortunately, they saw all Space Vikings—with the exception of the Trasks, who always treated them with respect—as enemies.

Morland agreed they weren't likable, but he thought that a lot of the Space Vikings' antipathy came from the fact that the Gilgameshers were their toughest competitors. With their self-image as tough, fearless raiders, Space Vikings didn't like to admit the truth, which was that they traded more than they pillaged. Part of it was necessity; some planets were difficult to raid because their valuable products weren't centralized. It was also good business because typically the richer planets were the more civilized ones, and raiding civilized planets that had contragravity and nuclear weapons was a great way to get killed. In many cases, it was easier, and more profitable, to trade with them.

Whatever one thought of a Gilgamesher's personal beliefs, they would go anywhere in the galaxy to trade. They had probably visited more worlds than even the Space Vikings, and each ship carried a great deal of information, if you could afford to pay for it.

Morland's tearful reunion with his family was noted with surprise from his crewmen who viewed him only as a remote and stern captain.

"You said you were going to take care of your family—and you did," Laz Rivera remarked.

In unloading the cargo brought back on the voyage, they learned that DeBorder had not been exaggerating; most of the equipment supplied by King Alwyn was used and worn. However, DeBorder had also used some of his remaining personal funds to purchase some of the necessary items that the King did not provide.

"It hit me when we got to Joyeuse that since you've done most of the thinking for us, that I should contribute something to this venture," DeBorder told Morland.

Morland protested he should have used the funds to pay off more of his loan. DeBorder disagreed, saying that he was sure that he could take care of the rest of the loan in the future. Despite all the equipment he had brought with him, there were still some items that they needed.

Vann Stenger, whose first trip as captain had been delayed by the *Pay Dirt*'s arrival, stayed around long enough to catch up on all the gossip, then he said his goodbyes and left on the *Faerie Queene's* maiden voyage.

III

As he entered the office at the top of the Old Airlines Building that functioned as his headquarters, Morland wondered about the look on Stenger's face. Clearly there was something Vann wanted to discuss that he would not mention over the communication screen during his normal-space journey to the Litchfield spaceport. He had just returned with the *Faerie Queene* from Vishnu after being gone for almost two thousand hours.

"What's wrong?" Morland asked as he walked through the door. "Did you run into any problems with the ship?" He had been on Koshchei starting up a new project when Stenger returned from his trip.

Vann Stenger mission had been to visit Vishnu to sell loot and pick up some needed machinery and equipment for the new shipyard. On the way he had stopped at a planet called Ashtereth to give the new recruits some relatively easy combat experience. According to previous intelligence, Stenger had expected Ashtereth to be only a chicken-stealing world, instead he had spent over a week raiding and had come away with loot valued at about twenty million stellars, declaring it was now a Civ-Level 5 world.

"Everything went fine," Stenger replied. "The *Faerie Queene's* a great ship. It's everything I've ever wanted, just like I told you over the radio. The crew, including the new recruits from the Sword-Worlds and Poictesme, did well. We practiced several different types of raids to get them some experience. Ashtereth wasn't a real tough test, but that's why we chose it first."

Morland nodded, having done the same thing on the *Skull Splitter's* shakedown cruise.

"Well, guess who was in Ashtereth system about a hundred hours before I got there?" Stenger asked.

"I have no idea." Morland shrugged.

Filling two glasses with melon-brandy, Stenger handed one to him as he continued. "We took a couple of prisoners, for reconnaissance purposes like your Historians suggested; and guess what they told us?

Morland shook his head

"Captain Vandarvant and the *Challenger*, with another Mardukan ship, visited Ashtereth about six Galactic Standard months before our arrival. He was asking a lot of questions about a Space Viking ship—the *Skull Splitter*."

This could be a harbinger of real trouble, Morland thought. "Fortunately, I've never set foot on Ashtereth, but I don't like the fact that this damn Vandarvant is looking for me less than two hundred light-years away."

"I agree. It sounds like he's stalking you; I suggest you keep the *Skull Splitter* berthed here on Poictesme for the time being."

Morland nodded. "Not a bad idea. But we need to know more about Vandarvant: Who is he? What's his reputation as a captain? How important is his family back on Marduk? How much juice he has, et cetera?"

"Good questions, David," Vann Stenger said. "We've got a lot of trade goods piled up here in Litchfield. Maybe it's time one of us made a trip to a civilized world to maximize our profits, say Marduk?"

"Brilliant."

"Yes," Vann Stenger continued, "and probably the best ship to take would be the *Faerie Queene*, since it's a newly registered ship based on Poictesme. I think it'll pass as a heavily armed free trader, especially since it doesn't have a Sword-World pedigree."

"And, on the way back," Morland finished, "you can offload the rest of your goods at Tanith. I'll put together a dispatch for King Rodrik and hopefully he'll have some intelligence to pass on about the Mardukan situation."

Vann Stenger drained his glass. "Or maybe Vandarvant, as well." He refilled his and another glass with melon-brandy, which he handed to Morland. "Now a toast."

"To what?"

"Let me congratulate you on your promotion to Commodore," he continued. "It was long overdue."

They clinked glasses.

"Now that we have three ships," Morland said, "With so many captains, I thought it was time to promote myself to the next highest rank."

"I agree, but I don't think you went far enough—"

Morland shook his head. "To call myself Admiral of three ships is sheer vanity."

"That's not what I'm referring to, Commodore," Vann Stenger said. "We need to solidify our position on this planet. And I'm not the only one who thinks that way."

Morland had heard the same pitch from both Laz Rivera and Lord Ladbrok; both had suggested that he declare himself prince or king of Poictesme.

He shook his head. "There are only a little over ten thousand of us here. Right now, most of the locals like us because we've improved their lives and have asked little in return. We've acted as if we were a new business in town, not the new Grand Poobah. If we start throwing our weight around and claiming titles and obligations, then we'll need a large force and a ship here at all times to prevent a rebellion. That will reduce our ability to raid and trade."

The only locals who seemed to be really unhappy with them were the railroad companies and their employees, who were starting to suffer as more and more trade was conducted by contragravity ships. However, they were making up some of their losses hauling passengers to Litchfield, as people all over the continent tried to join his crew or sought the advanced training provided by the Sword-Worlders. His father, just barely days off the *Pay Dirt*, had returned to his profession of robotics instructor, saying he'd had a long enough vacation on the flight from the Sword-Worlds.

"But what are we now?" Vann Stenger asked. "Are we Sword-Worlders? Or are we citizens of Poictesme?"

Morland smiled and sat down. "What you are really asking is: Who's in charge? Who will make people do what they don't want to do, when it's the right thing, or do what we want them to do? I don't think we have to deal with those questions, at least not now."

"But shouldn't we be parceling out districts, states, provinces, baronies, dukedoms or something along those lines?" Vann Stenger asked. "How will we decide who gets what land? How will we collect taxes? Nature abhors a vacuum and if we don't fill it, someone else will."

"Why do we have to do any of that at all?" Morland retorted. "Poictesme allows people to claim vacant land or unused buildings. We can just work though their legal system, just as we did when we claimed most of that valley next door."

The valley to the west of Litchfield was almost uninhabited except for a small railroad stop and some scattered farms. They had taken over and repaired an old installation that had been a former military barracks and used the barracks and much of the valley to train new recruits as ground fighters, contragravity vehicle operators and other needed jobs.

"Let Lord-High Mayor Morgan Fitch worry about taxation and landholders. After all, that's why the citizens of Litchfield elected him."

Vann Stenger shook his head. "For a Space Viking, you sure have a contrary view on conquest and base worlds."

"Yes, we need a base world, a place to operate out of, but not one we have to baby-sit. If we let the locals run things, we're good neighbors and they welcome us. The minute we start bossing people around and demanding revenues, whether we call them tithes, taxes or levies; we're the evil and rapacious Space Viking conquerors."

"How will we provide for our rule without taxes?" Vann Stenger asked, bewildered. "What if our people want to settle down here and farm or raise cattle or run businesses?"

"This is a raiding base and I'm a Space Viking, not a land baron," Morland stated flatly. "That is how I intend to make money. As long as someone is a member of my crew, they are subject to my orders. If they want to quit and become a Poictesmian, they will be subject to Mayor Fitch's laws, or whomever's in charge. I will not try to stop them, nor protect them. My duty ends when they resign their commission and are no longer a part of the *Skull Splitter's* crew."

"How about those engineers and machinists we ferried from the Sword-Worlds to come and work for us?" Vann Stenger asked. "What about their obligations to us and to the ship?"

"The moment those workers have fulfilled their contract with us, which includes reimbursement for their transportation costs to Poictesme, they're free to work for whomever they want. I doubt that anyone on this planet can afford to pay them as much as we can." He could see it was hard for Vann Stenger, a child of the Sword-Worlds, to grasp the concept that these were workers under contract, not feudal obligation.

When you grew up on any of the Sword-Worlds, you were always aware of who were your superiors and who were your inferiors, as well as your place in the planetary hierarchy—your fealty to your local lord, the baron, count or duke above him, and the planetary king above them all. Some people were clearly going to have trouble adjusting to a less stratified social order.

The primary reason Morland didn't intend to return to the Sword-Worlds was that he was tired of being judged by who his parents were, where he was born and his position in the local pecking order. Being a Space Viking had allowed him to exercise talents far beyond the social limitations of his birth. On this voyage he had seen many of his crew do the same thing. He was no longer interested in what rank people were born with; he was interested in what they could do with what they had and how well they did it.

"As far as the crew, most of them have already more than earned their pay." Morland stated. "Those that left Joyeuse with us have enough bonus money to make something of themselves if they were to return to the Sword-Worlds."

"Yes, and most of them still seem to think that we are all going to return one day."

"Well, that's not part of our contract."

"But it is, and you have an implied obligation to take them there," Vann Stenger stated, a little stiffly.

"No, I only have an obligation to see that they are provided with return passage and their salary plus bonuses. Soon I will announce that I plan never to return."

"But you've sworn an oath to King Alwyn—"

"I'm only sworn to the Letter of Marque that I signed my name to. I will continue to send the King his share of any loot the *Skull Splitter* makes, but I will not return to Joyeuse in person. I expect that some of our crew will want to return. They can go with the *Pay Dirt* the next time it returns to Tanith. They can book passage, at my expense, from Tanith to anywhere in the Sword-Worlds."

Vann Stenger appeared to have a hard time digesting his ruling, or lack of ruling philosophy. To give him time, Morland decided to change the subject.

"Tell me more about the trip to Vishnu. How is our friend Vin Qual?"

Vann Stenger brightened. "He was very happy to see me. He said he was hoping that your visit wasn't a one-time thing. He bought everything I had with me with a minimum of dickering and gave us good prices on the equipment we needed. That pretty secretary of his was very unhappy you weren't there, though."

Morland smiled; he had fond memories of Nadira.

"The most important thing," Stenger continued, "was that he wanted a lot more of the melon-brandy."

"Wine-melon brandy? From Poictesme?" Morland asked, astonished. Most of the crew really enjoyed the local brandy. In fact he had heard spirited discussions as to how it compared with Excalibur red-whiskey, Nissaba pomegranate wine, Gram gum-pear brandy, and other shipboard favorites. "He didn't seem like a drinker to me. I don't even recall having a single drink with him while we were doing business."

Stenger chuckled. "He's a teetotaler, in fact. The reason he was interested is because you gave him a case of melon-brandy as a gift on our first visit and he passed it on to some friends. They went nuts over it and are begging for more."

Stenger went on to tell him about the drinking clubs on Vishnu that specialized in off-world specialty wines, liquors and distilled spirits. The people in these clubs were willing to pay more for a glass of alcohol from another planet, even if they admitted the differences in taste were often subtle. The taste of Poictesme melon-brandy, on the other hand, was incomparable to anything they'd tasted before.

"Vin said he'd buy whatever we had on hand," Vann Stenger continued. "We scrounged together all the unopened bottles on the ship; he paid us a premium price and threw in a couple of cases of the local whiskey, so we wouldn't go thirsty on the trip back. Also, Vin did some research on which luxury products and alcoholic beverages had been big hits in the past on Vishnu, but are no longer available. He gave me a list," he finished, handing it off to Morland.

Morland reviewed a list of several dozen products. They were all unfamiliar to him until he reached a familiar name. "Ammut sugar-plum rum? We raided Ammut last year. I don't recall any rum."

"Neither do I," Vann Stenger said. "We must have missed it. We'll have to make another stop at Ammut. And what about that Nissaba pomegranate-wine? I bet they'd love that, too."

Morland strode over to the large star chart that covered one wall of his office. It was a representation of the star region around Poictesme. It went as far as Odin and Vishnu, and well into the Mardukan five-hundred light-year zone.

"There's been a lot of new information added in the last few months," Vann Stenger noted as Morland made a note next to Ammut's place on the map. "I see Walt's been busy."

Walter Ovard, Senior Assistant Historian, had been exploring many of the nearby worlds to locate new targets for raiding and familiarize everyone with their neighborhood of nearby space. Morland brought Stenger up-to-date on what worlds had been rediscovered while he was gone, including DeBorder's raids on some nearby planets.

"Walter has mapped out a big raid," he concluded. "He says he's guaranteeing us at least a hundred million stellars on every world and several possibilities for additional bases."

Stenger raised his eyes, impressed. "When do we leave?"

Morland grinned. "Tomorrow. We've just been waiting for you to return."

"What about my trip to Marduk?"

"We'll be loading you up with trade goods tonight. You can pick up more during the first raid or two. Then you can leave for Imperial space."

LYONNESSE

I

"I'm really sorry, Commodore," Walter Ovard said, a wretched look distorting his normally pleasant face. "I thought...."

"Walt, that's enough apologizing. Any more and I'll throw you in the brig," Morland said sternly, until he couldn't hold it in anymore and grinned, while the rest of the bridge broke out in laughter.

"I think he bet money on his prediction, and he's more upset about having to pay it off than he is about being wrong," Tylor Ragnarsans crowed, drawing another laugh.

Ovard's guarantee of a hundred million stellars worth of plunder or more per world had held up during the first two raids. Sulsaga was a world of over three hundred million people with a Civ-Level 6 civilization. It also had the largest mountain any of them had ever seen, which Ragnarsans had gone nuts over. The top of Gudea Mountain was well beyond the oxygen level necessary to sustain life so no one was ever going to climb it. The historian's research had identified several depositories of gold and silver so between that and the big cities they had hit, they'd taken away about two hundred and fifty million stellars worth of loot.

The next world, Ningal, was one of the oddest he had ever encountered. It had a peculiar climate, with much of the world sheathed in a perpetual cloud cover. The largest continent was practically one big swamp. Normally, Morland wouldn't have given the world a second look, but Ovard had determined from old records that during the late Federation Ningal had been the source of a lucrative interstellar fur trade. Apparently the animals living there needed a lot of fur to stay warm and shed the constant moisture. They had raided all the major towns on the planet, and along with the furs had stolen a variety of luxury goods; the total estimated value was just over two-thirds of what they got from Sulsaga.

The world they just left, Parvati, had been relatively disappointing. Poorly populated and technologically backward, Ovard had recommended it due to its gem and mineral wealth, particularly a large platinum mine. They'd had bad luck, however, as the platinum mine was closed down due to a local war and had already shipped most of its inventory. They'd had better luck at some of the gem mines Ovard had located, but it was still short of the riches that the assistant historian had promised.

While lucrative target worlds, none of them had the assets Morland was looking for in terms of another base.

"Ovard, why don't you tell us about the next target world," Morland asked.

The historian brightened. "For this planet, I have much more recent information from a Gilgamesh trade ship that brought a load of champagne to Odin. Lyonnesse has about five hundred million people and it has a Civ-Level 7. There's one medium-sized spaceport, not too badly damaged, which may have possibilities as a base. The most interesting thing about our visit is that while we were in orbit examining the planet someone contacted us by radio."

"On the Sword-World frequency?" asked Rovard Harvan, now in charge of signals-and-detection since Gytha Valkanhayn's promotion to Second.

"No," Ovard replied. "But we were monitoring as many of the radio frequencies as possible to learn all we could about local politics, population concentrations, banking centers and military instillations."

"What did they say?" Second Officer Valkanhayn asked.

Harvan chuckled. "They seemed to think we were a ship called *Fairtrader* who had traded with them a few years ago. I said we weren't and they invited us down to trade anyway. I told them we were on a survey mission from Poictesme and that a trading vessel would return later in the year."

"*Fairtrader*," Laz Rivera mused. "That sounds like a Gilgamesher name."

"It is," Ovard said. "I looked it up. A ship of that name has traded on Tanith and Xochitl."

That caused a lot of discussion among the crew. Morland had been wondering why they hadn't seen or heard anything about Gilgameshers in this sector of the Old Federation. They seemed to be around everywhere else. If they traded regularly with Lyonnesse it meant there was something worth having on the world.

They took a pinnace down to the old spaceport on Lyonnesse. It had been called Melyodas Port and a portion of it functioned as an airport for the city next to it, which was called Launceston. Launceston was located on a large island, or small continent, depending on your viewpoint. It was the capital of Albion, which Ovard had identified as the most advanced nation of Lyonnesse. Morland was relieved to find that the more he listened to the radio chatter the better he could understand the local accent.

Accompanied by his aides and Rovard Harvan, Morland was ushered into the office of a man identified as Premier Mohammed Cohen, the elected leader-for-life of Albion. Cohen was dressed in a sky-blue formsuit that looked as if it had been imported from Odin about a decade ago. The room itself was palatial with local masterpieces on every wall. Obviously, what was good for the proletariat, wasn't quite good enough for their Premier.

After some conversation, Premier Cohen's face took on a suspicious cast. "You seem very different from Captain Obverjenn and the high priest of the *Fairtrader*. What are you here for?"

"Initially, we were interested in your champagne, Your Excellency," Morgan replied. "We sampled some on a layover at Odin."

"Ahh. At one time, it was renowned throughout the Federation. We can supply you as much as you require at a good price. But our champagne is not all that we have to offer." He went on to list a number of trade items that they customarily traded with off-worlders.

There was a lot of discussion back and forth about possible trade deals until Morland put his foot in it. "We did not detect any nuclear energy as we approached your planet. Would you be interested in nuclear power plants or nuclear weapons?

Morland wasn't really interested in trading nuclear technology. What he wanted to know was how much the Premier knew about it and whether they knew of any off-world sites of fissionable materials.

A look of horror sprang up on Cohen's face. "We are not ignorant of history, Captain. We are aware that Mother Terra was nearly destroyed by nuclear wars. Why would we want to bring that scourge to our beautiful world?"

Taken aback, Morland replied, "We know nothing about the political situation on your planet, Your Excellency. Some nations prefer to hold them as a last resort in case some other nation threatens them. If you have nuclear weapons and they do not, they would be less likely to attack you."

"Not, here," Premier Cohen said resolutely, "Launceston is the ancient capital of our world and it has always been the wish of our people to reunite Lyonnesse and restore Launceston as the capital. But I will not do it by conquest, only by persuasion."

"Of course, Your Excellency. I meant no offense."

Calming down, the Premier replied "No offense is taken. You obviously could not know my feelings on the matter." Standing up, he continued, "These talks have been fruitful. You have seen our list of trade goods. Please provide my aide with a list of your trading stock and we will continue our negotiations tomorrow. In the meantime I will be happy to arrange a tour of our city for you."

"Certainly, Your Excellency. I will send someone to your office with the information you requested."

Momentarily left alone after they were ushered out of the Premier's office and waiting for a tour guide to arrive, Harvan spoke in a whisper, "I detected four electronic devices in the walls of the Premier's office." He was wearing some sophisticated electronic sensors, well beyond Lyonnesse's technical ability to detect, in order to monitor and record information.

"Could they have been recording our conversation?" Morland asked. Seeing someone who looked like their guide coming toward them, Ovard moved to introduce himself and give them time to continue their discussion.

"With four devices?" Harvan replied. "I think it's more likely that someone was listening in on the Premier without his knowledge. I wonder who?"

Smiling as they walked over to meet their guide, Morland said "I have a feeling we will shortly find out."

His feeling proved correct. That night they were guests at a hastily arranged dinner party with several ambassadors from other nations. The food and wines had been excellent, especially since they had responded to Morland's request and served fish. He was especially taken with the local champagne. The ambassadors were carefully feeling him out when Premier Cohen launched into a long speech about the need for reunification of Lyonnesse.

Morland had assumed that the Premier had been lying earlier that day when he said he only wanted to reunite the planet by persuasion. When the Premier went on at length in the same vein, the ambassadors and other dignitaries' countenances had the studied look of people who were hearing something they'd heard far too often, he was forced to revise his opinion. The Premier was telling the truth; he was just politically naïve. Fortunately the Premier's Chief of Staff cleared his throat rather loudly, causing him to realize he had gone on too long and it was time to end his speech.

The depth of the Premier's naiveté was determined later when he compared notes with Ovard and Morrison. Representatives from several of the countries present that night had approached them about buying nuclear weapons.

"I think we shall accept all of the ambassadors' generous invitations to visit their countries and talk trade," Morland said.

"However, we're going to have to coordinate this precisely," Morland said to his officers. "It's clear that everyone here is spying on everyone else but Premier Cohen. We'll have to make our exchanges at the same time everywhere or word of what we're doing will leak out."

11

They spent a productive week traveling around Lyonnesse and discussing trade with all of the major nations. Every country except Albion wanted to buy nuclear weapons. Morland succeeded in getting everyone to bid against one another. He had also agreed to sell them to every one of the nations he had talked to, while convincing them that they were the only ones he was selling to.

"How do we know they'll give us the precious metals they promised us?" Ragnarsans asked.

"I had Harvan visit every country and verify the existence and location of their payment," Morland answered.

DeBorder grinned. "Then if they try to pull out of the deal at least we know where to raid."

The *Pay Dirt* along with the *Faerie Queene* had remained on the other side of one of Lyonnesse's two moons. The locals had no idea that other ships were lying in wait. Their strategy of making friends on the planet looked like it was going to pay off again, albeit in a way they hadn't intended.

"I wouldn't want to be on this world when everyone starts lobbing nukes at one another," weapons officer Mathes declared. Everyone nodded in agreement. Morland smiled to himself. He hadn't revealed that part of his plan to his officers yet.

As planned, the moment the transactions in the other countries were completed, Morland walked into Premier Cohen's office uninvited. "Is there something urgent?" Cohen asked, looking up from his desk where he was going over papers with his Chief of Staff.

"Yes, Your Excellency. I have just sold nuclear weapons to four of the other nations on Lyonnesse," he said, naming them.

Cohen's face drained of color.

"And, Your Excellency," Morland continued. "As of this moment, I am also having nuclear weapons delivered to your main military base."

"Why are you doing this?" the Premier cried. "Our world will be destroyed."

Morland gestured to the two men accompanying him. Holding electronic detectors they walked around the office, locating and tearing out differently shaped listening devices. The Chief of Staff, a look of panic on his face, reached for a device under the desk.

"Don't!" said Morland, drawing his gun. The Chief of Staff froze.

"What's going on here!" Cohen yelled, leaping to his feet.

"It is very simple, Your Excellency. Your enemies had listening devices planted in your walls and on your desk. They have been spying on you for years."

The Premier looked as if he were about to faint, catching the edge of his desk with his palm.

"I made that announcement," Morland said, "so your enemies would know that you have nuclear weapons, too. I had the listening devices removed so that you and I can talk in private."

Events were clearly moving too rapidly for Premier Cohen. "But everyone will try and attack each other first," he said, dazed and bewildered as he sat back down. "Especially now that they know other nations have nuclear weapons, too."

Morland smiled. He'd been looking forward to this. "Yes, they'll attack, but things won't go the way they planned. You see, Your Excellency, I sold them weapons with faulty triggers. They won't explode."

Cohen sagged back in his chair. "I don't understand. Why are you doing this?"

"Because, Your Excellency, I wish to trade with your world in the future and a destroyed world doesn't have anything to trade."

"But why the charade then?" Cohen asked. "You could have just refused to sell weapons to anyone."

Morland smiled again. He had to choose his words carefully because he did not want the Premier to realize how closely he'd came to duping them all. "I came here to make a profit, Your Excellency, and I'll be making a nice one out of this visit. You have been helpful to me and I decided to be helpful to you in return. The nuclear weapons I have given you are intact. They will work."

The Premier stood up slowly, resolution evident throughout his body. "No matter what, I will not use force to reunify our world."

"That's your choice, Your Excellency. However, if I were in your shoes, I would carefully consider the events of today: the spying devices, the invasions your fellow nations are launching at each other at this very moment and their willingness to betray your trust. I believe this will cause you to reevaluate your illusion that reunification can come without any pain and suffering."

"I've always known other nations were spying on us," the Premier replied. "We have our own spies in their countries, of course, but the fact that they were able to plant listening devices in my own office…" He turned to look at his Chief of Staff, now in handcuffs and seated on the couch flanked by two large Space Vikings.

"Not all of those devices were planted by other governments, Your Excellency," Morland said sadly. "Several were planted by one of your trusted associates."

The Chief of Staff twitched, turning his face away.

"No!" cried Cohen horrified, staring at his once trusted aide and head of the military. He appeared more shocked by this revelation than anything else he had heard. "Vincent, how could you?"

"Premier, Mo, I…I didn't do it willingly," his Chief of Staff babbled. "They promised me your job. How could I refuse, when you wouldn't listen to my recommendations? Your blindness to our enemies' machinations threatens us all!"

"Take him out of my sight!" Premier Cohen cried. "I must re-evaluate my staff, my everything— I've been a complete fool."

III

"Six hundred million stellars!" Laz Rivera announced to the stunned group. "All of it in gold, silver, jewels, or rare metals. All of our strongboxes are full. We had to put some of the loot in one of the small storage holds. On top of that, we didn't lose a single man, or spend one cartridge to get it."

The assembled officers of the small flotilla were holding a celebratory meeting in the *Skull Splitter's* command room. They had been stunned when Commodore Morland told them only two of the nuclear weapons would work.

"You gave him working nuclear weapons and you intend to come back to trade," DeBorder said, shaking his head in disbelief. "They'll take them apart and start building their own missiles. Next time we return we'll be greeted with a sky full of nukes."

"I told the Premier that the two bombs would explode if they tried to open them. Given his abhorrence of nuclear weapons, I don't think they'll try anything."

"Will they really explode?" Captain Ragnarsans asked.

Morland smiled. "Do you think I want to destroy a good trading partner? I want this world unified," he continued when they questioned him. "Of course, we'll examine all the other worlds we visit on this voyage before we decide whether Lyonnesse will make a good base world for us. But clearly, given the wealth of the planet, the large population and the advanced technical level of the people, it has a lot of potential as another base for our expedition."

DeBorder shook his head. "I thought we already had our base on Poictesme. What about that, Commodore?"

"The population base there is too small and uneducated. Poictesme is just our auxiliary base."

DeBorder exhaled loudly.

Laz Rivera looked puzzled. "What I want to know is, how is this planet going to become unified? Everyone's fighting each other," referring to the wars that had broken out shortly after they'd delivered the weapons.

"The fighting won't last long," Morland said. "Everyone's strategy was based on eliminating the other nation's army or their leadership with nuclear weapons. No one had any time to build up supplies and plan for a real invasion. Things will stall quickly."

Indeed, Premier Cohen had already started sending messages to other countries, offering his services as a mediator. This was after he recovered from the betrayal of his long-time Chief of Staff. Morland had brought a veridicator planetside; faced with no way to continue lying Vincent had talked. He had been spilling secrets to opposition politicians and building his power base in Albion for years.

"Since Albion is the only one of the major nations not to have attacked any other nation, they'll be well placed to try to resolve the fighting. And since Premier Cohen's had some of his naiveté knocked out of him, I think he'll be realistic enough to get things done. Plus, he has the only nuclear weapons on the planet."

"But everyone thinks all the weapons you gave them are duds," DeBorder said, referring to the vituperation streaming across the radio channels toward the Space Vikings once the other nations found that their nuclear weapons did not work.

"Yes, they do," Morland replied. "I suggested that Premier Cohen let the other nations know that he has working weapons, perhaps when they are gathered at Launceston for peace talks. There's a small uninhabited island in the middle of the southern ocean. He could set a nuke off there without harming anyone."

Morland stood and stretched. It had been a long day and he was tired. "When we come back in the future, we should examine that small island. If it's glowing, I think we will find we have a unified world to visit."

TASHMETUM

If Lyonnesse had been a dream of a raid, Tashmetum was the nightmare. Tashmetum was a planet of over two billion people, most of whom seemed to be attacking them the moment they came into the stratosphere. They had nuclear weapons and weren't afraid to use them by the handful. Morland could see several mushroom clouds in the distance. If his ships hadn't shot down the planes carrying those nukes, the *Skull Splitter* would have been part of one of those clouds.

"The biggest advantage we'll have," Walter Ovard had said, as the senior staff reviewed all the scouting reports from a few days ago, "is that Tashmetum has not yet mastered space travel or contragravity. They do have nuclear weapons and their primary delivery systems are airplanes, ground-based missiles and nuclear-armed artillery."

"Should we land and try to make friends again?" Haversham asked.

"Excuse me, sirs," a young man interrupted hesitantly. That was the Assistant Historian who had remained with the pinnace. Walter Ovard was now Ship's Historian on the *Faerie Queene.* Morland couldn't remember the young man's name at the moment. With him was a young Lieutenant from Excalibur who had commanded the pinnace.

"Yes. Go ahead, Alex," Ovard said.

That's it, Morland thought. *Alex Feraday is his name.*

"From everything we have determined," Feraday stated, "we think any landing attempt would be met with an instant attack. There are six major nations and two dozen or so minor ones. They are constantly at war or threatening to attack one another, so everyone is on edge." Seeing the quizzical expressions on their faces, he continued, "More importantly, they have a historical memory of being attacked from outer space."

That brought an instant reaction. "How long ago?" Morland asked.

"Space Vikings?" DeBorder queried almost simultaneously.

"I don't know; the attacks happened centuries ago. It could have been Space Vikings or it could have been raids at the end of the Interstellar Wars. But we've heard them mentioned a few times during the usual radio chatter and during some lectures that were transmitted on their audiovisual system. The menace from other worlds appears to be an important part of their psychological makeup. They're a rather paranoid bunch."

Morland looked at the Lieutenant, who nodded his head in agreement.

"All right," Morland declared, "If that's how they think, it's obvious we'll never be able to make friends with any of them. So there's no reason to examine any of the old spaceports." He shook his head in disappointment; Tashmetum had numerous spaceports and was heavily industrialized to boot. "We will raid only," he concluded. "This world appears to be almost as advanced as Mara. We had a rough time there, so we had better be careful here."

"I'll say," Ragnarsans said, holding up the arm that had been broken on Mara. "That was a bad one."

"Maybe you should wear armor this time," DeBorder joked.

"If I hadn't worn armor I'd be walking around with no legs," Ragnarsans had replied to general laughter.

They had divided the raid into six targets. Three were nuclear manufacturing sites with breeder reactors. Two pinnaces were assigned to each one. They would take only enriched uranium and plutonium there. Tashmetum had not yet rediscovered direct conversion of nuclear energy into electric current so there were no power cartridges. The reactors were built in isolated areas near the uranium mines. The other three targets were known banking and trading centers.

"Keep your people focused," Morland ordered. "We have to strike quickly and get out. Our problem on Mara was that we tried to raid one too many targets and they were waiting for us at the last one. It helps that we have an additional ship for this raid."

DeBorder looked worried. This was by far the toughest planet he'd ever tried to raid. He had grinned gamely at Morland, though. "It's a good plan, Commodore."

Now with artillery shells, tracer lines and explosions filling the air, Morland was glad for a moment that his fellow officers had refused to let him lead the attack in a combat car. He had required the other captains to stay on their ships as well. He forced his mind back on the task at hand, which was trying to locate all the sources of those artillery shells. Though the conventional shells had minimal effect on the collapsium plated *Skull Splitter*, they could damage the lighter armored combat cars, and if they struck an individual air-cavalry mount it was all over for the unfortunate rider.

The spaceships had taken out most of the nuclear missile sites at first launch and, so far, only a few of the smaller air vehicles had been hit by atomic missiles. The few missiles that had gotten through were of a low megatonage and had caused little damage to the starships. Fortunately, they only had atomic warheads, not thermonuclear ones.

With the missile sites destroyed or not firing, the remaining missiles were carried by airplanes, most of which they shot down well before they reached the target areas. The problem was there were so many of the damn jet fighters they were like bees in flower field!

Fortunately, the raids on the nuclear refineries were going well. Lacking contragravity and advanced robotic machinery, the locals hadn't envisioned the removal of plutonium as anything other than a slow and cumbersome process; therefore, those sites had few defenders or hardened missile sites.

The three big cities were much better protected. The *Skull Splitter, Faerie Queene* and *Pay Dirt* had each taken one city, knocking out the military airfields around them as they went in. The *Skull Splitter* hovered over a city called Rondonia according to Records, firing on any military units or armed resistance they could detect. The two pinnaces were down on the ground, being loaded by a steady stream of contragravity lifters from banks, stores, and warehouses. A horde of combat cars and air-cavalry single-mounts surrounded them, trying to protect them from small arms fire.

"There, a dozen miles southwest," Rovard Harvan, the Fourth Officer yelled suddenly, calling out the location of an artillery battery.

Weapons punched some buttons on the main weapons console, sending off a thermonuclear missile. "That should do it," Mathes stated.

There was a sudden blast of light, shielded by the viewscreens which all turned gray. All of a sudden there were a lot fewer explosions in the immediate area. When the screens came up, they could see that about a quarter of the city had been leveled and that there were fires everywhere.

"This'll teach them to put their artillery so close to home," one of the communications officers said.

"Damage?" Morland asked.

"Minor," Valkanhayn replied, as she checked the instruments. "Most of their artillery hasn't even dented our armor. Even their atomic missiles have penetrated no more than one or two decks. Damage-control is sealing off those minor breaches."

"How are the ground crews doing?" he asked.

Laz Rivera smiled. "They've made some good finds. Banks, jewelry stores, two art museums, warehouses. Like the reports said, there's a lot of wealth here. Once again, your historians have stuck gold!"

Morland turned to the telescopic-screen. His crews were emptying what appeared to be a multi-story building while a screen of troops tried to keep the Tashmetum soldiers off them. He was happy to see that most of the crews exiting the building were towing small loads. He wanted the remaining storage space on the *Skull Splitter* filled with high value items, not bulk goods. As he watched, a combat car swooped down, firing missiles at a concentration of natives who appeared to be gearing up for a counterattack.

"What about the other ships?"

Rivera checked his console. "Stenger is reporting minimal opposition at New Cabinda. DeBorder's having a hot time at Dampier but says he's handling it."

"Airplanes, about twenty miles northeast," a signals-and-detection officer cried.

"I'm on it," replied Mathes, launching missiles and directing a combat car to follow up. After what seemed like many long hours, but what the ship's clock indicated was barely fifteen minutes, three messages came in almost simultaneously.

"They're finished at the nuclear sites," Rovard Harvan reported.

"More planes, about four hundred or so, detected about forty miles to the east."

"Armored columns about ten miles to the south."

"Sound the recall and bring everyone home," Morland ordered. "Keep those planes away from the collection areas."

"Casualties?" he asked when everyone was back on board.

"Eighteen dead, according to the monitors," Laz Rivera said, gesturing to the screens. "I don't have a count on the wounded yet."

The *Pay Dirt* reported similar success and casualties. Suddenly Morland's screen chimed. Vann Stenger's smiling face appeared on the screen. "Congratulations, Commodore!" he said. "Agni is no longer your best raid!"

The majority of the crew was, if not totally drunk, at least well on its way there. Morland hadn't observed the same exuberance after Lyonnesse. It seemed that it required being under fire and in mortal peril to make people really want to celebrate. *This,* he thought contentedly as he looked around the great room, *is one of the differences in the* Skull Splitter's *construction that I enjoy.* The *Prince of Thieves* did not have any large rooms, so there were always a number of parties after a successful raid going on at the same time which had encouraged the formation of little cliques on the ship.

The *Skull Splitter's* great room, on the other hand, could comfortably hold the entire ship's crew at one time and was the only party site. Since most of the crew was there, it was rather crowded. The air was hazy with smoke and the noise level was high, but that let everyone enjoy the celebration together. Not that he hadn't seen a few crew members pair off for a more private celebration.

They were still in the Tashmetum system, examining some of the industrial installations on the outer planets. Lieutenant Torran had discovered the installations on his initial examination of the system but had focused the majority of his time studying Tashmetum itself.

"Do we even need to continue?" DeBorder asked rhetorically. He and his officers had come over from the *Pay Dirt.* "Over two billion stellars on just one planet! More than three billion stellars on the entire trip. That's got to be the greatest raid in Space Viking history."

Morland agreed that was even a better haul than what the *Nebula* had taken off Agni.

Still, that statement drew a raucous response from those present as everyone was feeling pretty good. When the debate quieted down everyone looked at Ship's Historian, Ulrik Selner and Laz Rivera. Rivera was the most experienced Space Viking and usually accepted as having the final say on issues like this.

"Erlic Sanchez, the Planet-Buster's raid on Isis is usually considered the richest raid ever," Rivera stated authoritatively. "Of course if you figured in inflation you could make a case for Grosser's raid on Anubis and Inana, or the Trask-Harkaman raid on Amaterasu and Beowulf, or even Alywn Kintour's raid of Tiwaz, Sukhavati, and Kaltesh."

"Now I disagree," the Historian said. "How about Wulf Hellmut, the World-Smasher. He brought home a billion and a half stellars in the Sixteenth Century A.E., when a stellar was worth three times what it's worth today. And not a milistellar by way of trading!"

That brought calls of disagreement from Rivera and some of the other people at the table. If you wanted to start a good-natured argument in a Space Viking crowd, just ask who'd led the richest raid of all time. The only other subject to arouse such passion was which planet had the most beautiful women.

Lieutenant Torran and several engineers and technicians eventually returned from their examination of the other planets in the Tashmetum system. There were a variety of installations, some usable, some not. While the installations were nearly as extensive as those in the Gartner Tri-System, there was no world even close to Koshchei in usability.

As the Lieutenant continued with his report to Morland, Ovard left his card game to join them. He was anxious to press on, claiming that he had the coordinates to several worlds that were good raiding targets and potential base worlds. Morland wondered if he had another bet going, but agreed to continue the raid. He didn't see any reason to stop until all of the cargo holds were full or he found a likely base, whichever came first.

After their brush with the Mardukan Navy, Morland knew it was only a matter of time before the Mardukans came hunting for the *Skull Splitter* in force. Fortunately, only the *Skull Splitter* had actually fought in the space battle with the *Challenger* so it was unlikely that the Mardukans would send a fleet to hunt him down, maybe just two or three ships. However, even if they defeated that flotilla, the next one would be even larger.

Morland was either going to have to build his own space navy or spend the rest of his days looking over his shoulder. With Poictesme they had their own naval yard and the tools and equipment to build ships. *Now, all I need is time*, he thought. What was it the Pre-Atomic Era conqueror Napoleon once said? He'd read it in one of Harkaman's books. *Now, it's coming back*: "Strategy is the art of making use of time and space. I am less concerned about the latter than the former. Space we can recover, lost time never."

The End

www.ingramcontent.com/pod-product-compliance
Lightning Source LLC
Chambersburg PA
CBHW030825310726
48980CB00006B/646/J

* 9 7 8 0 9 3 7 9 1 2 1 2 6 *